ONE-EYED TOM

BRENDA CRISSMAN MUSICK

To: Jack
Enjoy!
Brenda Crissman Musick

ONE-EYED TOM

BRENDA CRISSMAN MUSICK

Published August 2013
Little Creek Books
Imprint of Jan-Carol Publishing, Inc.

ISBN: 978-1-939289-23-0
Library of Congress Control Number: 2013947856

You may contact the publisher:
Jan-Carol Publishing, Inc.
PO Box 701 Johnson City, TN 37605
E-mail: publisher@jancarolpublishing.com
jancarolpublishing.com

Dedicated to:

My husband, Jimmie, my forever love,
my encourager and my best friend.
His love and faith never cease to amaze me.

And in Honor of:

My mother, Mamie Stump Crissman,
who, at this writing is ninety-two
years young. Her incredible memory
has helped me beyond measure in the
writing of this novel. She is the epitome
of an Appalachian woman and an
icon for motherhood.

Her children rise up, and call her blessed; her husband
Also, and he praiseth her.

Proverbs 31:28

ACKNOWLEDGEMENTS

This book came together as a result of the influence of many people. My dad, Clarence Crissman, loved to read, write and teach; quite a testament to a man with only an eighth grade education. Dad was constantly writing stories and poetry and cherished his years as a Sunday school teacher. He also taught me daily about love and forgiveness. We lost him in 2004 to Parkinson's disease and dementia; but I know if he were here today, he would be my biggest fan.

I also owe much to my Reminescent Writers group at Southwest Virginia Community College; my wonderful support group. They have laughed with me, cried with me, encouraged me and critiqued me. Thank you, my friends.

Nothing can encourage writing like a good schoolteacher and I have had many. Among those were Dorothy Harrington, Ida McKinnon (both deceased) and especially Carroll Wolfe. All were, and are, fantastic teachers and role models.

I owe the greatest debt to God, who gives talents to all and expects us to develop them. I cannot imagine a day without His unconditional love and forgiveness. May this work be pleasing in His sight.

LETTER FROM THE AUTHOR

Dear Reader,

Our heritage is a precious thing, an integral part of who and what we are. To forget one's heritage is to forget a part of ourselves. I treasure my family and my roots, and I cherish the stories that have been handed down to me through the years; especially those from my mother. Stories of our lives and those of our Appalachian heritage are the greatest family heirlooms we can leave to our children. My reminiscent writing style has been a tremendous help to me in writing this novel. It is purely fictional, but derived from stories handed down on which I have put my own twist using this writer's imagination that lives inside of me. The names are fictional, but I have tried to stay true to names of the early twentieth century in the Appalachian Mountains. It has been a joy creating names to fit the characters, and it has been exciting to watch my characters develop and take on roles I did not foresee at the onset of the book.

As you read about Carrie, I hope you will see a little bit of her in yourself, and as you read about Tom, you might have to accept a little bit of him in yourself, too. You see, we all have our good qualities and our flaws. That's what makes us interesting, and that's what makes a novel interesting. We women have come a long way since the early 1900s, but I hope our hearts haven't turned away from the things that matter most, such as family and faith. We, too, are leaving a heritage. Let's make it one our descendants will smile about and continue to share with pride.

So, sit back, readers. Get ready to meet Carrie and Tom and immerse yourself in their lives. Enjoy.

INTRODUCTION

BY JAMES K. CRISSMAN

There are several novels that, even though they are fictional, provide an adequate depiction of Appalachian culture and the Appalachian family. Popular books such as Harriette Arnow's *The Dollmaker*, Jesse Stuart's *Taps for Private Tussie* and James Still's *River of Earth* come to mind. Brenda Musick, a lifetime resident of Central Appalachia has written a novel that ranks with the best in its portrayal of family life in the Virginia mountains, and the reader can easily relate to both the characters and their problems.

There is at least one "one-eyed Tom" in every hamlet in Appalachia. He is both likeable and easy to dislike. He cares about his wife and family, yet there is something inside that compels him to stray from the marital bond and risk losing his family. Carrie Ranes Swank, like most Appalachian women in the early 1900s, is strong both mentally and physically. She takes care of home and family and holds the family together while her husband strays. It seems also, that there is always a "Loose Lizzie" who can tear a family apart and doesn't really care who she hurts as long as she satisfies her own wanton desires.

Musick also adequately delineates the cultural problems extant in Appalachia during the early 1900s. Medical care was virtually non-existent, diseases such as pneumonia, tuberculosis, and influenza were ever-present, and deaths during child-birth and from accidents were common-place. Women like Carrie Ranes Swank, had to be strong to survive and aide their family members and friends in survival.

If you enjoy reading about Appalachian characters in their native milieu, *One-Eyed Tom* is an excellent book, written by someone who cares about Appalachia and its people. I look forward to reading another book by this author.

James K. Crissman is Professor and Chair of the Department of Psychology, Sociology, Criminal Justice, and Master of Science in Clinical Psychology at Benedictine University in Lisle, Illinois. In addition to numerous articles on Appalachia he is the author of Death and Dying in Central Appalachia *and one of the co-editors of* The Encyclopedia of Death and Dying.

A MOUNTAIN WOMAN'S PRAYER

She doesn't ask for much, Lord.
Luxury, she's never known.
She's had little of material wealth
And nothing to call her own.

Perhaps the love of a good man, Lord,
Hard-working, honest and true.
A little house to care for,
Nothing fancy, nothing new.

She's not afraid of hard work, Lord.
It's been her lot since birth.
She'd clean his house, fix his meals
And daily prove her worth.

Maybe a little family, Lord.
She has so much love to give.
Children to make a house a home
And life a joy to live.

A husband, a home, a family, Lord.
No wealth or fancy array.
Just look upon this mountain woman
And hear her as she prays.

— *Brenda Crissman Musick*

CHAPTER 1

"Carrie," her mother called. "You're going to make us all late for the corn shuckin' if you don't get a move on. The Hayneses like to get an early start!"

"Just a jiffy, Mama!" returned Carrie, giving her hair one last pat as she looked into her small handheld mirror.

Oh, my, she thought, staring at her vision, *why is my face so long and my nose even longer. Will Tom even notice a face like this?*

With a sigh, she laid down the mirror.

It was the second corn shuckin' Carrie had attended this fall, and her family would be having one of their own in a few weeks. It was a good way for the farm folks of Lacy Creek to get some work done and have a good time in the doing. The Hayneses would invite all the neighbors to the shuckin'. Each family would take a dish of food, and added to all that the Haynes women would prepare, there would be quite a spread.

Some families walked; others rode the family farm wagon, with mom and dad on the front seat and all the children in the back. No one in the area, up and down the hollows, least not farmers, had fancy transportation. When you had to scrape to put food in the mouths of your family, you had no thoughts of such foolishness. They would gather around ten in the morning and eat lunch about twelve. In those two hours, waiting for the food to be readied, the children played games, the men swapped knives or yarns, and the teenage boys and girls watched each other out of the corner of their eyes to see who might be there to swap a kiss with if they were lucky enough to find that special ear of corn.

After stomachs were filled and more yarns spun by the older generation, all of the men, children, and part of the women would begin the corn shuckin'. Some of the women would clean up after the meal and mind the food left for supper, keeping away insects, cats and dogs. As they shucked the corn, the men would continue their stories. Carrie loved to hear them, and she and her sister, Nora, would talk about them and retell them to each other for days. Nora and Carrie had a bedroom together and shared most everything. Her two older sisters Lily (Lie-lee) and Ellie also shared a room. There were eight children in her family, including four brothers. It was a house full, but Papa Silas and Mama Cynth took good care of them, though the living was not easy on their little farm back in the hollow. Mama Cynth was a midwife, and although most folks had no money to pay her, some often gave her a chicken, or a hunk of ham, or a poke of meal or flour. Mama would be gone sometimes two or three days birthing a baby and then taking care of the baby and new mother until she was sure everything was okay. Doctors were scarce, and even if there was a doctor nearby, most folks had little money to pay him. Carrie often resented her mother's absence from the home, but Mama Cynth reminded her of the importance of her work. She was proud of Mama, but she vowed at an early age never to become a midwife and leave her family.

"Coming, Mama!" called Carrie, breaking out of her reverie. She had spent just a little extra time "fixing up" this morning, feeling pretty sure a certain young man named Tom would be there. She had been noticing Tom for some time now, but she wasn't sure the noticing was mutual. He was such a good looking boy...dark hair, blue eyes, a certain sway to his walk that sent butterflies flitting in her stomach. He just seemed to have an "air" about him, even though he was short of stature and could never be called muscular. Tom and his family lived on a farm just over the hill from Carrie.

I wonder what it would be like to kiss Tom, Carrie mused. *I've kissed my hand before and even my mirror once, but I'm sure it's better than that.*

"It-It sure does," stammered Carrie, immediately feeling like kicking her own backside. Why couldn't she come up with things to say like some of the other girls?

"Are you gonna stay for the dancing after the shuckin's done?" asked Tom.

"I suppose so," answered Carrie.

"I suppose I might be asking you to dance," said Tom. "I might even find that red ear of corn, and then I might be asking you to take a walk."

"I would like that," replied Carrie, nervously winding a strand of hair around her finger.

"Hey, you-all!" called Sally. "Looks like lunch is being served, and I'm starved. Let's go!"

"Well, I-I best go," said Carrie, feeling like a dimwit.

"Hold up," said Tom. "How about we get a plate and eat with some of the others over there under that old sycamore tree? There's plenty of good shade."

"Okay," answered Carrie eagerly.

With that they all headed for the huge spread of food waiting for them. Carrie had to pinch herself to make sure she wasn't dreaming. Tom was so handsome and mannerly. She hung on to his every word, and he gave Carrie his full attention, making her feel special.

This is a day I'll never forget, she thought to herself.

Soon the corn shuckin' began and they all moseyed over to the huge pile of corn. Nate Swank, Tom's brother, was the first to find a red ear of corn just minutes into the shuckin'. He immediately handed it to his sweetheart, Charlotte, who blushed a beet-red, knowing that before the night was over Nate would be stealing a kiss.

As the shuckin' continued the men began once more to tell their stories. Most of the stories had been told before, but no one minded. Besides, the stories usually changed some with each telling. Soon another red ear was found, this time by a young wife who immediately handed it to her husband and received a big kiss on the cheek without delay. As everyone applauded he laughed, "Hey, no need to wait to kiss my sweet wife. I have a license, you know."

The afternoon wore on lightheartedly with a few more red ears, some kidding of the lucky finders, and then some more stories. The pile of corn was pretty well shucked and everyone was getting hungry again. Carrie was somewhat disappointed that her dashing Tom had not found a red ear, but all in all, she was just happy to be sitting next to him and enjoying the way he looked at her. He had even held her hand a time or two.

"No red ear for us it seems, Carrie," said Tom. "But I sure would like a dance later."

"I'd like that, Tom," replied Carrie, blushing again but boldly taking his arm.

"Okay folks," called Jed Haynes. "Looks like these gals have supper all ready here. Let's fill our bellies and then have some dancing."

And that's just what they did. Old Charlie Wade brought his fiddle and Billy Tatum brought his banjo to supply the music for some lively dancing.

Carrie had an unforgettable night, dancing and talking with Tom, who hardly left her side the entire night. During one dance Carrie watched as Lily and Corb Tyler slipped off behind the barn. They were gone for about thirty minutes. She was amazed and even disgusted when about an hour later she saw Lily slip off behind the barn with Corb's brother, Dent.

Pa ought to wallop her good, thought Carrie, *behaving like a hussy.*

But Carrie was determined not to let Lily's "carrying on" ruin her evening. She had Tom by her side and that was all that mattered. As the day wore down and her family rode home in the wagon, Carrie just savored the memories of the day and the warm feeling she had inside. After all, Tom had asked if he could come to court her next Saturday night. My, that seemed such a long way off. He hadn't kissed her yet...maybe Saturday night.

CHAPTER 2

As the weeks passed, Tom came a-courtin' every Saturday night and quite often on Sunday afternoon. He didn't kiss her the first week, but he did the second, and it was everything she thought it might be and more.

I'll never need to kiss an old mirror ever again, she thought with a sigh.

Carrie was head-over-heels, slapdab in love with Tom Swank. The only problem was, she wasn't exactly sure Tom felt the same way. He seemed to enjoy being with her, and he was always attentive and sweet, but he had never spoken of love. He had stolen a few kisses, but those kisses were never followed with talk of the future. Still, Carrie remained hopeful...yet...there was the time she saw him wink at Lily when he thought she wasn't looking. That didn't set well with her at all.

He didn't mean anything by it, Carrie told herself. *He's just being nice to my sister.*

The feeling of disappointment hovered, however...that nagging little let-down feeling that tiptoed up and down her spine. It didn't help matters to know of her sister's flirty ways with boys. Lily was seeing Reed Tyler pretty steady these days, and Carrie secretly hoped they might marry. Lily could use some "settling down."

It was Friday and Carrie and Nora were helping Mama Cynth do some baking for the weekend, a chore Carrie loved. She could even turn out a pie crust as flaky and tasty as her mother's. Nora wasn't quite as thrilled with it as Carrie, but she didn't mind, and she definitely loved being in the kitchen with her two favorite people. Ellie and Lily were supposed to be cleaning the living room and front porch, but there seemed to be more giggling coming from that direction than sounds of work. Company would be coming for Sunday dinner and, though it was mostly relatives, Mama Cynth expected everything to look its best. Mama and Papa always took the family to the old Primitive Baptist church every other Sunday. On Sundays off from church, they had company for dinner. On "off Sundays" after breakfast, Papa always gathered the family around the kitchen table to read from the "good book" and have prayer. If anyone had any sins to confess from the previous week, that's when Papa Silas expected them to do it, and Papa also seemed to know when there was some confessing to do, like the time he found the dead robin.

"Charles," he asked his son, "did I see a little bird lying dead under that sycamore tree last Thursday?"

Charles, his eyes toward the floor, just shrugged his shoulders.

"It looked a might like it had been killed by a sling shot," continued Papa. "Know anything about that?"

"Y-Yes, Papa. I killed the bird. I-I'm sorry," stammered Charles, head down clear on his chest. "I won't ever kill another bird as long as I live," he added.

"I believe you're a man of your word, Charles my boy," declared Papa. "I accept your apology and I believe when you pray tonight and tell God you're sorry, He'll forgive you, too. Just remember, God knows even when a sparrow falls...or a robin."

With that the matter was closed and was never mentioned again, nor did Papa find any more dead birds.

The Ranes home was not fancy, but it was always neat. Cynthia Ranes saw to that, as she believed in taking care of what God gave her. They lived in a log house with a living room, kitchen, and one bedroom downstairs. Upstairs consisted of two bedrooms that had later been partitioned off into four, giving more privacy to the occupants. The ceilings were low and the space was limited, but it served its purpose, and it was more than a lot of families in the little Appalachian area possessed. Water came from a little spring just down the hill and had to be carried in. Then, of course, there was the little two-seater outhouse out back. All in all, Carrie was very proud and thankful for her home, but most of all she was thankful for Papa Silas and Mama Cynth.

Her thoughts were interrupted by the sound of Old Jake barking. At the same time Ellie came running to the door.

"Somebody's coming, Mama!" she called. "Looks like old Marvin Herd!"

About that time they heard a wagon pulling up.

"Uh-oh," said Mama Cynth, heading out the door, wiping her hands on her feed sack apron as she went.

Marvin, his wife, and their nine children lived about a mile down the road and across a swinging bridge in a little clapboard house hardly large enough for two people, much less eleven.

"Maudie needs you, Miss Cynth. Can you come catch the baby?" asked Marvin, somewhat out of breath. "Don't reckon it'll be too long now."

"I'll be right there, Marvin," answered Cynthia, heading back into the house.

"Girls, it looks like number ten is on its way," she said to Carrie and Nora.

Carrie's face clouded over. "I wish that old man would croak so's they'd quit having young'uns," she grumbled.

Before she knew what was happening, Mama Cynth grabbed her by the shoulders and gave her a shake.

"God gives babies, and God says when to stop. Do you hear me, young lady?"

Carrie looked down at the floor, the shame of her words lodged crosswise in her belly. "Yes, Mama. I didn't mean it."

"I know you didn't," answered her mother, pulling her close for a warm hug and a loving pat or two. Then, just as quickly, she let go of Carrie and headed toward the wall shelf to fetch her worn black bag with all the things she needed for birthing.

"I'm depending on you girls to get the baking done for me. Fix your Papa and the boys a good supper," she said as she pulled off her apron, reached for a clean one and headed back out the door. "This is number ten so I don't reckon it'll take too long. I should be back tonight or early tomorrow morning. I'm counting on my girls."

"Ellie, Lily, I expect this house to be as clean as a fresh-washed sheet blowing in the breeze on a sunny day. Understand?" asked Mama as she made her way to Marvin's old rundown rickety wagon.

"Yes, Mama," they chorused.

Carrie watched forlornly as her mother rode away with Marvin Herd. She knew she should be proud of Mama...and she was...but she just hated it when Mama had to be away catching babies. She also knew that if any work was to be done in Mama's absence, it would be up to her and Nora. Already Ellie and Lily were headed to the old maple shade tree, whispering and giggling.

No matter, she thought, *I'll do what Mama asked me to do. Then I need to get myself ready for Tom's visit tomorrow night. This might just be the time...*

With that happy thought she began rolling out dough for two more pies, smiling to herself. Nora was busy fixing apples for the filling and watching Carrie's smile out of the corner of her eye. She knew what Carrie was thinking. A part of her wanted Tom to ask Carrie to be his wife, yet an unknown fear kept sounding an alarm. She had seen Tom flirt with other girls, and it made her uneasy. Nora certainly didn't want to see her sister and best friend get hurt.

"Please, God," she whispered. "Don't let my sister get hurt. You know her heart, God, filled only with good."

CHAPTER 3

On December 8, 1902, Carrie's eighteenth birthday, Tom Swank asked her to be his bride. She was beaming with a warm, expectant happiness as the wedding date was set for February 19th of the following year. It would just be a simple affair at Carrie's home with her family and Tom's.

Right now, though, Christmas was the focus of everyone's thoughts... well, except maybe for Carrie and Tom. Christmas was always special and exciting at the Ranes' home. It was not because they received an abundance of gifts; it was usually one homemade gift and some fruit and nuts in a stocking for each child. But, oh the cooking and decorating and cleaning that led up to the special event! There were oodles of cakes, pies, and other confectionaries. Papa brought in a big ham from the smokehouse, and Mama cooked it to perfection. Then a few hens made their way from the chicken lot to Mama's frying pan. Mama Cynth made the best fried chicken and gravy of anyone Carrie knew.

The Christmas tree was always an exciting event. Papa waited until two days before Christmas and then he and one or two of the boys went out and cut the loveliest cedar tree they could find. Cedars were in abundance on the little Appalachian hills, but finding one shaped just right took some walking and some looking. Soon the house was filled with the aroma of cooking and baking and the special scent of cedar. The tree decorations were all homemade. As soon as the tree was up, Mama popped corn and the whole family strung the corn onto heavy thread for ropes. Usually Mama had to pop several poppings because everybody also ate their fill. The girls would find the largest pine cones in the woods and hang them on the tree. Then they cut out cloth in the shape of Christmas bells and stars to add to the trimmings. In the top of the tree was a gold star made by Mama's mother, Grandma Rachel, who had died before Mama Cynth ever married. When finished, they all agreed each year it was the most beautiful Christmas tree yet.

For the Ranes family, though, Christmas was not just about decorations, gifts and food. It was about the birth of Christ. Papa always read the Christmas story from his old Bible on Christmas morning, and every year it was more beautiful than the year before. Sometimes the children even put on their own play about the nativity, with Papa always as Joseph and Mama always as Mary. Being the oldest son, Eb was always the donkey that carried Mary (Mama) in the play.

Mama would object, "I'm too heavy. I might hurt your poor back."

"Why, Mama," Eb would reply, "you're so light you could ride on a flea's back and he wouldn't pay it no mind."

With this, Mama would just smile and the matter was settled.

This year was especially exciting for Carrie. It would be the last in her parents' home.

Next year Tom and I will be decorating our own tree in our own home, she mused, getting goose bumps.

Tom was already working it out to buy a little house just across the hill that had belonged to his grandfather. It wasn't much...a board house with a living room, kitchen and two small bedrooms. It could be "built on to" Tom had assured her with a twinkle in his eye.

"How many young'uns we gonna have, Carrie?" Tom had asked her just last Saturday night. They had gone for a walk even though it was cold as ice outside. Tom was holding her hand as they walked, stopping to steal a kiss every now then.

"I don't know, Tom," answered Carrie shyly. "I'd like to have a big family like Papa and Mama have. Families are so much fun."

"Well, some families are fun, I guess," he replied with a smirk.

Tom was very close to his mother and father, but sometimes he and his siblings didn't see eye to eye. He was the oldest in the family and complained that while he worked, his brothers and sister seemed to get by with doing nothing. One brother, Ort, was already married with one child, and he and Tom hardly spoke.

"I want our family to always be close, Tom," whispered Carrie.

"I want their mama and papa to be close," said Tom, giving her hand a squeeze.

They walked in silence for a few moments before Tom spoke again, "I hear Lily and Reed are talking about marrying. Have they said anything about a date?"

"I think just after Christmas," replied Carrie, "and Mama and Papa are sort of relieved. Lily seems a little on the rowdy side, and I can see it's worrying them."

"Yeah, Lily's a good bit different from you," injected Tom.

Something in the way he said it gave Carrie an uneasy feeling in the pit of her stomach.

"Do you wish I was more like Lily, Tom?" she asked, studying his face.

Tom was quiet for a moment, and then replied, "I reckon you're you and Lily's Lily."

Somehow that wasn't the answer Carrie had hoped for, but her thoughts were muted as Tom stopped to steal another kiss.

In January, Lily and Reed Tyler were wed, and on February 19, Carrie married Tom. It was the happiest day of her life, and she couldn't wait to see what the future held.

After the wedding, they rode across the hill to their new home and set up housekeeping. Carrie was an excellent housekeeper, trained well by her mother, and she wasn't afraid of work, as Tom soon found out. Tom was a sweet attentive husband, but didn't much care for work, as Carrie soon found out. It wasn't so much that he was lazy. Tom just didn't believe in going out of his way to hunt work. He had saved a little money, but Carrie knew it wouldn't last long.

By early fall Carrie was expecting their first child. She was happy and anxious to be a mother and she breezed through the pregnancy, working as hard as she had before. Mama Cynth brought her some fabric and she was busy making diapers and gowns for the baby. For the first time, Carrie was glad Mama was a midwife, because she knew who would be delivering her baby.

Tom didn't say too much about the baby either way. On occasion, she had heard him bragging to the other men about it, but he seldom mentioned it to her.

"Which do you want, Tom, a boy or a girl?" Carrie asked, as they lay in bed one night.

"I don't reckon it matters much," answered Tom, yawning. "I guess it would be handy to have a boy to help on the farm some. I just hope it don't squawl all night like my brothers and sisters did. A man needs his rest." With this, he turned over and was snoring in minutes.

Luke Thomas Swank made his boisterous arrival June 16, 1904, with Mama Cynth right there to do the birthing. When Carrie first held him in her arms she thought he had to be the most beautiful baby in the entire world, and the robins in the cherry tree outside her window seemed to be in full agreement. Tom was right proud, too, declaring that he looked just like his Paw. He determined right then and there that his children would call him "Paw" and Carrie "Maw", and that is just what they did.

Luke was a good baby, but even good babies take a lot of feeding and caring. Carrie always tried to keep him fed and quiet at night so Tom could get his sleep. A few weeks earlier Tom had gotten a job on the Norfolk and Western Railroad, a job that would mean good money for his family, and it also meant Tom needed his sleep. Carrie had to work extra hard at the house, doing some of the things Tom used to do, but she knew God had been good to her and she would do the work and not complain. Sometimes Mama came over to help her with the wash, and sometimes Nora came over and tended the baby while Carrie worked in the garden or did some extra baking.

"I hope you and Tom and Luke can come over next week for a Fourth of July dinner," said Mama Cynth one day while helping Carrie with the washing. "I'm going to make some of my blueberry pies, and I know how much you love them. Your Papa says it's too dry for fireworks, but we'll still have some fun. It'll be your first time of visiting since little Luke was born.

"I don't know, Mama. I'll have to ask Tom," answered Carrie, looking away.

Mama noticed a little quiver to Carrie's voice that made her feel uneasy.

"Is everything alright between you and Tom, Carrie Tan?" she asked.

"Yes, Mama. Tom just stays tired lately since he took the job on the railroad. He even has to work overtime some days," explained Carrie.

At this revelation, Cynthia frowned to herself. She hadn't heard of any of the other men working overtime.

That night when Tom came home...late again...Carrie determined to ask him about going to her mother's for the Fourth of July.

"Now, woman," he barked, "I already made plans for the Fourth."

"What are we doing?" asked Carrie.

"It ain't *we*, it's *me*," answered Tom again, raising his voice. "I'm going to meet up with some of the men and *we're* going to do some celebrating and have us some fireworks. I think I deserve some time out as much as I work and slave around here. You just take the boy and go on over to your Maw's. I reckon I'll be out pretty late so why don't you just stay the night?"

Carrie fought against the hot tears in her eyes. She wasn't worried about Tom drinking. As far as she knew, he had never been one to drink. It was just the fact that he would rather be with the men than with her and Luke. She couldn't imagine Papa Silas doing such a thing.

I'm not right to feel this way, she scolded herself. *Tom works hard and he deserves some time to have some fun. It's not that he don't love me and Luke.*

At the same time, a small voice whispered inside her, *Why don't he think it's fun to be with his wife and son?*

Carrie arose early the morning of the Fourth, feeding the baby, milking the cow, feeding the chickens and slopping the hogs. Tom was sleeping late and she didn't want to disturb him. When he did get up, she fixed him a big breakfast of country ham with gravy and biscuits. Tom did love her biscuits. He was still there when Papa Silas came in his old wagon to get her and Luke but he didn't go out to speak to her father. Her brother Eb had promised to come across the hill this evening to do the milking and feeding. It was with a heavy heart that Carrie got in the wagon, leaving Tom behind. He had seemed rather testy lately, but Carrie kept telling herself it was the new job.

When she arrived at the Ranes' house with her Papa, all of her brothers and sisters were there and those who had families had brought them. Even Lily and Reed were there with their baby daughter Tiny, born just five months after their wedding. Nora had recently married and Ellie was soon to wed. Her two younger brothers had declared themselves forever bachelors, but with several girls "eyeing" them, no one believed that declaration would last.

As usual, Mama had outdone herself with the meal and everyone was "full to the brim." It was good for Carrie, talking with her family and swapping baby stories as well as learning from the other mothers some tips that would help her. Still...she missed Tom with a loneliness that pressed on her heart...and an uneasiness that refused to leave.

They were just heading out to the front porch to sit a spell when two men came running up the hollow. Papa immediately stood and walked out to meet them. He could tell by their pace that something was amiss.

"It's Tom!" shouted Corb Tyler, as he drew within hearing distance. He bent over, gasping for breath.

Carrie grabbed her chest. "What's happened, Corb? What's happened to my Tom?"

"There's been an accident, Carrie, with a firecracker. Tom thought it had gone out and it hadn't and he picked it up and it went off and..." babbled Corb.

"Slow down, young fellow," inserted Papa Silas. "We can't make out what you're saying. What has happened to Tom?"

"He picked up a lit firecracker, Silas," said the other man, a little more settled than Corb, yet still out of breath. "They took him to old Doc Whitt, but I'm pretty sure it got his eye."

"Papa, I've got to go to Tom," gasped Carrie. "Will you take me?"

"Come on, daughter. Of course, I'll take you. I'll get the wagon," answered Papa.

The ride to town was a short one, but to Carrie it seemed unending. As they stepped down from the wagon and walked toward the office door, she could hear loud guttural groans coming from inside.

"Oh, Doc," Tom was half groaning, half crying. "Oh, Doc, it hurts something awful. Can't you make it stop? Ohhh!"

As Carrie's knees went weak, Papa reached out his hand to steady her.

"Take a deep breath, Carrie girl," he said softly. "Tom will need you to be brave."

With this, she pulled herself upright, took a deep breath, and walked straight into the room where Doc was tending Tom.

"I'm here, Tom," she said, with not a quiver to be noticed. "I'm here and you're going to be alright."

As she looked at the eye it was all she could do not to turn and run outside. The food in her stomach threatened to come up at any moment as she prayed for help. It was a horrible bloody sight with burn marks over his entire face, and as Doc Whitt tried to clean the injury, Tom's head was thrashing from side to side.

"Oh, Doc! Oh, Carrie!" he screamed. "Please make the pain go away!"

Tom lost his eye that day. The bright, alert blue eye would forever be replaced by a white ball that filled his eye socket, never seeing, only occupying a space. It was weeks before he could work again, and Carrie had to keep the eye clean in order to keep down infection. There was pain, and it was a hideous sight to look at, but Tom refused pain medication. Instead, the days were spent with his groaning and complaining and his constant demands for Carrie's time and attention. Between taking care of the house, the farm, Luke and Tom, she was bone weary, praying daily for strength.

Tom changed after that, and not for the better. It wasn't a change that Carrie could put her finger on; it was just there. He finally went back to work, wearing a black patch over his eye to protect it from infection. No one seemed to think any differently of Tom. In fact, if anything, he became something of a hero. "One-eyed Tom", they called him, and Tom seemed pleased with the name and the attention.

By Christmas Carrie realized she was once again in the family way. When she told Tom one night after he came home late again, he simply nodded his head and began eating his supper. He didn't seem glad, nor did he seem mad. Carrie could have handled one or the other, but his indifference saddened her. It just didn't seem to matter to him.

This pregnancy wasn't as easy as her first one as Carrie was sick every morning when she awoke, and her energy just wasn't the same. She tried not to let it show when Tom was there. Mama and Nora came over to help her when they could and it was on one of those days that she overheard Nora talking to her mother.

"Why can't that lazy Tom Swank help out more around here? Carrie has far too much to do. No wonder she's tired all the time," Nora was saying.

"Now, Nora, that's not for us to say," replied Mama. "We'll just keep helping out all we can. The Good Book says not to judge."

"Well, it's hard not to judge when all you hear is talk of One-eyed Tom hanging around that old trollop, Lizzie Willis," stated Nora, with an angry shake to the sheet she was hanging on the line. "She's got five kids and not a one knows who its daddy is."

"Nora, that's gossip," warned Mama.

"Ben saw him at her house with his own eyes, Mama," argued Nora. "I don't think he was there sipping tea. Sally saw him, too, and she heard her folks talking and they said Tom was with her and showing off when he got his eye put out. Serves him right!"

"What does the Bible say about vengeance, Nora?" countered Mama.

With that Carrie went back into the bedroom to check on Luke. She just couldn't listen to anymore as tears streamed down her face.

Is it true? she asked herself. *Does Tom have another woman? Is he tired of me?*

As she changed Luke, defiant tears soaked her cheeks, but she briskly wiped them away so that Mama and Nora wouldn't know she had heard.

She was determined to confront Tom when he came home that evening, but for some reason Tom was in an unusually good mood. He even brought her some stick candy. Folks in the Appalachians didn't get store bought treats very often, and Carrie loved sweets. Not wanting to destroy this close family time, she just stowed away the questions, telling herself that Nora must have been wrong.

CHAPTER 4

Belinda Nora Swank was born at 9:25 P.M., August 6, 1905, with Mama Cynth again doing the birthing. Carrie had a whole new appreciation for Mama's midwife talent now. She knew it was a true gift God had given her and she was so proud of her mother. Belinda was a healthy baby, just as Luke had been, and Carrie was beholden to God for that.

Tom was right there waiting when the baby arrived. When he came into the room and looked at his baby daughter, Carrie could have sworn she saw a tear in his eye.

"She looks just like her pretty mother," he said to Carrie, smiling. What did you name her?"

"I named her Belinda Nora after my sister," replied Carrie. "Do you like it?"

"I reckon it's just fine," Tom answered, "but I think I'll call her Beanie." And that's what she was called by everyone from then on.

For a while Tom seemed his old self again. He came home on time, did a few more chores around the farm, and even took some time to play with Luke. Since he was doing more of the chores, Carrie had time to regain her strength and was soon back to normal. Tom even went to church with her a few Sundays. Lately he'd been talking about building onto their house. Two more bedrooms would make such a difference, and with his job on the railroad there was enough money to do it. He had even talked about an enclosed back porch with a system of water boxes in which water from the nearby stream would run into the house and then flow through concrete boxes or troughs. Not only would they have indoor water, but Carrie would have a way to keep her milk and butter cold without having to carry it to and from the old spring house down the hill. Tom talked with excitement about these ideas, an excitement he hadn't shown in months. Carrie would always remember it as a very special time in their marriage.

Carrie was thankful for Tom's job on the railroad. The pay was good and there was talk he might soon make section foreman. That would mean even more money. She was thankful Tom didn't work in the coal mines like so many of the men in the area. She watched them come home each night, so black all you could see was their eyes and even those were encrusted with the clinging black dust. What washings their wives must have! She noticed as the men walked with stooped shoulders and stiff knees from crawling in the mines to dig out the coal. Many of them had persistent coughs, and young men seemed old in no time. Carrie's brother Eb and her brothers-in-law, Reed and Henry were coal miners, and she saw what it was doing to them. Reed, just a young man, wheezed with every breath.

Tom could have worked at the Big Tree Lumber Company in Haymaker, the little town joining the Lacy Creek community. The "big men" from Pennsylvania had come down and opened the sawmill just a few years back, providing jobs for many men in the little Appalachian area and an alternative to hillside farming and mining. That's where two of Carrie's brothers and Nora's husband Ben worked. She could hear the whistle blow three times a day from the sawmill. It provided decent jobs for the community, but still it didn't pay as much as the railroad. Carrie's brother, Sile J. worked for a logging company that provided logs for the sawmill and it paid well but was a dangerous job. She heard frequently of men who were killed or maimed by trees falling on them.

Thanksgiving was coming up soon and Mama and Papa had invited them home for the Thanksgiving meal. Carrie, with some trepidation, decided to approach Tom about the matter.

"Tom," she began. "Mama and Papa have asked us to come over Thanksgiving Day for dinner. Do you think we can go?"

Tom's face clouded for a moment, but then he replied, "I reckon as to how we could make it. Then maybe that Sunday afternoon we could ride over to Mam and Pap's for the evening meal. Pap was just saying the other day they would like to see the grandbabies."

Carrie's mouth almost fell open, but she shook herself quickly. Tom seldom ever mentioned going to visit his folks. Carrie really liked his mother, Izzy, and his father, Charles, but for some reason, Tom just never wanted to visit. He still didn't get along with some of his siblings, although he and his sister Nannie were close. He hardly spoke of his brothers, Ort and Nate, and of his brother who lived over in Kentucky. Charles and Izzy went to the same Primitive Baptist church that Carrie attended, so she usually saw them there every other Sunday, as they were "No Hellers" also. In the little country church the "Hellers" held church one Sunday and the "No Hellers" the next Sunday. Mama said she was a "No Heller" because she believed one gets his hell here on earth and she had seen a many a people getting it.

"Why, I think that would be right fine, Tom," she offered enthusiastically. "I haven't seen your folks in a long time except at church, and I want Luke and Beanie to get to know them."

"Then I guess we got it all settled," said Tom, scooting over to give her a kiss, seemingly pleased with himself.

They welcomed Thanksgiving with beautiful weather, just warm enough to be outside some, yet cool enough to make it feel like fall of the year. Tom arose early that morning to do all of the outside chores while Carrie fixed breakfast, got the children ready and finished the food she was taking to Mama and Papa's. She was taking her rhubarb pies, one of Tom's favorites. By eleven o'clock they were ready to leave.

As usual, all of Carrie's siblings and their families were there. The grandchildren just seemed to grow in number and size every year. Eb and

Maggie had two and Maggie was expecting again. Lily and Reed were there with their two, but from what Carrie had heard they were having some marital problems, with Lily being the reason. She just couldn't seem to settle in to family life. Will and Sally had finally "got hitched", as Will put it, just two months ago, but her other two brothers still clung to their bacherlorhood.

"Ain't no woman gonna tie this man down," bragged Charles. "I like being free."

"That's cause no one will have the old clod hopper," teased Will, good naturedly.

The Thanksgiving meal began with a thank you to the good Lord from Papa Silas, followed by a chorus of "Amens". Then it was every man for himself as the food was passed around. Carrie didn't know which there was more of...eating or talking. Everyone seemed in such a jovial mood, and she noticed Tom talked and ate just as much as anyone. Carrie also noticed Papa and Mama as they seemed extra quiet, just enjoying the presence and good fellowship of their children and grandchildren.

"Thank you, dear God," she whispered silently, "for my sweet Papa and Mama."

After stomachs were full, everyone began to move outside to enjoy the beautiful sunny day. Luke and Beanie had fallen asleep during the meal, as had two other little ones, so they carried them all and laid them side by side on Mama and Papa's bed. Maggie carried little Molly to the rocking chair on the porch, hoping that soon she would also be napping.

The men soon began a game of horseshoes, but the women were content just to sit on the porch and visit, swapping recipes, stories of their children, and maybe just a little gossip. As Maggie rocked little Molly, three-year-old Tiny played at Mama Cynth's feet.

"I dearly love being a wife and mother," said Carrie, with a sigh of contentment.

"I'm finding it to be mighty satisfying myself," added Nora.

"Humph!" injected Lily. "If you ask me it's nothing but work, work, and more work!"

"But don't you just love having Tiny and James?" asked Carrie. "With children there's never a dull moment."

"Or a peaceful one," grumbled Lily.

"I guess I'll soon find out which one is right," announced Ellie. "Henry and I are going to have a little one come spring."

"Oh, praise God!" exclaimed Mama Cynth, clapping her hands. "Another precious grandchild!"

"Which do you want, Ellie, boy or girl?" asked Carrie.

"It don't really matter to me," replied Ellie, "but Henry's got his heart set on a boy."

"Well, I'm just glad it's you and not me," huffed Lily.

Nora and Carrie exchanged sad looks. They just didn't understand their sister.

Deciding to move to a lighter subject, Mama asked, "What patterns do you girls plan to use for your first quilt this season?"

For folks of the Appalachian Mountain region, quilting was a natural part of the winter season. While quilts were a necessity for cold drafty winters, the women took pride in their beautiful patterns and their tiny stitches. Poor people found beauty any way they could and were thankful when they found it.

"I have a new star pattern called the Bright Star," spoke up Nora. "I'm kind of anxious to try it. Ben's mother gave me the pattern and several swatches of her cloth to use in it. Maw Ramsey is so good to me."

"I have a new Dresden Plate pattern," offered Maggie. "It belonged to my Aunt Thelma, who gave it to my mother, and she gave it to me. It's just a bit smaller than the other Dresden Plate I have, and I thought it would look right nice on Molly's bed when she gets a little older. I'd be glad to make you all a pattern from it if you want."

"Oh, I'd love to have it," said Carrie. "I have a pattern called Polly's Pinwheel I'd like to try if I can get enough material. It calls for just three colors, so I'll have to have enough of each color. I've been thinking of looking at Berke's Mercantile to see what they have and if I can afford it. What about you, Mama? What are you going to try this year?"

"Well, I just might try a quilt or two for my oldest grandchildren. I thought this year I'd make one for Eb Jr. and one for Tiny. Maybe even one for Luke. Then, each year, one for the next oldest until I have a quilt for each of my precious babies. I just haven't decided which pattern I'll use."

"What about you, Lily?" asked Carrie. "Are you going to try a new pattern?"

"Girls, I'm just not into all of that quilting and sewing," stated Lily. "What's wrong with just going to the mercantile and buying some good sturdy blankets?"

"It's all about *joy*, Lily girl," answered Mama. "It's all about *joy*."

With this the subject ended. Carrie, Nora and Ellie rose from their chairs, stretched, and began to move toward the yard to watch the men playing horseshoes.

CHAPTER 5

At Christmas things were still going well between Tom and Carrie. Tom had made section foreman and had to be away from home overnight every now and then, but most of the time he was home right on time, helping with the chores and even playing some with the children. They all decorated a tree together and Carrie constantly made treats for them to enjoy in the evenings when the toils of the day wound down. Tom bought her a new butter churn for Christmas as well as a beautiful cameo brooch. There was a stuffed bear and clothes for Beanie and a rocking horse to thrill little Luke. Carrie had made Tom two new shirts and he seemed right pleased with them. It was a special time.

Christmas day was once more spent with Papa Silas and Mama Cynth. Everyone was there except Lily and Reed. Lily was again in the family way and not one bit happy about it, as she and Reed were still having marital problems. Reed worked in the coal mines and that didn't set well with Lily. She hated all of that dirty wash and she hated "tending to brats all day" as she told anyone who would listen. According to whispered information from Nora, Carrie learned that Reed had come home early a couple of times lately and discovered "gentlemen callers" in his home. He had ordered them to leave his home and never to come back, and he had also threatened to leave. Although Lily wasn't happy with her life, she certainly liked the paychecks Reed brought home, so it seems she was now on her best behavior.

"Oh, Nora," exclaimed Carrie. "Why can't she appreciate what she has? Reed works hard to provide and he seems like a good man."

"I've never understood our sister," replied Nora. "She's just never satisfied with what she has."

"I would never treat Tom like that," said Carrie. "He's been so good to me lately, and I cherish every moment we have together."

"He does seem more attentive," affirmed Nora. "I'm glad to see you happy and smiling, Carrie. I love what you and Tom have done to your home, and that system of water boxes is simply genius. I wish Ben would build one for us."

"It's really helped out with my work and in keeping my milk and butter cold," stated Carrie. "It's so nice not to have to make that trip down to the spring house with two little ones to tug along."

During the winter months Carrie and Tom talked about things they wanted to do to the house and farm. Tom planned for a front porch spanning the entire front of the house.

"We'll put banisters all around it and a gate at the top of the steps," said Tom. "That way Luke and Beanie can play out there while you enjoy some fresh air. Maybe we can even get you a rocking chair. How would you like that, Carrie?"

"Oh, I'd like it just fine, Tom," Carrie answered, tears of joy glistening in her eyes.

"Maybe we'll buy a couple of horses so I won't have to borrow Pap's or your Paw's," added Tom.

"Sounds good to me," said Carrie with a happy sigh. "I'm really looking forward to spring, Tom, with a garden and flowers. Spring is my favorite time of year."

And so the winter went. They were happy times for Carrie. Yet, as it is with life, happy times just never seem to last. There's always another trial over the next horizon, and so it was for Carrie.

By spring, Carrie and Nora acknowledged to each other that Mama Cynth was just not well. She always seemed tired, and her color was not good. She would leave to deliver a baby and come home so exhausted that she would have to take to her bed for a few days.

"The light has gone out in her eyes," sighed Nora. "Remember the spark that has always been there, Carrie? It's just not there anymore."

"I've tried to ask her about it," said Carrie, sighing, "but she just says warm weather will do her old bones a might of good."

"Papa Silas is worried, too," said Nora. "I can see it in his eyes when he looks at Mama."

"Perhaps we need to go over and help her out more," thought Carrie aloud. "I don't have a lot of time, but I'm sure Tom wouldn't mind me going once or twice a week. He loves Mama Cynth."

"I'll talk to Ben tonight," stated Nora. "I'm sure he won't mind either. Maybe seeing her grandbabies more often will help Mama."

That very night Carrie talked to Tom, but she was surprised to see the frown on his face.

"What about your own family, Carrie?" he asked gruffly. "Ain't we what you need to be thinking about?"

Fighting away tears, Carrie answered, "Oh, Tom, you know you and the children are the most important things in the world to me. I'll be taking Luke and Belinda with me and I'll be home in plenty of time to fix your supper. I just feel that Mama needs me, too."

"I can't come in after working all day and do all the chores," grumbled Tom, a pout on his face. "A man needs his woman home taking care of things."

"If you don't want me to go, then I won't, Tom," sighed Carrie.

Tom saw the sadness in Carrie's eyes. "Oh, go on," he said. "We'll try it once a week, but no more than that. I need a wife who's at home."

"I won't let things go down here, Tom. I promise," said Carrie quickly. "Thank you, Tom."

And thus began Carrie's life for the next months. She went over to help Mama Cynth every Tuesday and Nora helped on Friday. Some days Eb's wife Maggie went to help, but with her two little ones and the third due shortly, her help was limited. Will's wife Sally helped from time to time, but she, too, was in the family way and daily dealt with morning sickness. Ellie came sometimes, but she lived farther away than the rest and it was hard for her to get there, not to mention the fact that her baby was soon due. Lily, as usual, seemed to have no desire to contribute.

In May, Maggie gave birth to a fine baby boy and she now had her hands full at home. Later that month, Ellie and Henry welcomed a little girl into their home, and in June, Lily gave birth to another girl who Reed named Belle. Lily refused to name her and stated emphatically that there would be no more. By this time Mama Cynth spent most of her time in bed. On warm days Carrie and Nora tried to coax her to sit in her rocker on the front porch.

"I thank you, darling girl, for all you do," said Mama to Carrie one day, "but it just takes too much out of me to make the effort anymore. Your old mama won't be here much longer, Carrie, but don't you fret. I've got a mansion waiting in Glory. My Jesus said so."

"Now, Mama, don't you talk that way," gasped Carrie. "I know you're going to be well."

"No, sweet girl," whispered Mama. "God has other plans for me. Now you just be strong so I can be strong. Carrie, I need you to be especially strong for your Papa. Men don't handle things like dying very well and they don't show their feelings. They just hurt inside, and that's the worst kind of hurting. Me and your Papa have had a good, long, happy life together, and that's more than enough to thank the Good Lord for. Just be there for your Papa, Carrie, because he won't let you know how much he's hurting. Be strong for him."

"I will, Mama. I promise," said Carrie softly, placing her hand on her mother's cool, wrinkled old cheek.

"And Carrie," Mama continued, as though it must be said, despite her waning strength. "Carrie, you are a special young woman. Don't ever let anyone or anything make you think you're not. Forgiveness is good, but a woman needs to believe in herself...in her worth. God made you Carrie, and He made you special. Do you hear me, girl?"

"I hear you, Mama, and I promise to remember," answered Carrie, tears flowing unchecked down her cheeks.

With that, Mama Cynth drifted off to sleep. Carrie sat beside her bed, holding her frail little hand and pondering what Mama had said.

In July, Will's wife Sally gave birth to a son, William Silas.

In August, Mama Cynth passed away. Carrie remembered what Mama Cynth use to say, quoting from her Bible, *To everything there is a season...a time to be born and a time to die.* It was William's time to be born...it was Mama's time to die.

Carrie, Nora and Papa Silas had sat by her bed all night long, praying, yet knowing it was her time. The boys sat quietly on the front porch... waiting. At daybreak, Ellie and Henry came. Mama Cynth's breathing was uneven and, at times, raspy and labored. From time to time she would open her tired eyes and look at her family, her love for them shining forth like a noonday sun as her frail, limp little hand lay on her cherished Bible. She opened her eyes one last time and looked at her darling Silas.

"Been good," she whispered with her last breath.

"Yes, Cynthi," whispered Silas, tears meandering down his rough old cheeks, as he looked at the precious face now at rest. "It's shore been good."

With that, Papa stood. Weakly he walked over to the old clock and stopped its hands at 6:31 A.M. Sile J., who had been standing just inside the door, picked up the black cloth from the back of Mama's rocking chair and draped it over the mirror on the living room wall.

Papa walked from the house and toward the barn. No one followed him. This was his time and they would respect it.

It was a time of unfathomable sadness for Carrie. She had just lost her dearest friend. As she sat beside the bed, bereft of strength, she reflected on all the years she had been blessed to have her dear mother. Mama had taught her everything she knew. What would she do without dear Mama Cynth? Who would she talk to about things she couldn't share with anyone else? Most of all, who would birth this new life growing inside her that she hadn't even yet told Tom about?

One by one, the boys left. Eb went to fetch the neighboring women who always helped to prepare the body. Sile J. left half-heartedly to spread the word of Mama Cynth's death and to purchase a coffin. Charles walked up the hill to the little cemetery where he knew neighboring men would be coming soon, offering their help in digging the grave. Will fed Papa's livestock and then left to check on his wife and new baby.

By this time Lily had shown up and, with sad hearts and little talk, the girls began to prepare the house. It would be a busy place for the next few days, and Mama Cynth would want it sparkling clean...every nook, every piece of furniture, every dish, every board of the floors held memories of Mama. Even Lily seemed sad, and from time to time Carrie could swear there were tears in her eyes. They cleared out a place where the coffin would sit, and as he returned from his time in the barn, Papa brought the old sawhorses on which the coffin would be placed. All of the women of the small community would be bringing food throughout the day and for several days ahead, so the girls began clearing space for all of that. Everyone, far and wide, knew and loved Cynthia Ranes. She probably birthed half of them or more and kept a good number of them fed when they fell on hard times.

Two men showed up in their wagons with extra chairs, on loan from the neighbors, for many people would be "sittin'up" all night with the family tonight. They would extol the wonderful virtues of "Aunt Cynth", as they called her, and tell stories of her life as well as other stories of the hollows, while one or two of the women stood over the body and fanned it. It was a hot August day and it would be important to keep the body cool and the flies away. Besides, it made them feel they were contributing something during this sad time. The Appalachian folk might have disagreements from time to time, but they were fiercely loyal and inherently kind.

Within an hour, two neighbor ladies arrived to prepare the body. As she heard them pull in, Carrie went to the closet where Mama and Papa hung their meager wardrobe of clothes. She took down Mama's one good dress, a black one with the white lace collar. Oh, how many times she had seen her Mama wear that dress...to the Primitive Baptist meetings... to funerals...all kinds of special occasions. Mama looked beautiful in that dress, and now she would wear it one last time. Carrie held it to her face, feeling the nearness of her mother as her tears fell on the old cloth.

"Oh, Mama, I'm going to miss you so much," she whispered.

Her remembering and mourning were brought to an abrupt halt by the sound of a loud voice outside.

"Where's Carrie?" It was Tom's voice speaking to someone outside and he sounded very upset. Carrie placed the dress on the bed and hurried outside.

"Here I am, Tom," she called.

Tom came toward her, a scowl on his face. He was half leading, half dragging little Luke and carrying Beanie under his arm like a sack of potatoes.

"Have you forgotten where you live, woman?" he demanded loudly. "You've got a home and family, you know." With this he roughly deposited Beanie in her arms.

"I'm sorry, Tom. I left them with your sister Nannie. She said she didn't mind watching them for me," answered Carrie.

"Well, what are you doing over here so long?" growled Tom.

Carrie's face was beet red by now, as everyone could hear, although they were trying not to stare.

"Tom, Mama died just a little while ago," said Carrie, wiping her cheeks. "I've been sitting by her bedside until the Lord came for her."

Tom's faced blanched. "I didn't know."

"I told Nannie it was Mama's time. Didn't she tell you?" asked Carrie in a low voice.

"She just said you came over here to sit with your Maw. How was I to know?" pouted Tom. The wind had been knocked out of his sails and he was trying to recover without looking like the scoundrel that he was.

"I need to stay here for now, Tom," replied Carrie, straightening her shoulders and looking him in the eye, daring him to forbid it. "Just leave the little ones with me. I can mind them and do what needs to be done here."

With this she took Luke by the hand and walked toward the house, back straight and head held high. Tom stood watching her, knowing that all eyes were on him.

As Carrie walked into Mama Cynth's living room, Nora stood there, arms crossed.

"That man's got the devil in him, for sure. I declare, Carrie, I don't know how you put up with him. He thinks the world was made just for him."

"Not now, Nora," whispered Carrie. "We have too much to do to think about my life right now. We have to make things right for Mama."

"You always made things right for your Mama, Carrie," said Papa Silas. "She was always proud of you."

Carrie was taken by surprise. She had not realized Papa was standing in the doorway of the kitchen. Blood rose to her face, a declaration of the embarrassment she felt. She had talked many times with Mama Cynth about her life with Tom, but never once had she even hinted of the marital discord to her father. He knew, though. She could see it in his eyes.

A wagon pulling into the yard saved her from more explanation as neighbors had already begun to bring food. Carrie and Nora quickly made room for it and Tom was forgotten as thoughts returned to the business at hand.

Bessie Seavers and her daughter climbed down from their wagon and began to unload dishes of food. They knew Cynthia's body was not yet prepared, and out of courtesy for the family, they brought the food only to the doorway and handed it to Nora and Ellie.

"So sorry 'bout your Mama," said Bessie, with tears in her eyes. "She was a mighty fine woman. Birthed all six of my children. When Mary here was born, she stayed three days helping Joe and the little ones until I got back on my feet. A mighty fine Godly woman. Is there anything you need or that Mary and me can do?"

"Thank you, Bessie," answered Nora. "This is very kind of you. I think we have everything underway right now. I'm not thinking too clearly. We surely do thank both of you for all this food.

As the women climbed back into the wagon, Ellie and Nora carried the food to the table and covered it with a white cloth. Papa Silas had already taken Luke outside to play, and Beanie, thumb in mouth, was fast asleep on the rug near the hearth.

"Are you alright, Carrie?" whispered Nora.

"I'm fine," answered Carrie softly. "Thank you, sister. The main thing right now is to take care of the next few days. I'll think about Tom later, but right now he's just not important."

With this, they both went to work.

CHAPTER 6

The day of Mama Cynth's funeral was a beautiful sunny day, not too hot, not too humid as Tom, Carrie and the children arrived just past daybreak. Tom had been extra attentive and comforting since he had behaved so foolishly. He seemed to have the decency to at least be ashamed.

As Carrie climbed down from the old wagon, he held Beanie.

"I'll just hang onto the kids for awhile, Carrie, so you can help your Paw," he said.

"Thank you, Tom," she replied.

At that time Nora and Ben pulled into the yard also. She went straight to Carrie and the two clung together trying to sedate each other's sadness, but after a moment, each sister straightened her shoulders, put a smile on her face, and turned to face the day at hand. The other siblings were also arriving, and Nora and Carrie were determined to be strong for their sake.

The house and yard were full for the funeral. Brother Jonas from the Primitive Baptist Church in Haymaker presided over the service. As with the old Baptists of the time, the service was lengthy, leaving nothing unsaid, and some things repeated. Will's wife Sally, in her beautiful soprano voice, sang Mama Cynth's favorite song, *Rock of Ages*. Brother Jonas lined some of the old Baptist favorites as the folks joined in song. Mama Cynth loved good hymn singing, and though sad, it was also soothing to her family. Papa Silas sat with his head bowed, his hand on Cynthia's coffin.

After the funeral ended, the family and most of the friends and relatives walked up the hillside to the little cemetery at the top. There, near her mother and father and other relatives, Cynthia Ranes' body was laid to rest.

Tom carried Beanie and helped Carrie back down the hill. Little Luke walked with Tom's Mam and Pap. Sadness and fatigue prevailed as they made their way in silence. Back at the house neighboring women had set out a meal and were ready to serve. It was the custom for everyone to stay for a meal and fellowship with the family of the deceased.

The children ate quickly and began playing in the yard, forgetting sadness as children are blessed to do. The men gathered in the shade of the old sycamore tree to praise "Aunt Cynth" and to talk of others who were gone on to their heavenly reward. The women gathered in the many chairs on the front porch, sharing their sadness as women do with one another.

"Your Mama was one fine woman, girls," Bertha Reed declared, "one fine woman."

"She birthed more babies than you can shake a stick at," added another.

"And she didn't lose many of those babies she caught either. She sure knew her birthing," added another neighbor.

"That's because she always took the Good Lord with her when she went a-birthing," commented Mae Tyler. "Cynth always had the Good Lord right by her side."

Carrie loved listening to the women talk about her mother. She was so blessed to have had a mother like Mama Cynth...and to still have a father like Papa Silas. She glanced across the yard to see how Papa was holding up. He was surrounded by good neighbors who were trying to take his mind away from his sorrow.

It's good of them to try, she thought, with a sad smile, *but Papa's going to have sorrow for a long, long time.*

As the sun began to set, families took their leave, heading home to their farms and household chores. They had bid a loving farewell to a neighbor and friend, but now life must go on. Carrie's siblings also began to leave...first Lily and Reed, who had put aside their problems for the day, followed by Ellie and Henry, and then the boys and their families. Nora looked so sad and exhausted as she and Ben were loading their things into the wagon to take their leave.

"Carrie, I'll get over one day next week to check on Papa," she said. "Maybe you can come over that day, too."

"I'll sure try," replied Carrie. "We need to help Papa with the house."

Soon Tom and Carrie took their leave. Sile J. and Charles would be there with Papa Silas, so he would not be all alone. Yet, Carrie knew that he would be alone no matter how many people were around him. She looked back at her childhood home as they rode away, knowing it would never be the same again.

"Bye, Mama," she whispered one last time. "I'm sure gonna miss you."

In the weeks ahead Carrie and Nora went to Papa's once a week to help out with the cooking and cleaning. Tom had not objected, still ashamed of the way he had acted before. Sometimes Ellie joined them. No matter the sadness, no matter the pain, life has a way of continuing on its course. Carrie was having more difficulty with this pregnancy, and she looked forward to holding this new life growing inside of her.

In October Sile J. and Lula were married. They decided to live on with Papa Silas for awhile to take care of him. This would be a blessing because Lula was very good to Papa and every home needs a woman to care for it. Carrie and Nora would be free to take care of their own families, and this was good because Nora was also again in the family way. Charles had recently begun paying visits to Lucinda Banerd, the seventeen-year-old daughter of a merchant in Haymaker. Carrie and Nora liked her already and secretly were hoping they might soon have another sister-in-law.

It was a week before Thanksgiving, and Carrie was just sweeping the front porch when she saw Nora coming up the hill. She quickly set her broom aside and went to the gate to meet her sister.

"Nora, what on earth brings you out walking on this nippy day?" she asked.

"Whew, just let me catch my breath," gasped Nora.

The sisters walked up the steps to the front porch and sat in the rockers facing each other. Carrie could tell something was wrong.

"Oh, Carrie," cried Nora, "I just had to tell you what's happened with our sister. I'm so sad and, at the same time, mad and ashamed."

"I presume you mean Lily," replied Carrie. "She's the only one I know who can arouse such mixed emotions. What's she done now?"

"Reed has left her," declared Nora.

"Oh, no," gasped Carrie. "But then again, I'm not truly surprised."

"Well, the reason may not surprise you either," said Nora, fists clinched. "Reed came home unexpectedly and caught her with Bert Holson."

"What do you mean...caught her with Bert Holson?" asked Carrie.

"Sis, you know good and well what I mean," answered Nora. "Do I have to spell it out? They were where they shouldn't have been, doing what they shouldn't have been doing!"

"Oh, my dear heavenly Father," cried Carrie. "What has come over Lily?"

"The pure old devil, that's what," declared Nora. "Oh, thank God Mama is not here to see this. Lily's always been up to some kind of no good, but this is awful, even for her."

With this Nora pounded the banister in front of her.

"Now calm yourself, Nora," soothed Carrie. "You don't want to hurt the baby."

"I know, I know," replied Nora. "I'm just so upset with her."

"What did Reed do?" asked Carrie.

"Well, according to Ben, he just turned around and walked out, and no one has seen him since. He didn't even take his clothes, and that's been three days ago. Ben just heard about it yesterday from some men at the sawmill. I'm sure it's all over Haymaker and half the countryside by now. I don't know which I fill the strongest...sad, mad, or ashamed. I think I even fill a little murder in my heart."

"No, Nora," said Carrie, patting her sister's hand. "There's no murder in your beautiful heart."

When Tom came home that night Carrie determined to talk to him about Lily, but she knew it would be better to wait until supper was over and the children were in bed.

"Tom, have you heard any talk about Lily and Reed?" she asked quietly, later that night.

"Such as..." Tom replied.

"Well, Nora heard that Reed walked out and left Lily," responded Carrie.

"Ahh, he's a no-good anyway," sneered Tom.

"But had you heard about it?" continued Carrie.

"Yeah, woman, I heard about it. It's the talk all over," answered Tom, nonchalantly. "Lily's just as well off."

"But Tom...Reed caught her with another man in a...well a...well, doing something she shouldn't have been doing," said Carrie, her voice quivering.

"Listen, Carrie Tan," replied Tom. "Lily has her ways and you have yours. According to that fine, upstanding church you like to go to, it ain't your place to judge her. Now can't a man have a little peace after a hard day's work?"

With that, Carrie knew the matter was closed. Yet, she just could not understand Tom's attitude. It was almost like he was taking up for Lily. He didn't seem to see anything wrong with her behavior. Carrie was confused, and yes, a little hurt by Tom's reaction.

Thanksgiving of 1906 came and went. They gathered again at Papa Silas' house, and it was a good family get-together, but it was just not the same without Mama Cynth. Sile J. and Lula were taking really good care of Papa. The house was clean as a whistle, Lula was a good cook and Papa's clothes were clean. Carrie was thankful for all of that...yet she missed Mama. Charles and Lucinda were there with the announcement they would wed before Christmas, bringing joy to everyone's heart, as they all loved Lucinda. Carrie's other siblings were there with their families. Ellie's husband Henry was limping from a recent accident in the mines. The only one absent was Lily. Reed had still not returned and no one knew his whereabouts. Rumor was that Bert Holson was spending quite a bit of time there, as was Dent Tyler, Reed's cousin.

Carrie looked forward to Christmas, but, at the same time, dreaded it. Change was always difficult for her, but the change of being without Mama was almost more than she could bear. She was determined, however, to make it a special Christmas for Tom, Luke, and Belinda. Remembering her own childhood Christmases, Carrie wanted to make wonderful memories for her children.

Tom had been rather distant and irritable lately. Why? Carrie just didn't know. She tried to tell herself it was his job, but was not convinced. He did his chores at home but seldom gave any attention to his children, and Luke especially seemed to miss having his Paw play with him. Carrie tried to compensate, but with the household chores and the pregnancy she had very little time or energy.

Seeing her sister in deep thought one day as she was visiting, Nora asked, "Carrie, is everything okay with you and Tom?"

"Why, why sure," stammered Carrie.

"You seem sad lately," replied Nora, "and Luke said his Paw doesn't play with him anymore. What's happened?"

"Nothing I can put my mind to," answered Carrie. "I think he's just tired from his job and his chores here at home. He won't tell me anything."

"Carrie, I don't want to nose into your business, but you're my sister and I love you," said Nora cautiously.

"What are you trying to tell me, Nora?" asked Carrie, a gray cloud enveloping her eyes.

"Well, it may just be rumor...no, no it's not rumor. Well, here it is, Carrie. Ben has seen Tom at Lily's house several times lately. Did you know about it?"

Carrie paled and reached for the back of the wooden kitchen chair. "No. No. Tom has never mentioned stopping by Lily's," she said almost inaudibly. She sat down quickly in the chair.

"I'm so sorry to upset you like this, Carrie," said Nora, taking her sister's hand, "but I feel that you should know."

"What does Ben say about it?" questioned Carrie.

Nora paled and did not answer.

"Tell me the truth, Nora," said Carrie.

"Ben confronted Tom about it, Carrie, right in front of Lily's house," responded Nora. "Tom told him to mind his own business. Lily was there right beside of Tom at the front gate. She told Ben anytime he wanted to pay her a visit she would make it worth his while."

Putting her hand to her face, Carrie let out a moan. Nora quickly knelt down and put her arms around her.

"I hate to cause you pain, Sister," she said.

"It's not you causing the pain," cried Carrie, through gritted teeth. "I don't understand Tom, and I certainly don't understand that Jezebel sister of ours. She doesn't care who she hurts. I don't think she has a heart. Nora, you are so blessed to have a good man like Ben Ramsy."

After Nora left, Carrie sat for a long time just staring into space. She was brought back from her dark thoughts by the sound of Belinda's voice.

"Maw, I'm hungry," she said softly.

Pulling her into her lap and hugging her, Carrie answered, "I'm sure you are, my precious. Let's see if we might just find you a molasses cookie to satisfy you until supper."

Carrie knew she had to put thoughts of Tom and Lily out of her mind for now to take care of her children and see to her household chores. They were more important right now.

The holidays were upon them before Carrie could catch her breath, but she did all that she could to make it a special time for her family. Tom seemed more like himself again, but an uneasiness still lingered inside of Carrie. He bought her a new sewing machine for Christmas, something very few women in this little area could boast of. He also bought her a new pair of gloves and she was delighted with both gifts. He bought a toy rifle for Luke and a beautiful doll and new mittens for Beanie. He even bought a blue and pink blanket for their unborn child, the first real interest he had shown in it. On Christmas morning he played with both children as Carrie fixed breakfast and cleaned up the Christmas wrappings. The laughter of their children warmed Carrie's heart.

Later, when they went to Papa Silas' house, Tom was more sociable with her family than he had been in a long time. Carrie was thankful that, once again, Lily did not join the family. She did, however, wonder about Tiny, James and little Belle. Was Lily taking good care of them? How were they getting along financially?

Maybe Ben was wrong, considered Carrie. Yet the thought did little to ease her doubt.

Carrie had not questioned Tom about the things Nora had told her. She just couldn't bring herself to mention it. Maybe it was easier just not knowing.

CHAPTER 7

On a cold snowy day in March, Carrie went in to labor. Having been through this twice already, she immediately recognized the situation. It was ten o'clock in the morning and Tom had long ago left for work. She was alone with Luke and Beanie, and although she did not panic, Carrie knew she had to come up with a plan. The baby would most likely not hold off until Tom got home from work. How would she get word to someone?

She walked out onto the snow encrusted front porch, where she could see for a great distance. There was no one in sight. By noon Carrie knew she had to do something soon. The pains were stronger and coming more often. She began to bundle up Luke and Beanie in their winter coats. Somehow she would have to walk to the bottom of the hill and then to the Malerds, the nearest neighbors. Just as she was buttoning the last button on Beanie's coat, a powerful pain overtook her. She cried out, scaring Beanie, and the little one began to cry.

Oh, dear Jesus, I need your help in a most powerful way, prayed Carrie silently. *Please give me strength and don't let anything happen to this unborn baby or the two you've entrusted to me. Keep them safe, dear Jesus.*

With this she opened the door and stepped again onto the snow laden porch, one child on each side of her. She was just about to step onto the top step, when she heard a voice.

"Carrie, wait!" someone called.

Carrie squinted in the bright snowy light to see what help the Lord might have sent. It was Nora's husband, Ben.

I praise you and thank you, dear Lord, she whispered.

Ben was coming up the steps.

"Carrie, is it your time?" he queried.

"Yes, Ben, and I think this baby is in a hurry," she answered.

"Nora has been anxious about you all morning and couldn't find any peace until I told her I would come check on you," said Ben. "Go back into the house and I'll go get Widow Thomas. I promise I'll hurry."

Carrie thankfully led the two little ones back into the house and took off their coats and scarves. The pains were coming more quickly.

Lord, you said you would never leave us or forsake us, again she silently prayed, *so I place it all in your capable hands and I'm trusting in your word.*

With this, a peace came over Carrie as she found toys to occupy the children. Within twenty minutes Ben was back with Widow Thomas and her daughter Eliza.

"Carrie, I'll just put their coats back on and take the kids to our house," said Ben. "We'll take good care of them."

Reaching for their coats, he said, "Hey, you two, Leona needs some playmates today. Want to go over to play with her for awhile?"

"Yes! Yes!" they chorused. Then remembering their manners, they turned to Carrie. "Can we go, Maw?"

"I think that's a wonderful idea," she laughed. "Bless you, Ben. God truly sent you here today."

"God and Nora," laughed Ben, as he walked out the door carrying Beanie and leading Luke.

Ady Rose Swank arrived that afternoon at two twenty-five. Widow Thomas hadn't arrived a moment too soon. Carrie was thankful for her birthing help, but a tear ran down her cheek when she remembered the other two births with Mama there beside her.

Widow Thomas noticed Carrie's teary face.

"Missing your Mama, Carrie?" she asked, with understanding eyes.

Carrie nodded. "I'm so grateful, Mrs. Thomas, but I do miss Mama."

"That's understandable, deary. No one can take the place of our Mamas," replied the Widow. "You just have yourself a good cry and then enjoy that new life God just gave you. She's a mite small and will need plenty of loving care, but she'll be fine.

"Thank you, Mrs. Thomas," whispered Carrie as she drifted into a few moments of sleep.

Carrie awoke a short time later as Eliza laid baby Ady in her arms.

"Maw says she needs to nuzzle," said Eliza quietly.

Carrie nestled little Ady Rose in her arms, smelling her sweetness as Eliza left them alone.

"I wonder what your daddy will think of you, my precious," whispered Carrie. "I hope he will love you as I do, and I especially pray that our family can be happy. Seems like our happiness just comes and goes anymore. That's not what I want for you, little one. That's not what I want for any of us. Oh, Mama, how I need you."

A short time, later, Widow Thomas came into the room.

"Ben sent word that the children can stay overnight with him and Nora," she informed Carrie. "I have to go home to fix my boy Rollen's supper now, but Eliza will be staying with you until Tom gets home. If you need me for anything, she can fetch me right quick."

"I do thank you, Mrs. Thomas," said Carrie. "God sent you just in time. In fact, God has sent two people just in time today."

By five o'clock Tom still wasn't home and Carrie was beginning to feel anxious.

"Eliza, I'm so sorry to keep you," she said. "Tom should be here soon. The animals have to be fed and Old Betsy has to be milked."

"Don't you worry, Miss Carrie," replied Eliza. "I'm just going to go right now and milk for you. If he's not here by the time I finish, I'll go ahead and do the feeding. I've already got beans on a warming and cornbread in the oven. Now you just rest."

"Bless you, Eliza," responded Carrie, tiredly brushing a strand of hair from her pallid face. Despite her happiness with little Ady Rose, she felt a tiredness and loneliness clear to the inner depth of her body, not to mention a gnawing uneasiness that she just couldn't explain.

It was almost eight o'clock by the time Tom arrived home. Eliza was cleaning up in the kitchen when he walked in. A look of surprise immediately showed on his face.

"Is something wrong with Carrie?" he asked.

"She's doing just fine now, and you've got yourself a fine new baby girl," answered Eliza. "She seemed to be in a hurry to get here. Now I'll just mosey on home and let you take over here. Luke and Beanie are staying with Ben and Nora for the night and your supper is in the oven. The cows have been milked and the animals are all fed."

"Th-thank you," stammered Tom, not knowing just what else to say.

Eliza took her leave and Tom walked toward the bedroom.

"Carrie," he whispered, unsure if she was awake.

"I'm awake, Tom," answered Carrie. "Come meet your daughter, Ady Rose."

Tom peeped in at the baby.

"Are you alright, Carrie?" he asked quietly. "Did you have a hard time?"

"Not so hard," responded Carrie. "This little girl just got in a hurry. She's small, but Widow Thomas says she seems to be healthy enough. I was worried about you, Tom."

"Just had to work over a little," replied Tom, avoiding her eyes. "Think I'll go eat a bite of supper now."

With that he turned and walked out the bedroom door.

"Well, I guess that's that," whispered Carrie to little Ady Rose. "Happiness comes and goes."

The next morning Tom was out and gone by five o'clock without a word of concern or an offer to stay home and help. Carrie awoke again at six. She slowly, and somewhat painfully, maneuvered her way out of bed. The pain in her body was not nearly as bad as the pain in her heart.

Tom just didn't seem to care about his new daughter, she thought to herself. *Nor did he take much thought to me.*

She made her way to the kitchen, knowing Luke and Beanie would soon be awake and hungry. Then she remembered, as though in a fog, that her children were with Nora. No sooner had she lit the oil lamp in the kitchen than she heard a knock at the door.

"Miss Carrie," said Eliza quietly, "Momma saw Tom leave out this morning and she sent me over to help out today. She says you need at least this one day in bed. Now you scat back to that warm bed and I'll take care of breakfast. But first, I'll see if our new little girl needs a dry diaper."

"I-I don't know how to thank you," said Carrie, tearfully.

"No thanks needed. Now scat with you," answered Eliza with a sweeping motion.

After Eliza changed Ady, Carrie fed her. The next thing she knew it was eleven o'clock and there were voices in the kitchen. She arose slowly, put on her old shabby robe and made her way to the kitchen.

"Sister, are you okay?" asked Nora, with a worried look on her face.

"I'm fine, Nora. Eliza and her mother have taken real good care of me, and it was so good of you and Ben to take the children. Where are they?"

"They're still at my house," replied Nora. "Sally and little Will came over to stay with them while I came to check on you. We'd like them to stay one more night if that's okay with you. Widow Thomas says you could use some mending time."

"Oh, I'll be fit as a fiddle in no time, Sister Dear," said Carrie. "It would be a blessing though if you could keep Luke and Belinda one more night. Seems like I'm just tired to the bone."

"Did Tom finally make it home?" questioned Nora in a disgusted tone.

"He got here about eight," replied Carrie. "Said he had to work over. I was just too tired to care."

"He oughta be here with you today," grumbled Nora. "I'd like to take a stick to that man sometimes."

Carrie, eyes fixed on the table, made no reply.

After staying just a while longer, Nora took her leave, promising to bring the children home the next morning.

"I'll stay part of the day with you, too, just to make sure you are back on your feet and doing okay," promised Nora. "Now, back to bed with you!"

"Come on Miss Carrie," urged Eliza. "Miss Nora is right and we're gonna let her be the boss today. You need all the rest you can get. I'm fixing supper so you don't need to think about anything except feeding little Ady Rose and getting your strength back.

Tom did make it home by five thirty that afternoon. He seemed more himself as he came into the bedroom to check on Carrie.

"You okay?" he asked gently.

"I'm doing alright," Carrie answered. "I slept most of the day. Don't know what's come over me. I didn't act like this with the other two."

"Maybe we'd best wait awhile before having more young'uns," said Tom. "I'm going to eat a bite and then milk and feed. Do you need anything before I go?"

Just then there was a light knock on the bedroom door.

"Miss Carrie?" called Eliza in a quiet voice.

"Come on in, Eliza," answered Carrie.

"I brought you something in here to eat so you won't have to get out of bed. You haven't eaten much of anything today and you need to get your strength back so you can take care of them three precious little ones. I've got Mr. Tom's supper on the table, and now I'll be running home."

"How can I ever repay you, Eliza?" asked Carrie. "I don't know what I would have done without you and your mother. God surely has blessed me with good neighbors like you."

"I'll be back to check on you in the morning," replied Eliza, "and I'll stay until Miss Nora gets here. Bet I know two little ones who will be glad to see their Mama."

As she left the room, Tom rose from the side of the bed.

"So I guess the nosy sister will be coming tomorrow," he growled in a low voice.

"She'll be bringing our children back that she's been tending to," replied Carrie, making no attempt to hide her irritation.

"Back where they belong," replied Tom. "They should have been back already."

"And who would have taken care of them? You, Tom?" questioned Carrie, looking him in the eye.

Without an answer, Tom strode from the room and Carrie didn't see him again until he turned in for the night. He was gone again the next morning without a word.

The next weeks and months took on a pattern. Tom left early and came home late. He ate, did chores, slept, and left again. He had very few words for Carrie and no time for the children. Nora came by frequently with little Leona, helping with Carrie's three and just spending time with her sister. Her baby was due in mid June.

On one of her visits, Nora seemed extra happy. "I have some good news, Sister," she said.

"Well, tell me. Don't keep me waiting," urged Carrie.

"Our sister Ellie is also going to have another little one. It's due this October.

"Wouldn't Mama be so happy," sighed Carrie. "She did love her grandbabies."

"This will be good for Papa Silas," said Nora. "Sile J. says he is having a hard time without Mama. Maybe new grandbabies will cheer him up."

"I don't mean to change the subject, but have you heard anything of Lily recently?" questioned Carrie.

"Nothing good," Nora answered. "With our sister it's never anything good. Mama would turn over in her grave at that girl's shenanigans."

"What is it now?" asked Carrie.

"Well, Ben says Dent Tyler has moved in with her," whispered Nora. "On weekends they throw a party and everyone there drinks heavily, including Lily."

"Oh, no," gasped Carrie. "How can she do that? What about her children, Nora? Who takes care of them?"

"That's the worst of it," answered Nora. "The children are right there in the middle of it. I've heard the neighbors have been threatening to go to the sheriff about it all."

"Oh, Nora," cried Carrie. "I can't tell you I like our sister much. I'd be a hypocrite to say that. But I do pray for her, and I do pray for those three innocent little babies and even for Reed, wherever he is."

"Better make those prayers for four innocent babies," said Nora.

"What do you mean?" asked Carrie.

"I saw Lily at the mercantile last week," answered Nora. "I'm pretty certain she's in the family way again."

"Oh, dear Jesus, have mercy on our sister," gasped Carrie, "but keep those babies especially in your loving care."

CHAPTER 8

By early June Carrie had regained her strength and, though still tiny for her age, Ady Rose seemed to be healthy. She still wasn't sleeping through the night and Carrie was up with her a lot, trying to make sure Tom wasn't awakened. The week before, Nora had given birth to a little boy, so this put a stop to visits from Nora for awhile and Carrie really missed her sister.

It was a warm, sunny, "just right" day and Carrie had finished the breakfast dishes, dressed the children, and settled down with them on the front porch. Luke and Beanie were playing with some old wood blocks and Ady Rose was fast asleep in her cradle. Carrie was relaxing in her rocker with some mending when she heard the sound of a siren. At first she thought it might be from the sawmill, but soon realized it was much too loud and continuous and not the right time for the sawmill whistle. She saw the neighbors down the hill come out in their yards looking all around. The siren continued on and on...until it suddenly dawned on Carrie just what it was.

"Oh, no," she cried, wrapping both arms around herself, feeling a deepening chill on this warm June day. "It's the siren from the mines. Something has happened."

A wagon stopped in front of the house of her neighbors, Harold and Nancy Moser. She watched as Harold and Nancy went over to the wagon to talk. Other neighbors, including Widow Thomas and Eliza came running over to the wagon. She shivered as Widow Thomas began to scream. The wagon drove away as Eliza led her weeping mother back toward their little house. Harold, Nancy, and the others remained in the yard talking.

Able to stand it no longer, Carrie walked down the steps of her porch, closing the little gate behind her. She walked part way down the hill and called down to the neighbors.

"Nancy, Harold, what's happened?"

Harold left the others and walked quickly up the hill so Carrie wouldn't have to go farther from her children.

"It seems there's been a cave-in at the mine, Carrie," he said, gasping for air after the swift climb up the hill. "They say several men are trapped."

"Oh, no," cried Carrie. "Do they know who is trapped, Harold?"

"I haven't heard any names yet," he replied, shaking his head.

"Will you let me know when you hear more, Harold?" asked Carrie. "I have to get back to the babies."

"I sure will, Carrie," Harold assured her. "In the meantime, just pray for whoever may be trapped. I know you're a praying woman."

"God is our refuge, Harold. He is my refuge on a daily basis, and he'll see us all through this," answered Carrie. "I will most assuredly be praying. So many of our neighbors work in the mines. Ellie's husband Henry is off this week because his father is real sick and he's helping his mother, but I'm pretty sure my brother Eb is working today. I don't know what Maggie and the children would do if anything happened to him, and yet I know it would be just as bad for our neighbors to lose someone. I'd best not be borrowing trouble, though."

"You're a good woman, Carrie...just like your mother." With that Harold set off back down the hill.

Carrie spent most of the morning on the front porch, leaving only to get snacks for the children. She had many chores to do, but she just couldn't seem to do them. People walking, riding horses, or in farm wagons, continuously made their way toward the town of Haymaker. The siren had long since stopped, but the sound still resonated in Carrie's ears. As she rocked or played with the children, she constantly prayed for the men trapped and those who would be trying to rescue them. She prayed for the families waiting to hear news of their loved ones.

By noon she had to go in to fix the children some lunch and put them down for a nap. She had just fed Ady Rose and put her down with the other sleeping little ones when she heard a light knock at the door.

As she walked toward the screen door, she was surprised to see Papa Silas standing there.

"Papa!" she exclaimed. "It's so good to see you. Are you alright?"

"I'm alright, Carrie Tan," he assured her. "Have you heard about the mine cave-in?"

"Yes, Papa," she replied. "Oh, Papa, are you bringing bad news?"

"Eb is one of the men trapped, Carrie," replied Papa, wiping a tear from his old wrinkled cheek. "I knew you wouldn't have any way of knowing about it, so I rode the old mule over to tell you. I stopped by on the way to tell Nora."

"Can you stay with me a while, Papa?" asked Carrie.

Seeing the plea in her eyes, he answered, "Of course I can, girl. What's a Papa for anyway?"

"Let's go sit on the porch, Papa," said Carrie, feeling an extreme relief wash over her. "I can hear the children if they wake up but I think they'll sleep for awhile."

By four o'clock there was still no news. Carrie had spent a soul-quenching afternoon with her father, talking about the cave-in, about Mama, and even about Tom. Papa knew more about Tom's ways and their problems than Carrie had ever imagined.

"I don't know what gets in to some men," declared Papa. "They have everything anyone could want, and they just ain't never satisfied. Don't know where Tom gets his ways from. He's got a good Maw and Paw, and his brothers and sister are good family folks. I just don't understand him. But then, your Mama was the salt of the earth, and look how our Lily has turned out. I just don't understand."

"It's not all bad, Papa," said Carrie. "We have our good times, too."

"That's not enough, Carrie my girl," he replied. "The Good Book says a man is to love his wife just like Christ loved the church. Good times now and then is not what the Good Book was talking about. Your Mama and

I had a marriage like God intended a man and woman to have, and that's what I wanted for my children."

Their conversation was interrupted as they saw Nora's husband Ben coming up the hill at a fast pace. Carrie's heart did a tremendous lurch as she gripped the arms of the rocking chair and looked over to see that the children were occupied. As Ben neared the yard, Papa Silas arose from his chair, but Carrie could not find the strength to get up from the rocker.

"Hey, Silas!" Ben called. "Didn't know you'd be here. I came by because I knew Carrie would be worried about all the goings-on."

"Is it bad, son?" questioned Silas, his voice quivering in spite of all he could do.

"I don't know all of it yet," replied Ben. "I did find out that Eb is okay. He made it out with just a broken arm. Maggie was at the opening of the mine with the other families and he went on home with her after Doc Whitt set his arm."

"Praise God!" said Silas as he sat back down in his chair. "Come on up Ben and rest yourself a spell. Have you told Nora yet?"

"No, I'm just on my way, and I knew Nora would want me to stop by and ease Carrie's mind," answered Ben. "I really need to get on home, but I will sit long enough to catch my breath."

As she finally found her voice, Carrie asked, "Ben, what about the others? Do you know anything?"

"Not much, Carrie," he sighed. "I know Widow Thomas' son, Rollen, is alive but has a broken leg and some broken ribs. They took him on over to Doc Whitt's. Corb Tyler is alive, but just barely. Don't know if he will make it or not. They're still digging for the others, and they're a mite sure there's about six others still in there."

"Those poor men," said Carrie, "and their families. We need to pray powerfully for them."

"Well, I'd best be getting on home to Nora," said Ben. "With the little one just here, she's got enough without extra worry."

"Carrie girl, I'd best be getting on, too," said Papa Silas, rising from his chair. "I don't want to worry Sile J. and Lula. It's not for me to tell, but Lula just found out she's in the family way. Now don't you let on that I told you."

"Oh, Papa!" squealed Carrie. "That's just the kind of news I needed to take the edge off this day. I'm so happy for them, and I'll keep your secret. Papa, you're going to have more grandchildren than you ever imagined."

"Can't think of anything I'd like more," declared Papa.

After goodbyes from the children, he and Ben took their leave.

At six o'clock Tom had still not made it home, so Carrie fed the children and took all three of them with her to the barn. She made a little play area for them, placed Ady Rose on a blanket, and then set to milking. She needed something to keep her busy, and there was just no telling when Tom would find his way home. He most likely was at the mine, waiting for word.

After milking, she carried the milk bucket in one hand as she carried Ady Rose in her other arm. Beanie walked beside her mother with one hand clutching Carrie's dress as Carrie had taught her to do and Luke walked on the other side of Beanie holding her hand. He was such a good big brother and was becoming a big help to his mother.

At seven thirty that evening there was a knock at the door. When Carrie answered, Eliza Thomas stood waiting, her forehead wrinkled in worry.

"Miss Carrie, Mama sent me to check on you. We hadn't seen Tom come home and we just wanted to see if you needed anything," said Eliza.

"Oh, Eliza, you and your mother are so thoughtful," declared Carrie, with a catch in her voice. "I could use one favor. I've already milked, but could you watch the children while I run and feed. I just don't know when Tom will get here."

"I'd be most glad to," responded Eliza emphatically. "I always love being with these three little angels."

Carrie went to feed, so thankful that Eliza had shown up. *God always provides*, she thought with a sigh.

It took her only a short time, but it was something she could not have done with the three little ones, and Carrie would never leave them for that long, feeding or no feeding. She returned to find Eliza with both Luke and Beanie on her lap and baby Ady in her cradle as she told them a story that certainly kept their attention. Carrie looked on with a smile.

"Eliza, you are so good with children," she said. "I hope someday you will have some of your very own. By the way, how is Rollen?"

"He's doing just fine," answered Eliza. "We are just thankful to the Good Lord for watching over him. We just heard a few minutes ago that two other men were brought out of the mine. They didn't make it, Miss Carrie."

"I'm so sorry," sighed Carrie. "Did your family know them, Eliza?"

"Mama and me didn't, but Rollen did," replied Eliza. "He said one was just nineteen years old and still lived with his folks over in Roan Junction, but the other one had a wife and four little children. Whatever will they do?"

"Are there still some men trapped?" asked Carrie.

"We don't know for sure," Eliza answered. "They say there's still three that they can't count for. Well, I'd best be going. Mama is still a little shaken by all of this."

"I surely do thank you, Eliza, and thank your mother, too," said Carrie.

It was eight thirty when Tom finally came home. All three children were fast asleep, but Carrie just couldn't seem to find comfort in anything she did. Her heart ached for those who had lost loved ones.

"Tom, are you okay?" Carrie asked.

"I'm tired to the core, Carrie," he answered. "I'm as hungry as a bear, but I don't know if I have the energy to eat."

"Just sit down and I'll bring you a plate. You need to eat," coaxed Carrie.

"It's been a bad day, Carrie Tan," said Tom quietly. Carrie felt her heart jump a bit as he used the name Mama Cynth had always called her.

"We just never know when it's going to be our time," said Tom. "Makes you think about your life, Carrie. It sure does make you think."

"Do you know if all of the men have been found, Tom?" inquired Carrie.

"They brought the last three out awhile ago," he replied. "All three were dead. Do you remember Ned Haynes' boy, Arvil? He was killed. Left a wife and three little girls. Do you remember Sam Karvey that married Alice Wheaton? Alice is expecting a baby any day now."

Tom paused for a minute, swallowing as though a big lump was lodged in his throat.

Carrie spoke. “You said three men, Tom. Who was the third man?”

“The last one brought out was my brother Ort, Carrie,” he rasped.

With that, Tom laid his head down on the table and Carrie watched as his shoulders shook.

“Tom, I’m so sorry,” Carrie whispered. She put both arms around him as she leaned down against his back. Sorrow swept over her entire body, squeezing her heart like a wood vice...sorrow for Tom and Tom’s folks, and for Ort’s wife and two children.

CHAPTER 9

The following week was filled with funerals and sadness. In all, six men were dead. Corb Tyler had died three hours after they brought him out of the mine. Everyone seemed in a daze, as each had been touched by the horrible cave-in, whether through family or just as a neighbor. Hearts ached for the families and fear grappled within those who had husbands, fathers, sons or brothers who would soon be going back into area mines to work... going in and maybe never coming out. It was a fear mining families lived with day in and day out, but a tragedy like this ignited that fear, choking them in its intensity.

Ort's death had hit Tom hard. He talked to Carrie in a way he hadn't talked in a long time.

"You just never know, do you?" he said to her. "You just don't know when you walk out the door if you'll ever walk back in again."

Carrie said nothing, but simply held Tom's hand. He needed to talk and she was ready to listen.

"I should have made up the differences between me and Ort, Carrie," he went on. "Now it's too late, and to beat it all, I don't even know what our differences were. Mam and Pap are gonna have a hard time with this, not to mention Betts and the two little ones."

"The Lord will see them through, Tom," said Carrie soothingly.

"I think I'll go over to Mam and Pap's today and see if there's anything I can do to help," said Tom. "Do you mind, Carrie?"

"Of course I don't mind, Tom," Carrie assured him. "I put a cake in the oven this morning and just as soon as it cools, I'll put the icing on and you can take it over to them."

"You're a good, caring woman, Carrie," stated Tom, with tears in his eyes. "I don't deserve a woman like you."

With that, Tom made his way to the door and out to do the chores. Carrie stood with her hand to her chest as tears ran unhampered down her face.

Tom returned from his Mam and Pap's in a somber mood. Carrie had just never seen him look so forlorn as he walked back toward their home. She went out to the porch to meet him.

"Come sit on the porch with me, Carrie Tan," he said, falling into his rocker with a sigh as though he couldn't go another step.

"Are your folks getting' on, Tom?" Carrie asked quietly.

"No, I can't say they are," he replied. "Mam has taken to her bed and Pap says she ain't quit crying since they brought her the news. She couldn't even talk to me, Carrie."

Tears rolled down Tom's cheeks as he wiped at them with the back of his hand.

"Pap says Betts and the two little ones have gone to stay with Betts' maw and pa. Betts is in a bad way and just can't take care of the children by herself. They won't even remember their paw, Carrie, being just mites."

Again Carrie simply sat and listened, allowing Tom this time to talk and release the awful hurt gnawing at his insides.

He continued on, "Pap talked about what a good man Ort was, Carrie. He said he was a fine son and a good husband and father. He talked about how Ort worked in the mines all day, came home and did his chores, and still helped Betts with the children."

Carrie continued to sit quietly, rubbing Tom's hand.

"It's true, Carrie. Ort was a good man. I just wonder what Pap would say if it had been me. I wonder what anyone would say. The truth is, I ain't been a good nothing. I ain't been a good son. I pert near never go see Mam and Pap, and I don't even talk to my brothers. I ain't a good husband. God knows I ain't, Carrie. I ain't a good Paw. Some days I don't even see my own children."

"Don't take on so, Tom," said Carrie, taking his hand in both of hers. She couldn't deny the truth of Tom's words, but it broke her heart to see him in such a bad way.

Tom began to speak again. "Carrie, if you'll just give me a chance, I promise things around here will be better. I'll be a better husband and father, and I intend to be a better son. I'll spend more time with you and the young'uns, and I'll go see Mam and Pap more. I'm even going to see Nate and have a talk with him. We shouldn't be having hard feelings between us."

"I think that's a fine idea, Tom," Carrie said, her voice loving and soothing. "The kids and I will love seeing more of you, and I know your Mam and Pap would welcome more visits from you and from their grandbabies. Things will be okay, Tom."

"We need to get this farm in better shape," continued Tom, as though just talking and planning erased some of the pain he felt. I'm going to build you a new chicken coup and get you them new chickens you been wanting. We could use some more. The house needs some work done, too, and we'll just do it. What do you say we take the kids into town and get them some new clothes this weekend, Carrie? How does that sound?"

"That sounds right good," she replied, tears meandering down her cheeks.

"Then how about if we go see Mam and Pap this Sunday?" he asked. "Seeing them grandbabies might just be the tonic Mam needs to get her out of bed."

"That's a good idea," Carrie answered. "Maybe I'll make a couple of pies and take over, or maybe I'll even take some fried chicken. I'm sure your mother isn't up to cooking.

In the next weeks and even months, Tom seemed determined to keep his word. He was home each evening by five thirty, came in, set his lunch bucket down, hugged Carrie, and spent about thirty minutes having fun with the children. Then he went outside to do his chores, even taking Luke with him much of the time. When his outside chores were done, Carrie had supper on the table. Supper had become a special time, with Tom poking fun at the little ones and telling Carrie about his day at work and stories about some of the men he worked with. After supper, while Carrie did the dishes, Tom played with all three children and some evenings Tom and Carrie sat on the porch and talked while the children played. Other evenings Tom worked on projects such as the chicken coup.

By August the chicken coup was finished and Carrie had her new hens she had longed for. Tom had fixed up a bedroom for Luke and Belinda next to his and Carrie's bedroom. Both children were sleeping through the night now, and even Ady Rose wasn't waking as much. Carrie didn't know when life had been better. She had the husband she had always dreamed of, and nothing meant more to her than Tom and her little family.

The first week in October Lily gave birth to a little boy named Homer, and a week after that Ellie gave birth to a son. Papa Silas said they were coming so fast he couldn't keep up with them. Then in late October, as fall was in it colorful array, Sile J.'s wife Lula gave birth to a little boy, Woodrow Silas. In addition to all his other grandchildren, Papa Silas now had one living in the same house with him, and little Woody became the light of his old age. Lula always said she never had to hunt a babysitter, for Papa Silas was always there and willing to spoil his latest grandchild.

It was decided that Thanksgiving would again be held at Papa Silas' house. Lula loved the whole family there almost as much as Mama Cynth had. Thanksgiving Day arrived with a beautiful autumn sunshine, and by the time Tom, Carrie and the kids had the wagon loaded and headed out for Carrie's homeplace, it was already sixty degrees. It had all the makings of a wonderful day. All of Carrie's siblings were there with their families, including Lily, her children and Dent Tyler. Dent was a likeable sort and seemed to fit right in with the family. He could spin a yarn, as Mama Cynth use to say, "a mile long and half a mile wide." He kept everyone laughing and even Lily seemed more agreeable than she had in ages.

After everyone had eaten their fill of all the good food brought by each family, the men went outside to play horseshoes, whittle, and spin more yarns, and, as usual, the women went out to sit on the front porch where they talked and watched the children play. The smallest ones were again fast asleep on Mama and Papa's bed. Carrie couldn't help but think of her mother and how much Mama Cynth had enjoyed times like this. Her reverie was interrupted by Lily.

"I guess you all heard about Reed, didn't you?" she asked.

All of the women looked at each other.

"What do you mean?" asked Nora.

"Why, Reed died two weeks ago," replied Lily in a tone void of emotion.

"What happened?" asked Maggie.

"Well, I didn't even know about it until he was buried," answered Lily, "and me his wife. His mother and the rest of his family just had his funeral and buried him over in Kentucky where he was living without even saying dog to me. They all hate me."

"Lily, what did Reed die of?" asked Ellie. "Had he been sick?"

"Yeah," Lily replied. "You know how he used to wheeze like a worn out whistle...got on my nerves to no end. He died of some kind of lung disease. Just couldn't get his breath any longer. I'm sorry for his folks, but it was over between me and him a long time ago. Now at least I won't have to divorce him. He did send the kids some money every month by way of his sister Bonnie and I don't know how I'll take care of them now, but me and Dent's getting married pretty soon. We just have a few things to take care of first. "

There was a long period of silence as each of the women digested all that Lily had just revealed. Then Carrie decided to change the subject. They talked of the children, of harvest, and of Christmas, which was "just around the corner." About four o'clock each family began to take their leave.

Riding home, Carrie told Tom all that Lily had said.

"Did you know about Reed dying?" she asked.

"No, I sure didn't," he responded. "No one seemed to have heard from him since he left here. I can't say I much liked the man, but I'm sorry for his suffering."

Carrie felt extremely proud of Tom at that moment.

Tom really has changed, she thought to herself.

The next year was one of contentment, as Tom seemed to be a truly changed man. He was home on time, played with the children, and showed a genuine interest in his home and family. In January he had been given a good pay raise by the railroad, and with it he bought Carrie a new wash tub and washboard so that she had a tub for washing and a tub for rinsing, making the chore an easier one. He continued to visit his parents often and to help them out when they needed him. His mother was back on her feet and coping better with Ort's death. Tom and his brother Nate were also on good terms and sometimes worked together to help their parents.

Carrie's brothers and sisters were all doing well, except maybe for Lily. Dent moved out, then back in, then back out again. He was in and out so much that Carrie couldn't keep up with the situation. She did hear from Nora and Ben that men were constantly visiting at Lily's house. It just seemed Lily would never straighten up. Carrie prayed for her constantly and especially for the four little ones.

The last time Carrie visited Papa Silas he was the happiest she had seen him since Mama Cynth died. He adored little Woody and Woody adored Papa. The light was back in her father's eyes and that pleased Carrie greatly. Lula happily informed her that Charles and Lucindy were expecting a baby around Christmas and Eb and Maggie were also awaiting a little one in early December.

Carrie's hens were laying so well that she started selling eggs to Berke's Mercantile in the town of Haymaker. This allowed her a little extra spending money.

They spent Thanksgiving with Papa Silas again and the following Sunday with Tom's folks. At the Sunday dinner with Tom's folks, his mother Izzy told them that Ort's widow Betts was going to marry again. It seemed a little soon, but they knew she needed someone to support her and the two children, and Charles and Izzy liked the man she was going to marry. He was a widower just a few years Betts' senior, and he loved her children as if they were his own.

The first day of December Eb's Maggie gave birth to a son, and a week before Christmas Lucindy gave birth to little Grace Katherine who immediately received the nickname "Katie." All seemed to be right in Carrie's world. She thought of Mama Cynth and how happy she would be with all of these grandchildren.

The year 1909 began with promise. It was a mild winter, everyone was well, and Carrie's little family was all she had ever hoped for. By February she was pretty sure she was pregnant again. She had always wanted a large family, and so she was happy, yet a little hesitant to tell Tom. Things had been going so well, and she didn't want that to change, but by the first of March she finally got the courage.

"Tom," she began one night after the kids were all tucked away. "Tom, I have something to tell you, and I hope it will make you happy."

"Did you win a million dollars, Carrie?" Tom asked with a twinkle in his one good eye. "If you did I'll just quit that old railroad job and become a man of idle ways. I'll just buy me some fancy cigars and sit on the front porch and smoke 'em and talk to my darling wife."

"No. No million for us," countered Carrie, joining in his light mood. "No cigars either," she added, wrinkling her nose.

"Well, then what is it, my woman?" he asked, sitting back peacefully in his rocking chair.

"Tom, we're going to have another baby," said Carrie weakly. "I hope it makes you happy like it does me."

For just a moment Tom said nothing, and Carrie held her breath. Was he going to be mad? Would this change the way things had been going? Carrie was so afraid.

"Well, woman, I guess it's about time for another one," Tom said.

"Then you're happy about it, Tom?" asked Carrie.

"Why wouldn't a man be happy that he's going to be a paw again?" laughed Tom. "Now it would be good if we had another boy. We fellers are sorta getting outnumbered around here."

"Then I'll just ask the Lord to give us a good healthy boy," responded Carrie. "Unless," she slowly added with a mischievous twinkle in her eye, "unless the Lord wants to give us a good healthy little girl."

"That's right, Carrie Tan," said Tom softly, leaning over to give her a kiss. "We'll take just what the Lord gives us."

Carrie smiled contentedly. She had never felt so at peace and so loved.

CHAPTER 10

It was a beautiful spring; a happy spring. Carrie couldn't remember ever being more content. But disruption has a way of nipping doggedly at the heels of contentment.

It was one of those warm sunny days in May when it just felt good to breathe in deeply. Flowers were blooming, potatoes had been planted and the temperature was just right. Carrie was making dough to set aside and have its time to rise so she could make bread for her family and to send to Tom's mother. The children were playing on the front porch with some spinning tops Tom had bought them. Luke, who would soon turn five, was becoming quite the little man and a big help to Carrie. Each afternoon he would carry in firewood when it was time to start supper. Tom had bought him a little broom just his size and once a week he swept the outhouse and the front porch. It was a help to his mother and it made Luke feel like a grown-up. He was also good at gathering the eggs...not one bit afraid of the cantankerous hens. Lately he had even been taking Beanie with him as she carried her little basket she had gotten for Easter. Luke would put some of the gathered eggs in her basket and she was very careful not to break them. Carrie often stood in the doorway and smiled as she watched her two oldest coming back from the henhouse, each carrying their baskets and Luke protectively holding Beanie's hand. As Carrie put her dough in the big bowl and covered it with a feed sack towel, she pondered on these things, praising God for all that He had given her.

Just as she was washing her hands, she heard the screen door close. Little Ady Rose, now a rosy toddling two, came running to the kitchen.

"Thumbody coming!" she lisped excitedly.

"Who's coming, sweet baby girl?" inquired Carrie.

"Wooks wike Aunt No-wa," Ady Rose replied.

Sure enough, as Carrie looked out the door, Ben and Nora were just coming into the yard. Carrie immediately knew something was astir. Nora was out of breath and white as the flowers on Carrie's snowball bush and Ben had a troubled look on his face.

"Luke, you mind your sisters for me while I talk with Ben and Nora," said Carrie.

Seeming to know that something was wrong, Luke just nodded his head and looked toward Ben and Nora with worry on his little-boy face.

"Come on in and sit down," said Carrie. "I know something's wrong, but catch your breath first."

Ben and Nora each pulled out a chair at the kitchen table.

After a brief pause, Nora gasped, "Carrie, you've got to come with us to the train station."

"The train station?" questioned Carrie, hand to her mouth. "Oh, no. Is something wrong with Tom?"

"No, Carrie," replied Ben placing his hand on her shoulder in a calming manner. "It's not Tom at all."

"It's our sister, Carrie. It's Lily," cried Nora, still out of breath. "Carrie, you've got to come with us to stop her."

"Stop her from what, Nora?" asked Carrie. "You have got to calm down. You're not making any sense."

"She's giving her children away, Sister!" exclaimed Nora.

Carrie sat down in a chair, the air completely leaving her lungs. "What do you mean, giving her children away? You don't just give your children away."

Trying to make more sense, Ben replied, "Lily is on her way to the train station in Haymaker. She is to meet some people from the orphan-age over in Grinslow. She's going to send all four of her sweet children to the orphanage. Nora wants you to go with her to try and talk some sense into her."

Without hesitation, Carrie went to the front porch.

"Luke, I want you to do something for Mama," she said quickly. "I want you to go down the hill to Widow Thomases house and ask Eliza if she can come and sit with you and your sisters for awhile. Can you do that? I'll stand and watch you all the way."

"I can do that, Maw," Luke answered matter-of-factly.

Luke headed off down the hill, and Carrie called to Ben, "Ben, go hitch up Tom's wagon. With the baby, I can't walk real fast and the wagon will be easier for me and get us there quicker."

"Oh, Carrie," said Nora, "I hadn't thought about you being in the family way. Maybe you'd best stay here."

"I'll be fine," assured Carrie. "We've got to stop that crazy sister of ours."

In no time at all Ben had the wagon ready and Luke was back with Eliza. The children loved Eliza and Carrie knew that she was very trustworthy. After a few instructions to her and the children, the three were off to Haymaker and the little train station.

As they arrived, there seemed to be a crowd there, which was quite unusual for a week day. They spotted Lily and her four children right away. Homer was just a baby in her arms and Belle was no bigger than a flea. She stood with her older brother and sister, James and Tiny, clinging to their mother's dress and crying. Reed Tyler's mother and father, Lorris and Bud Tyler, were talking to Lily.

"Lily, don't do this awful thing," begged Lorris. "Me and Bud will take the children. We don't have much and we ain't young anymore, but we'll love them."

"It is already settled," answered Lily angrily. "You hated me when I was married to Reed, so why would you want my children. The last one ain't even his."

"That don't matter," pleaded Bud. "You just can't give them away like they're nothing a'tall. Look at them. They're scared to death."

"I told you the matter is settled," began Lily, but stopped as she spotted Ben, Nora and Carrie coming toward her.

"Lily, what are you doing?" asked Carrie, so out of breath she could hardly get the words out.

"Now, Carrie, just don't mix into my business," answered Lily. "My mind is made up. I can't take care of them anymore and I've already signed the papers to send them over to Grinslow. They'll get folks to adopt them and they'll have good homes. Now just let it be."

Tears were streaming down Carrie's cheeks as she tried to talk to her sister. "Is it money, Lily? Tom and me can lend you some money, and I'll even keep the children for you awhile until you get straightened out."

"I'll keep part of them, Lily," inserted Nora. "Maybe Carrie could take two and I could take two until you get on your feet."

"It ain't about my feet," stormed Lily. "I just wasn't cut out to change diapers and wipe snot, and I ain't gonna do it no more. Now just leave me be."

The more Lily stormed, the more the children cried. Everyone standing around Lily was crying, and it became even worse as they heard the train whistle blow, announcing its arrival at the little train station.

"Lily, don't do this, please," begged Lorris Tyler.

"Lily, let us take them," pleaded Carrie.

"Look at them, Lily," cried Nora. "They are absolutely scared to death. Don't you know what this is doing to them?"

Lily ignored them as two matronly women stepped from the train and walked to her.

"Mrs. Tyler, I am Agnes Waller and this is Pearl Banes. We are from the Home of Hope Orphanage. Are the children prepared to go with us?"

"They're ready," answered Lily, without any semblance of emotion. "They have their belongings in their bags."

As Carrie and Nora looked on they noticed that each child had a paper bag with their meager belongings in them. Tiny was holding two, one of which must have been for Homer. Was that all Lily was sending with them?

The train whistle blew. The two women from the orphanage looked at the children with cold emotionless eyes.

"Pearl, you take the baby," commanded Agnes Waller. Looking at the others, she said, "Come children, we can't keep the train waiting."

She tried to take Belle by the hand, but Belle pulled away, crying and holding to her mother's dress.

"Please, Mama," begged Tiny. "Don't send us away. We'll be good and stay out of your way. Please don't send us away."

"If you don't want us," added James, "let us go with Aunt Carrie and Aunt Nora. You heard them. They'll take care of us."

"Or even Maw and Paw Tyler," added Tiny. "They want us, Mama."

Little Belle said nothing, but cried as though her heart would break.

"Now listen," said Lily, addressing the children sternly. "It's all settled. You're going to a nice place where you'll have lots of other children to play with. You'll have plenty to eat and they're gonna find you a good home to live in. Now go on nicely."

Sobbing uncontrollably, the children walked to Agnes Waller, heads down and shoulders slumped. They seemed to know their fate had been decided. Without blinking an eye, Mrs. Waller half led, half dragged the children toward the waiting train. Everyone standing around the station was crying. Even the conductor of the train wiped at his eyes with his handkerchief. Many onlookers had stopped by to see what all the commotion was about.

"Lily, please don't do this awful thing," begged Carrie. "You'll regret it the rest of your life. What would Mama Cynth say if she was here? What will this do to Papa? Please, Lily, don't do this. Let me and Tom take them."

With an evil glint in her eye, Lily responded, "Wonder which one Tom would want, Carrie?"

Then she simply turned, stiffened her back, and walked away, not even waiting for the train to pull out. About half way up the steps to the train, Tiny stopped and looked back. All she saw was her mother walking away. With a sad look of resignation, she proceeded on and took her seat.

With a gush of steam, the train pulled out. As loud as the train was, everyone standing at the station could hear the children crying. There was not a dry eye to be seen, and some of the people were complete strangers in the little community.

"May God have mercy on her soul," whispered Lorris Tyler. "What will become of those poor children?"

"Whatever it is, it will be better than living with a mother like that," spat out Bud Tyler. Then looking around at Carrie and Nora, his face paled, "I'm sorry, girls," he said.

"You don't need to apologize, Mr. Tyler," said Carrie. "Right now my thoughts of Lily are not too Christian-like either."

"I guess you have more reason than any of us to have ill feelings toward her," said Lorris, looking sadly at Carrie. Then she turned and walked away.

What did she mean by that I wonder? Carrie asked, but only to herself.

CHAPTER 11

Carrie wasn't there when they told Papa Silas about Lily and her children, but Nora said Sile J. had come by their house the next day. He said Papa sat down and just cried like a baby. Then little Woody cried because his Grandpa was crying. Carrie, herself, had cried for days. She had told Tom about it that same night, after the children were asleep.

"Tom," she asked, "how could a mother give her own babies away?"

Tom just shook his head. "Lily is just cut from a different cloth, Carrie. I may not understand her, but it ain't my place to judge her."

Carrie didn't pursue the topic any longer. Tom was right; it wasn't her place to judge Lily, but she just wished she could understand her. She couldn't even fathom giving her children away. Her family meant everything to her, and now she was going to have another baby...a baby Tom was happy about. Still, Lorris Tyler's words kept haunting her...*I guess you have more reason than any of us to have ill feelings...*

The summer was gone before she knew it, and in September Carrie gave birth to a son, Jessie Silas. He was a fine, healthy boy and Carrie immediately wrapped her love around him. Tom seemed pleased, too, and continued to be the husband Carrie always knew he could be. She just couldn't believe how God had blessed them…four beautiful children, a nice home, and peace and tranquility. Tom even got another raise and the money was spent on some new fixings for the house and some clothes for the children. Luke especially was growing faster than his clothes could keep up with, and he just couldn't seem to keep the knee in a pair of overalls for more than a week. Carrie was sewing patches over the patches. Luke loved to follow Tom around on the farm and do everything he could to help out and to win his Paw's approval. Most of the time Tom was good to him, but his patience was somewhat lacking. On occasions, when the patience was at a low level, he would yell at Luke or criticize him. Luke would drop his head and his chin would quiver, but then he would just try harder.

Christmas came and then was gone. It was a good Christmas. Tom bought toys and clothes for the kids, a new dress and coat for Carrie, along with some much needed pots and pans. Carrie couldn't complain at all…yet something kept eating at her. It was something she couldn't explain, even to herself. There were little changes in Tom…changes that perhaps only a wife would notice.

"Where are your thoughts tonight, Tom?" she asked one spring night after the children were tucked away in bed. He had been sitting for almost an hour just staring at the little pot bellied heating stove, seemingly lost in thought.

"What do you mean?" Tom answered, a little more brusquely than he realized.

"I didn't mean anything bad," replied Carrie. "You just seemed a million miles away. I was afraid you might be fretting over something."

"I was just thinking about work," said Tom. Then looking at Carrie out of the corner of his good eye, he added, "Looks like I may have to work late a few evenings a week. We're a little shorthanded right now."

"Why are you shorthanded?" questioned Carrie. "Did someone quit or get sick or something?"

"I don't know, woman!" he answered irritably. "I just work there. I don't question what the big bosses say. I just do it. Now let's go to bed."

With that the conversation was over, but Carrie's thoughts were not.

He may be telling me the truth, she thought to herself, *but this is one time I won't just take his word. I'll find out what's going on."*

So with determination, but also a heavy heart, Carrie went to bed.

Her determination was to be put aside for awhile, however, A week after their conversation, Beanie became sick. It started with, "Mama, my tummy hurts."

Carrie was used to tummy aches and thought little of it at first. By nightfall, though, Beanie was running a high fever. Her stomach was hurting worse and she had both vomiting and diarrhea. All night and all the next day, Carrie worked nonstop trying to get the fever down. She knew the fever was dangerously high, so hot to her touch, and Beanie could keep nothing on her stomach. Little Luke did all that he could to help, fetching water and keeping check on the other little ones, though Carrie feared that he would come down with what Beanie had.

Thankfully, Tom came home on time that evening. She met him on the front porch to stop him before he pulled off his boots.

"Tom, you've got to go get Doc Whitt," she cried. "Beanie's really bad off and nothing I do seems to help."

"I'll go," Tom assured her. "Try to calm yourself, Carrie."

Tom was back with the doctor within forty minutes, but to Carrie it seemed like hours. By now Beanie was too weak even to cry. Carrie didn't miss the concerned look on Doc Whitt's face as he immediately began his examination.

"Doc, what is it?" asked Tom, as the doctor seemed to finish.

"Well, Tom, Miss Carrie," he said, addressing them both. "I'm pretty sure your girl has the flux."

"Just what is that, Doc Whitt?" asked Carrie. "I've heard of it but I can't say that I know much about it. Is it bad? Do you have something for it? Seems I recall Mama Cynth talking about people dying from flux when she was a girl."

Doc Whitt rubbed his chin. "I won't lie to you," he said. "It is very serious, and she's not the only one who has it. I've treated five other cases of it just in the past few days. We've got to get the fever down and the dysentery stopped. I'll give her some paregoric for the vomiting and dysentery. It will help. Do you have any peppermint, Carrie?"

"Yes," answered Carrie. "I always keep some aside."

"I want you to make some peppermint tea then," instructed Doc Whitt. "I want you to give her some of that as often as she can take it, starting with teaspoons full, and I'll write down when to give her some more paregoric. You need to keep bathing her in cool cloths to get the fever down. If necessary, put her in a tub of water...whatever it takes to cool her down. I'll check back tomorrow and I'll bring some fermented rhubarb. That soothes the intestines and will help with the wasting. She may be better in a few days, but I can't say for sure."

"What about the other cases, Doc?" questioned Carrie. "Are they getting better?"

Doc Whitt looked away as he answered, "Two seem to be mending. Two are touch and go."

"And the fifth one?" ventured Carrie.

"That was a little five-month-old across the mountain," answered Doc. "He passed away this morning, I'm sorry to say. But that doesn't mean your little girl won't make it. She's strong, and she has a mother and father who will do everything in their power to take care of her. Now leave your worries to the Good Lord and just get through the night."

With that the doctor took his leave with a promise to return the next morning. Carrie whispered a prayer as she continued to bathe Beanie. After eating a bite and tending to his chores, Tom bathed Beanie with cool cloths while Carrie made the peppermint tea, fed the other children, and put them to bed. Carrie knew it would be a long night.

By morning Beanie was no better and Ady Rose was complaining that her tummy "hurted." Soon her temperature was rising also and the diarrhea had begun. Carrie and Tom worked together, taking care of their little ones, fear lodged in their inner being with no time to give way to it.

"Mama, what can I do to help?" Carrie looked up from wetting a washcloth to see Luke by her side.

"Luke, you've already helped, sweet boy," replied Carrie, stopping to give him a hug. "You are always a big help to your mama. I just pray you won't get sick."

"I feel fine, Mama," he answered. "Are Beanie and Ady Rose going to die, Mama?"

"They are going to be fine," said Carrie, with as much confidence as she could muster. "You go check on little Jessie, and say a prayer for your sisters. Okay?"

"But Mama," his little-boy voice quivered, "I heard Doc say last night that somebody died from what Beanie and Ady have. If somebody died, couldn't they die, too?"

Carrie realized that Luke must not have been asleep the night before, as she had thought, and he had heard the conversation with Doc Whitt. She bent to look into his face.

"Luke, your sisters are going to get well. It may take a few days, but they will be well. Now quit fretting and help your mother by checking on little Jessie."

Luke reluctantly did his mother's bidding, but Carrie could see the worry on his face. Her heart ached for him, but right now the girls needed all of her attention. Tom had gone out to do the morning chores, and as she heard a door open and close, she assumed it was him.

"Miss Carrie?" came a whisper from just outside the door.

"Why, Eliza," said Carrie. "What are you doing here? You might not want to come any further. I don't want you to catch what the girls have."

"I'm here to help out, Miss Carrie," answered Eliza. " Doc stopped by last night and told us about little Beanie, so Maw and me decided I'd best come give a hand. The Lord will take care of me as he sees fit."

"Bless you, Eliza. I can never repay you for all the good you have done us," said Carrie. "I sure won't turn down your help now."

It kept both of them busy taking care of the two girls. They tried to feed them as much peppermint tea as they would take, but it seemed to come back up as soon as it was swallowed. Tom took Luke outside to do some more chores, and when the baby needed Carrie, Eliza took over the care of the sick ones. Carrie was trying to keep Jessie as far away from the illness as she possibly could.

About ten o'clock Doc Whitt returned. Carrie could have hugged him from the relief she felt, but the look of concern on Doc's face soon stole any bit of encouragement she might have felt.

"Their fevers are just staying too high," Doc said, almost to himself. "Carrie, I'm going to try some of this fermented rhubarb. It has been known to help in times like this, but there are no guarantees."

As each girl took a dose of the rhubarb, Carrie and Eliza bathed their faces, praying it would stay down. Beanie seemed unaware that anything was going on, while Ady Rose whimpered each time she was moved. Both were obedient in swallowing the foul tasting liquid.

"Doc," questioned Carrie. "Are there any more cases of this flux right close besides what you told us about last night?"

"I'm afraid so, Carrie," he replied. "Your brother Sile's boy came down with it last night, and Eb's little Molly and Robert are sick now. Two other families have the sickness in their homes. But, praise be to God, no one else has died."

"Are there any older people with the sickness?" asked Carrie.

"Not yet," he answered, "but I'm afraid it may happen. This flux seems to be partial to children and old folks."

"Papa!" gasped Carrie. "If little Woody has it, then Papa could get it, couldn't he Doc? Oh, I pray Papa won't get this."

"Now, Carrie," admonished the doctor, "don't go borrowing trouble. You've got enough on you. Just take care of your little girls and turn the rest over to God. Besides, Silas Ranes is healthier than all the rest of us put together."

"Miss Carrie!" called Eliza from the bed across the room. "Miss Carrie... Doc...come see about Beanie. I don't feel no breathing!"

They both hurried to Beanie's side. Doc examined her and checked for a pulse as Carrie held her breath.

"Doc?" gasped Carrie.

"Now, now," answered Doc. "There's a pulse. It's just very weak. Bring some cool water. Eliza, pour plenty of water in that tub. We need to get her in there immediately."

Eliza rushed to do as the doctor ordered and soon Beanie was in the cool tub of water. So ill was she, that she made not even a whimper. Carrie knelt beside the tub and prayed as Eliza and Doc bathed her.

"Please, God," cried Carrie. "Don't take my baby. I still need her, God. I still need her."

But in a second Carrie added, "Yet not my will but thine be done, Lord."

Ady Rose whimpered from her bed and Carrie moved to soothe her. She gave her a teaspoon of peppermint tea as the fermented rhubarb had remained inside her. Carrie was afraid to get her hopes up, but it seemed Ady Rose's skin was a little less hot to the touch. As the little one dozed off, Carrie went to check on Jessie. As she entered his room, there sat Tom holding little Jessie as Luke was singing ever so quietly to him. Tom looked up with concern at Carrie.

"I ain't much good at taking care of the sick," offered Tom, "but I can take care of the well. Does that help you, Carrie Tan?"

"Yes, Tom," answered Carrie with tears on her cheeks. "It helps more than you can know, and I thank you, my dear husband and son."

Carrie and Eliza continued to care for the two little girls throughout the day. Beanie's breathing was quite shallow but her temperature was not as high after the third tub bath of the day. They had been able to get a few teaspoons of the fermented rhubarb into her and the diarrhea was not as severe. Still, she seemed so lifeless, almost like a small corpse lying in her bed. Carrie's heart ached for her. Ady Rose had improved more and was taking larger doses of the rhubarb and paregoric. Her diarrhea was gone, yet her temperature was still high. She would sleep for long periods and Carrie knew that was good for her.

As nightfall came, Carrie tried to persuade Eliza to go home.

"Eliza, your mother and brother need you," Carrie insisted.

"I'm right where Maw would want me to be," responded Eliza. "She and Rollen can take care of themselves. Besides, with the girls improving maybe you and me can take turns through the night. You need some rest, Miss Carrie, so's you can take care of the other two little ones as well as the sick. We don't know yet, God forbid, but what Luke or baby Jessie could come down sick."

"I know," said Carrie, with a catch in her voice. "I'm praying as I work that they won't get sick, but I know God's will is perfect, and I just have to keep holding on to that."

By morning Ady Rose was much improved. She even announced that she was hungry for a pancake.

Carrie laughed, "I'm glad to see you hungry, little one, but I think we'd better start out with a little bit of dry toast. Your stomach may not be quite ready for pancakes."

Unfortunately, Beanie was not faring so well. Her temperature was only slightly elevated and the diarrhea was gone, but she seemed in a faraway world, not focusing or even aware of her surroundings. She just lay there like a little limp ragdoll.

Tom had decided he had better go back to work, so as soon as he finished the morning chores, he headed out. Carrie understood and at the same time was hurt that he would go and leave them at a time like this. However, she had little time to dwell on the matter. She was very thankful neither of the boys had yet shown any signs of illness. It would have been especially hard on one so small as Jessie.

She finally persuaded Eliza to go home for awhile.

"Just go get some rest," Carrie pleaded. "You haven't had an ounce of sleep since you came to help. We don't want you getting sick."

"I will go," consented Eliza, "but I most certainly will come back this afternoon. Then you are going to take a nap while I take care of these fine young'uns."

CHAPTER 12

Ady Rose made a quick recovery and the boys never came down with the illness, yet Beanie barely clung to life. Doc Whitt came by several times the next week, but he could do nothing for her.

"I just don't know what the problem is," said Doc, shaking his head. "All of my other patients have mended, except for the three who passed on. It's like the sickness has damaged something inside of her. We just have to keep doing what we've been doing and praying a little harder, Carrie."

The illness seemed to be dying down in the community but there had been two more deaths, one a baby and one a seventy-five year old grandmother of that same child. Eb and Sile J.'s children were well again, and Papa Silas had not come down sick. They were all thankful for that.

"Eliza," said Carrie one day when her neighbor had come to help a while, "I just don't know why Beanie won't mend. I've done everything I know to do, but she just lies there like she's alive but not alive."

"I know, Miss Carrie," answered Eliza. "It breaks my heart to see her this way, so I can imagine what it does to you. Maybe she just needs more time. We just have to trust our sweet Jesus."

Beanie wasn't the only trouble Carrie was dealing with. Almost as soon as Tom went back to work he started coming home late. Carrie confronted him.

"Now listen, woman," he responded with irritation, "I missed some days of work and the least I can do is to try and make it up. Looks to me like you'd be thankful I have a good job."

"I am thankful, Tom," said Carrie. "It's just that I could sure use your help here with Beanie still being sick and all."

"I still do my chores," countered Tom. "Looks like if I work at a job all day and still do my chores, you could at least take care of the young'uns without me doing that, too."

"I don't mind you working regular hours," answered Carrie. "But for just a little while couldn't you come home on time?"

"I'll be here when I get here," he retorted. "Now let me be, woman."

With this Tom stomped out the door and didn't return until bedtime. He didn't speak another word to her that night, and the next night he worked late again. Tears streamed down Carrie's face as she fed the children their supper and prepared them for bed.

"Maw, why are you crying?" asked Luke, placing his hand on his mother's arm.

"Oh, I just have something in my eye," answered Carrie.

"But you have a sad look on your face, too," said Luke. "You're sad because Paw's not home yet, ain't you?"

Carrie wanted to protect Luke, but she knew she couldn't lie to him. "Yes, Luke, I guess I am," she answered, giving him a hug. "I just like it better when we're all here together."

Luke looked up at his mother. "I can help out around here a lot more if you let me. I'm not a baby anymore, you know. I can help take care of Ady Rose and Jessie, and I can sing to Beanie and tell her stories. I can sweep and carry in wood and feed the chickens and even wash dishes. Maybe then Paw won't talk mean to you. Just don't cry no more, Maw."

"What a treasure of a son you are," laughed Carrie, hugging him closely. "You've always been my little man. Now off to bed with you. You need plenty of rest if you're going to do all of those chores."

When Luke, Ady Rose and Jessie were tucked in, Carrie went to Beanie's bedside. She sat there looking at her daughter and running her tired hand across Beanie's forehead, willing her daughter to respond.

"Dear God," she whispered. "I don't know what else to do for her. I want her to get better. You already know that, God. You know my heart. I can't help her, but you can, so God, I just place her in your hands. I accept your will, because I know you know best. If you need to take her, I'll still love you and trust you. If you plan to heal her in heaven, then I know she will be powerfully healed. Help me to be strong and to be a good mother to my children, Lord. And God, will you please be with Tom? Help him to live for you and to get rid of anything that might interfere with that. I do thank you, God. Amen."

With that, Carrie felt a new lightness of heart. She scooted down beside of Beanie and fell fast asleep. She didn't know when or if Tom came home. It was after daylight the next morning when she awoke. She immediately jumped to her feet, realizing she had not fed little Jessie. As she peeked into his bed, she was stunned to find that he was sleeping like a lamb all cuddled up to his special blanket. Luke was sitting up in his bed across the room.

"He's alright, Maw," Luke whispered. "I kept an eye on him all night but he didn't wake up a time."

"Praise be to God," sighed Carrie. "He gave all of us a good night's sleep."

Just then she heard a voice. "Mama? Mama?"

Carrie and Luke looked at each other. "Is that Ady Rose?" asked Carrie.

"I don't think so," replied Luke.

With that they both took off in a run to Beanie's bed. Her eyes were open and seemingly alert.

"Mama, I'm thirsty," she said.

"Oh, my darling girl," cried Carrie, "what a joy it is to see your beautiful eyes and to hear your voice."

As she looked around, Luke was already bringing a glass of water.

"Was I sick all night?" asked Beanie, weakly.

"Great day, sister," laughed Luke, "you've been asleep for two weeks."

With big round eyes, Beanie looked at her mother. "Luke's silly, Mama. You can't sleep for two weeks."

Carrie laughed out loud with pure joy and happiness. "The main thing is you are awake now, Belinda Nora...and God is so good."

Carrie fixed breakfast for ALL of her children with a lightness of heart she had not felt in a long time. She rejoiced when Beanie ate a whole piece of toast and drank her water thirstily. After breakfast she sent Luke to tell Widow Thomas and Eliza the news. He returned with Eliza by his side.

"I just had to come and see this miracle called Beanie," said Eliza. "Oh, ain't she the prettiest sight I have seen in a long time."

"Yes, she is," laughed Carrie, "and she owes a lot of it to you, Eliza. You have been such a good friend and neighbor. You are a true example, Eliza, of what God wants a neighbor to be, and I do thank you from the bottom of my heart."

Although Beanie did recover, it took months for her to get back to the happy, energetic little girl she had been before the illness. In fact, they would later find that the illness had weakened her heart permanently. Luke became her self-appointed caretaker. Wherever Luke was on the farm, there you would see Beanie. Luke always made it a point to return to the house with Beanie once or twice a day, insisting that his sister take a nap, and it wasn't hard to persuade her as her body still required a good bit of rest. When Luke began school in September, she was like a little lost lamb, following every step Carrie took. She was always standing on the front steps waiting for Luke to return each day, and until bedtime she never left his side. If Luke ever felt smothered by her attention, he never showed it. His patience and love brought roses to her wan cheeks and a happy little hop to her step.

One warm day in early October while Luke was at school, Carrie decided to take Beanie and Ady Rose to town as a special treat, and the girls were filled with excitement. Eliza agreed to take care of Jessie.

"What will we buy, Maw?" asked Ady Rose, skipping along as she held her mother's hand. "Can we buy some stick candy?"

"I think we just might do that," laughed Carrie. "What would you like, Beanie?"

"I think I would like some licorice sticks," replied Beanie. "Can we get some for Luke, too?"

"That sounds like a good idea," answered her mother. "We might even get one for Jessie to suck on."

Ady Rose giggled at that idea. She just couldn't imagine her baby brother with a licorice stick.

It seemed like a perfect day with no time for worldly cares as Carrie and the two girls entered Berke's Mercantile. She had a small list of needed items, but mostly this was a just-for-fun excursion for her and the girls. They had handled the two-mile walk into town splendidly, and Carrie wanted the entire trip to be a happy experience for them. She also intended to buy dress goods to make each of them a new dress, and she was going to let them pick it out.

"Good morning, Miss Carrie," greeted Mr. Faller, as they entered the door. "And who are these fine young ladies you have with you? My, they're might nigh grown and as pretty as a June bug. I hear they've been right sick, but I sure don't see any evidence of it."

This, of course, made Ady Rose giggle again. "We have been sick, really," she said.

"Mr. Faller," said Carrie, "I believe we need something for a sweet tooth. The girls will tell you just what they want. Then I believe we need some dress goods because they are growing so fast I plan to make each of them a new dress."

"Oh boy! Oh boy!" shouted the girls in unison, clapping their hands. "A new dress for us!"

After the girls picked the candy each wanted, Mr. Faller took them over to the cloth section of the store.

"Girls," said Carrie, "I want you to pick the cloth you want for a new dress. You stand here and look and make your choice and I'll go get a few other things I need. Now don't touch the material with those sticky fingers."

The girls stood licking on their candy as their mother walked to the grocery side of the store. Two women in the corner did not see Carrie as she came their way, but she could hear their conversation.

"Did you see that ole One-eyed Tom over at Loose Lizzie's last evening?" asked one of the women, her voice dripping with disdain.

"Huh, it wasn't just last evening," snorted her companion. "He's been there more than he's been home lately...and with that sorry woman when he has a jewel of a wife."

"Every day right after work, I'm told. It's just an out-and-out crying shame for him to act that way," retorted the first woman, shaking her head from side to side. "That Loose Lizzie is just after his money...money he should be spending on his own woman and children. If my man acted like that, I'd get me a butcher knife."

"You ain't by yourself on that," agreed the short, little round woman.

Carrie felt the life drain out from her. She turned on wobbly legs and moved away before they could see her, knowing she couldn't stand her humiliation or theirs either. As she turned, she looked straight into Mr. Faller's eyes, realizing he had seen and heard it all. He ducked his head and moved back over to where the two little ones were still deciding on their choice of material. Carrie moved in the same direction.

"Well, girls," said Mr. Faller, in a jovial voice, "have you made up your pretty little minds yet?"

As Carrie walked to their side, Beanie replied, "I think I like that blue with the little flowers in it. If I had a dress out of that, it could be flower time all year round."

"I believe that's a good choice," answered Carrie, with a wobbly voice, as she tried to smile through moist eyes. "What about you, Ady Rose?"

"I want the wed and white squares," stated Ady Rose with conviction, still unable to say her r's.

"It's called red and white checks," corrected Beanie.

"Okay, then I want wed and white checks," said Ady Rose, nodding her head.

"Mr. Faller, if you will just cut me two yards of each of those, I will be much obliged," said Carrie in a voice only slightly stronger.

As they moved to the cutting area of the store, Carrie came face to face with the two women she had overhead. Both had the decency to blush as they quickly moved on to another section.

Carrie paid for the cloth and other items she bought in a dark fog. She and the girls took their leave and headed toward home. As the girls chattered happily about their purchases, Carrie's mind struggled with its painful maze of questions.

Who is Loose Lizzie? she asked herself. *They said Tom's been going there... more time there than at home...giving her money...why does he give her money... last evening...* The thoughts went round and round in her head.

Tom was late that night as usual.

"Tom, how much longer are you going to have to work overtime?" asked Carrie.

He stopped in the midst of biting off a piece of bread and glared at Carrie. "I guess I'll work as long as the bosses tell me to work, woman. You want food on the table, don't you?"

Though stung by his words and glare, Carrie was determined not to be put off. Just as a spoonful of potatoes went into his mouth she asked, "Tom, who is Loose Lizzie?"

He turned pale as a ghost, and swallowing deeply, quickly reached for his glass of milk.

"Where did you hear a name like that, woman?" he asked, avoiding her eyes.

Carrie looked straight at him, although his eyes were still on his plate, "Oh, I just overheard some women at Berke's Mercantile talking about her...and that she has a lot of visitors. Do you know her?"

"Never heard of her," he replied gruffly. "How has Beanie been today? Can you tell a big difference in her? What would you think about taking the young'uns over to Mam and Pap's this Sunday?"

Carrie knew the subject was closed for tonight, but she would not let the matter drop. She intended to find out who this Loose Lizzie was, and what Tom had to do with her. A man doesn't look that caged unless something is hitting close to his backyard.

Two days later, Nora and her children came for a visit. It was good to see her and to catch up on all the latest family news. Ellie and Henry had moved to Kentucky for a better job for Henry. Ellie had recently written to Papa Silas and he had relayed all the news to Nora. Ellie seemed very happy in her new home and Henry was making more money than he had at the mines near Haymaker. He was still with the mines, but it was a much safer job. All three children were thriving in their new environment. Sile J. and Lula had another son, Orin Tate, and now Papa had another grandchild in the home with him.

"There are so many babies I've lost count of them," laughed Carrie. "But the Bible says to be fruitful and multiply, and I guess that's just what Mama and Papa's children have done. I do enjoy my babies, Nora. They're the light of my life."

"I know just what you mean, Sister," replied Nora. "They're a lot of work, but even more joy. I still think about Lily and the sweet children she gave away. Sometimes I have nightmares about it. I have the children by their hands, but the train keeps moving away until I have to turn loose."

"I wonder what has happened to them," sighed Carrie. "Do you think they are treated well? Do you think they'll find homes where they are loved?"

"I pray that they will," answered Nora. "I surely pray that they will. I haven't mentioned this to a soul, Carrie, but Ben went over to Grinslow and tried to find out about them, but the orphanage said they couldn't give him any information."

"I guess we may never know," said Carrie, "but we can pray."

Both sisters sat quietly for a few minutes, wrapped in their own thoughts. After a bit, Carrie looked at Nora. "Nora, do you know of a woman named Loose Lizzie?"

Nora's head jerked up quickly. "Why do you ask about her?"

"Then you have heard of her?" questioned Carrie.

"Why, Carrie," replied Nora, "I thought everybody in the country had heard of Loose Lizzie. You mean you haven't?"

"Well, I have now," said Carrie. "I overheard some women in the mercantile talking about her last week. Who is she and why is she called that?"

Nora sat quietly for a moment as if in thought. "Her name is Lizzie Willis. She lives in an old rundown yellow colored house as you go into Haymaker. She's a daughter of Matildy Willis. Matildy had a house full of kids and none of them know who their daddy is. I doubt even Matildy knows. I don't mean to sound gossipy, Carrie, but the truth's the truth."

"But why do they call her Loose Lizzie?" asked Carrie again.

"Because, sister, she's just like her mother," replied Nora. "The apple don't fall far from the tree. She has loose morals. She entertains men for money. It's her way of making a living, and from what I hear she entertains some uppity-ups that you just wouldn't imagine going there."

Again the conversation lapsed. Nora looked at her sister, studying her face. "Carrie, why are you suddenly asking about Loose Lizzie?"

Carrie didn't reply. Again Nora studied her face. "What is it, Sister? Tell me."

"I-I overheard some women in the mercantile talking about her," said Carrie, almost in a whisper. "They said Tom's been going there."

"Oh, dear Jesus," gasped Nora. "Surely he wouldn't, Carrie."

"That's what they said," affirmed Carrie. "You should have seen the look on Tom's face when I asked him who Loose Lizzie is. He almost choked. Then he changed the subject real quick like."

"You asked him about it?" gasped Nora, stifling an amused laugh with her hand.

"I just asked him who she is," said Carrie. "But, Nora, I will find out more."

CHAPTER 13

Beanie continued to improve and by Christmas, except for some persistent fatigue, she seemed to have made a complete recovery. Ady Rose, who had bounced back from the illness much more quickly, thrived in her newly found health. Where she had once been frail and prone to sickness, she began to grow and blossom. Carrie felt blessed by the Lord.

Only one thing cast a shadow on her life. Tom came home late almost every evening from work. Sometimes it was after the children's bedtime when he came in, and although Carrie had saved his supper, he often declared he wasn't hungry. He had very little to say, and when they went to bed he turned away from Carrie and fell asleep almost instantly. She lay awake for hours with a sadness so deep she could not even begin to describe it. Something was terribly wrong and she made up her mind to find out what it was. She knew, however, that it would have to wait awhile. Christmas was at hand and there was much to do.

Carrie and Tom had shared many joyous Christmases together since they wed, but this was not one of them. Tom continued to be subdued and irritable. He was especially cantankerous and impatient with Luke, bringing tears to the little boy's eyes on frequent occasions. It seemed Luke could never please him, although he tried constantly.

On Christmas Eve the children were filled with excitement. Carrie tried to make everything merry for them, even though inside she was anything but merry. Tom had made her do all the buying for the kids, whereas in years past he had always had a surprise of his own.

"Tom, they always like the special presents you come up with for them," said Carrie. "Can't you find the time for just one gift for each of them?"

"No, I can't," he growled. "Buying presents is a mother's job. That is, if she's any kind of a mother. Now either you buy it or it won't be bought."

So Carrie, heavy of heart, had bought each of them a special gift from Tom, hoping they would never know it wasn't their dad who did the actual buying.

Tom did make it home on time Christmas Eve. Carrie had a special supper cooked and on the table as soon as he and Luke had finished the outside chores.

Suddenly she heard voices from outside.

"Can't you ever do anything right?" Tom stormed.

Carrie opened the kitchen door to see him standing over Luke, who had fallen and spilled most of a bucket of milk. Luke's head was bowed low and Carrie could see that he was trying not to cry.

"Set that milk on the porch," ordered Tom. "Then you go down to that willer tree and cut me a switch."

"Tom, no," gasped Carrie. "He's just a little boy. He didn't mean to spill the milk."

"You get inside, woman!" demanded Tom, his face red with anger.

Carrie stood there, refusing to move as Luke returned with a switch.

"Now, I'm gonna whip this boy, Carrie, so's he never spills milk again," said Tom, his voice firm and his eyes narrowed. "If you get in my way, I'll whip you, too. Understand?"

Carrie could not speak or move.

"Maw, it's okay," whispered Luke.

"She don't need you to tell her what's what, boy!" yelled Tom, as he came down with the switch on Luke's back. Luke yelped in spite of his attempt at bravery. Tom continued to bring the switch to his back and his rear, until something in Carrie snapped. She picked up the broom standing by the door, and went toward Tom.

"That's enough, Tom!" she shouted. "Do you hear me? That's enough!"

Tom stopped, the switch in mid air, his mouth agape. Sanity seemed to return as he let go his grip on Luke's arm. The switch dropped to the ground. Tom stood there a minute longer and then turned and walked slowly away.

Carrie ran to Luke and enfolded him in her arms as his little body shook with sobs.

"I try to be good, Maw," he sobbed, "but he hates me. Why does Paw hate me so?"

"Let's get you inside and clean you up," coaxed Carrie, avoiding the question he had just asked. "Come on, my precious boy."

She had cleaned Luke's back and put a clean shirt on him, and they had just sat down to supper when Tom walked in the kitchen. His face was pale and he couldn't look her in the eye as he sat down in his usual place.

"I'm sorry, boy, that I whipped you so hard," Tom said to Luke. "I'm not sorry I whipped you, but I shouldn't have been so hard. Your Maw has made a sissy out of you and you've got to grow out of it." With this he looked at Carrie, his face telling her that the matter was settled and she had best let it be.

Supper was eaten in silence. Luke and the girls did not lift their eyes from their plates. Even little Jessie was quiet as Carrie fed him, seeming to sense that something was wrong.

When supper was finished, Luke took Jessie to their bedroom to play while Carrie and the girls did the dishes. Tom went to the living room and sat, just staring into nothingness.

When the kitchen was tidied, Carrie went in to see about Luke and Jessie, while the girls quietly went to their room. Luke was on the floor building a castle of blocks for Jessie, his eyes red with damp trickles shimmering down his little-boy face. Carrie's heart ached for him.

"Luke, are you alright?" she asked, almost in a whisper.

"I'm okay, Mama," he replied. Luke seldom called her "mama" anymore, as he considered himself too grownup for that term. Just hearing him call her "mama" showed Carrie what a state he was in. He was a little boy who needed someone to hold him and tell him how much he was loved. Carrie took him gently in her arms as Jessie looked on quietly, sensing that his big brother needed his mother right then more than Jessie did.

"Luke, I'm so sorry your daddy whipped you like that, and I'm sorry I didn't stop him sooner," said Carrie, hoping Luke could feel the depth of her love for him. "You did nothing wrong, sweet boy. It's not you; it's your paw. He has problems right now and he seems to take them out on you. I don't know what is troubling him, Luke, but I intend to find out. In the meantime, could you pray for your Paw, Luke? I think he needs our prayers. Can you do that?"

"I don't think I can pray for him tonight, Mama," answered Luke, his innocent eyes lifting to hers. "I'll try to pray for him tomorrow. Is that okay?"

"That will be just fine, sweetheart," affirmed Carrie. "I'm not sure I can pray for him tonight either. Now do you want to go in to the tree and open one present?"

Straightening his shoulders like a little man, Luke answered, "I guess we'd better, Maw, or the girls and Jessie will be disappointed."

Carrie didn't know when she had ever felt prouder than she did at that moment of her precious son. Nor did she recall a time when she wanted to throttle Tom Swank more.

Luke moved about stiffly for the next several days, and Carrie kept his back well tended to keep down any infection. She was thankful he wouldn't be having school for another week due to Christmas break. It hadn't been much of a Christmas, but Carrie had tried to make it as good as possible for the sake of the children. She and Tom had hardly spoken. He walked around like he was mad at the world, what little time he was home, for working late had become a habit for him. Luke still helped his paw with the chores, but he always walked a few steps behind Tom, eyes to the ground, and never spoke to his paw. Where he had once been full of questions, he simply did what he was told. This didn't seem to matter to Tom who was always in his own little world. Carrie knew something had to change, but she didn't know just how to handle the situation. Although she didn't realize it at the present, she would look back and know that the night Tom whipped Luke so brutally was the night their marriage and family life changed. It was a marriage already with troubles, but that night a coldness settled in and remained.

As she pondered the matter one day when the children were asleep and she was quilting, an idea began to form in her mind. She had to know about this Loose Lizzie and what connection, if any, she had to Tom. As soon as the weather let up a little she would begin to check things out.

March of that year came in with unusual warmth. The skies were sunny and the daily temperatures pleasant. The first week of the month Nora and Ben welcomed a new daughter, and all were doing well. Soon it would be planting time, and Carrie knew it was time to put her plan to work.

One day while Luke was in school she asked Eliza to sit with the little ones so she could make a quick trip into Haymaker. Nora told her where Loose Lizzie lived, and the first step in her plan was to find out what this woman looked like. She made her way down the hill and turned toward the small town. Lizzie's house was only about a mile and a half away.

Soon the house was in sight...a small yellow house, not exactly rundown, but a house that had received little care. Carrie slowed down, trying to decide just how to go about the idea woven into her mind. What if no one was at home? But she was in luck. Just as she neared the house, the front door opened.

"You come back real soon, Sugar Plum," she heard a woman's voice say.

"You betcha, Lizzie," laughed the man. "I'll be back *real* soon. You just be waiting."

As the man left, Lizzie stood on the small front porch watching him go up the road. She was in a red shiny bathrobe, her hair undone and tangled. It was a reddish-brown color and her makeup was easily seen from a distance. As she turned with a laugh to go back in the house, she caught sight of Carrie.

Bracing herself and straightening her shoulders, Carrie waved to her and called, "Hello. I don't believe we've met."

Lizzie stopped, but didn't respond. Carrie walked on up to her front steps.

"Isn't this March weather wonderful?" she asked, forcing a smile to her face.

"Yeah, I guess it is," replied Lizzie, eyebrows making a tent, seeming rather at a loss for words.

Carrie continued, "I'm Carrie Swank and I live just about a mile and a half back on Lacy Creek."

"I'm Lizzie Willis," responded Lizzie, sizing Carrie up with her eyes. "What can I do for you *Mrs. Swank?*"

"Oh, you know that I'm married?" queried Carrie innocently. "I guess married women do have a certain look about them, come to think of it. Are you married, Miss Willis? I guess I can't tell by looking."

A scowl came over Lizzie's face. "No, I am not married," she huffed, "although I guess a lot of women around here wish I was." She laughed loudly.

Carrie blushed in spite of herself. "Well, I'd best be getting on to town. I have to get back to my little ones and *my* Tom will be home for supper before you know it. Nice talking to you, Miss Willis. Oh, I saw Thad Baker leaving as I came by. I guess he's a friend of yours, too. He's an elder in the church where my family goes and has been a friend of mine and Tom's for years. We love his wife Millie and their five children. Well, I'll see you again. Now that we've met I'll be watching for you whenever I go by."

With that, Carrie waved and continued on toward Haymaker, her legs trembling so badly she could hardly walk. She could not believe she had mustered the gall to do what she had just done, but at least now she knew what Loose Lizzie looked like. That was a beginning. She had also seen one of Lizzie's callers, Thad Baker, better known apparently as "Sugar Plum." A part of her was amused, but an even greater part was sick to her stomach. How dare this woman do what she was doing, and how dare Thad Baker treat his family this way. Was Tom coming here, too? The thought chilled her through and through, yet a little voice inside her whispered, *It's true, Carrie. It's true.*

CHAPTER 14

By the end of April, Carrie knew that she was expecting. A part of her rejoiced at the thought of another precious baby, yet another part felt sadness at bringing a child into such a troubled marriage.

Tom's lateness in coming home at night and his attitude toward Carrie and the kids had grown worse. The children tiptoed around in fearful silence when he was home. Though he had never beaten Luke again the way he had on Christmas Eve, he constantly fussed at him and criticized him, sometimes kicking him for some small mistake. He never raised his hand to Beanie or Ady Rose, but neither did he seem to acknowledge their existence, and he constantly cast his mean, one-eyed glance toward Jessie.

Papa Silas had begun dropping by more often, and Carrie wondered if he realized how bad things were. Jessie adored his grandpa. One day he was bouncing Jessie on his knee and playing "horsey."

"I'll bet your paw bounces you higher than this, don't he?" laughed Papa Silas.

"Paw don't like me," avowed Jessie, "and I don't like him neither."

Papa looked at Carrie and Carrie looked back at Papa, yet neither said a word. What was there to say? From that day forward, Jessie, who was just a toddler at the time, left no doubt about how he felt toward his father. Even Tom could look at his face and see the anger.

It was summer before Carrie told Tom she was pregnant. He simply nodded his head and walked out to do his chores. He did come home earlier for awhile, seeming to at least have the conscience to realize she needed extra help. By this time, however, the three older children had become her helpers. Luke was a man before his time, seldom laughing except when he played with his younger siblings. Beanie and Ady Rose helped Carrie cook and clean when most children their age were playing. It made Carrie sad to see their childhood pass from them, but she was also proud of each one.

Clay Isaac was born a week before Christmas. He was a strong, robust baby with an equally strong set of lungs. Carrie loved him from the beginning, but she vowed silently to herself that this would be the last child she had with this man who didn't love her. All of the children loved little Clay, but two-year-old Jessie adored him. He hovered over him constantly, talking to him as he would a child his own age. It was the beginning of a brother relationship that would last the rest of their lives.

The year 1912 made its entrance with blustery winds, cold temperatures and heavy snows. It was a difficult time to do outside chores and most of those fell to Carrie and Luke. It troubled Carrie to watch seven-year-old Luke try to do the work of a man when it was so cold his little gloves froze as he fed the livestock and carried wood. Beanie and Ady Rose were now able to watch Jessie and little Clay for short periods of time, allowing Carrie to milk and help Luke. Jessie was such a well-behaved little boy, seeming to know that his mother needed him to be so, and Clay was a healthy contented baby, especially when brother Jessie was nearby. Carrie's heart ached for her little family, but she knew God was watching over them and that gave her the reassurance to go on.

Tom hardly acknowledged Clay. He seldom came home before eight o'clock, ate, barked out a few orders to Luke, the only child still up, and then went to bed. He was usually snoring by the time Carrie got to bed.

She was thankful that he was asleep, and yet she lay awake aching for the life of which she had once dreamed. She prayed constantly for Tom, and sometimes thought the praying was all that kept her from hating him.

Somehow they all made it through a difficult winter, and spring rolled around as it has a way of doing. April arrived with moderate temperatures and daffodils giving their spring greetings in yards everywhere. Carrie longed to see the buttery daffodils in Mama Cynth's yard. Something about spring made her long for Mama Cynth. She had not been to visit Papa since Christmas, although he came by to see her and the children at least once a week. It was one such gorgeous spring day when she was sweeping the porch that she looked up to see him coming up the hill. A smile wreathed her face. Something about just seeing Papa made her world a calmer, happier place.

"Hi, Papa!" she called, as he neared the gate. "Have you ever seen such a glorious day?"

"Don't know that I have, Carrie girl," he replied. "Springtime is just a special time. It was your Mama's favorite time of year. She said everything came to life again, just like the Good Lord was doing his creating all anew."

"Mama had a way with words, didn't she?" laughed Carrie.

"Yes, and a special connection with her Maker," added Papa.

"What brings you out today, Papa? Are little Woody and Orin alright?" she asked.

"Oh, yes, they're fine," said Papa. "They keep us all hopping."

Carrie pulled a rocker over for Papa to sit. It was just too nice to go inside. She could see the children playing just inside the door, and five-year-old Ady Rose was a very reliable babysitter. Luke and Beanie were at school. It was hard to believe Luke was in second grade and Beanie in first at the little one room school in Haymaker.

"Have you heard from any of the family, Papa?" inquired Carrie, always anxious for news of her siblings. With the cold, snowy winter she had had very little contact with anyone.

"Well, there's news of your sister Lily," replied Papa.

"Oh, no. I'm afraid to ask," moaned Carrie.

"It's not so bad this time," responded Papa. "At least considering it's Lily we're talking about. It seems she and Dent went out and got married this past weekend. That's better than living the way they've been living."

"You're right, Papa," agreed Carrie. "I just wish she hadn't given those sweet children away. I still grieve over that."

"Well, there's more to the news," said Papa. "It seems Lily is in the family way."

Carrie's hand flew to her chest. "Papa, tell me she won't give this one away!"

"I don't think she will," replied Papa. "From what I'm told, she seems a mite happy about this one."

"I'll be praying extra hard that is true," sighed Carrie.

"I also heard from your sister Ellie," said Papa. "I'm afraid Henry is not well. Ellie said he has consumption. The doctor won't even allow him to be around their kids. They say it's catching, so he has to keep away from everyone as much as possible, but of course, Ellie has to take care of him. There's no way around that. There are places they keep people like him but Ellie won't hear to it. Can't say as I blame her."

"That must be so hard on Ellie," said Carrie, "taking care of Henry and the three little ones, too. Oh, Papa, you can always see others who are much worse off, no matter how bad your situation seems to be."

"Things no better between you and Tom?" asked Papa Silas.

"About the same," sighed Carrie. "We don't see much of him, to tell you the truth. He don't see the children, except for Luke, from Sunday night until the next Saturday morning."

"Don't he do any of the chores?" questioned Papa.

"Mostly on the weekend," answered Carrie. "Luke and I do them during the week. It's so hard on a boy not quite eight, but Luke is a man before his time. I'm truly proud of him, and yet my heart breaks for him. He needs to be running and playing, not slaving on this farm."

Changing the subject, Carrie asked, "How about you, Papa? How are you these days?"

"Oh, I can't complain about my life," sighed Papa. "Sile J. and Lula are good to me, and I love those two little boys, but I sure do miss your mama. She was the darling of my life, Carrie girl."

"I know, Papa. I know," whispered Carrie, feeling the moisture in her eyes.

It was soon time for Papa to take his leave, and Carrie went back to her children and her chores. Her heart seemed a little lighter after having someone to talk to. She had just finished feeding the children and cleaning up the dishes when there was a knock at the door. Ady Rose raced to answer it.

"Miss Liza is here! Miss Liza is here!" she called.

She came back into the kitchen with Eliza Thomas holding her hand and laughing.

"It's good to see you, Eliza," exclaimed Carrie. "We haven't seen you much this winter."

"I know," replied Eliza, "and I have missed these little ones sorely. Did I say little ones? My, they are half grown."

"I'm getting bigger and bigger," boasted little Jessie, with his chest puffed out.

"You certainly are," replied Eliza. "Why, you're almost a man, Jessie."

Carrie laughed, "You sure do know how to win him over, Eliza. They have missed you, too."

Well, that's really why I'm here," said Eliza. "Maw and I were just saying that you haven't been out of this house for months with the bad weather and all. Why don't I keep these wonderful children tomorrow and let you get out awhile."

"My, my, Eliza," answered Carrie. "That would be a real treat...for me and the children. I have some things I need from the mercantile, so I believe I'll just say yes to that offer."

"Then it's settled," said Eliza. "I'll come up about ten in the morning and you can have all day if you want it. I can catch up on everything with these youngsters before they've off and married."

With this the children broke into giggles.

The next morning she was there right on time. The children were so excited to be spending the day with "Liza".

"Now, Miss Carrie," said Eliza, "you just have yourself a good day and don't hurry back. Me and these three folks will have us a good time. I think I just might have a few stories to tell them if they are really, really good."

"We'll be good!" chorused Ady Rose and Jessie. Baby Clay contributed with a gurgle.

"I'm going to get some things I need at the mercantile," said Carrie. "Then, I'm thinking I just might go visit my sister Lily. Papa Silas says she and Dent got married and I think it's time two sisters got together. I don't always like what Lily does, but she is still my sister, and if she can get her life straightened out, I need to be helping all I can."

With this, Carrie took her leave. She was glad she had worn her wrap, because it was a bit nippy in spite of the azure blue sky and sunshine. As she neared town and passed by Loose Lizzie's house, she tried not to let thoughts of the woman spoil her day. Upon entering Berke's Mercantile, she met Bessie Seavers and her daughter.

"Why, Carrie," cried Bessie, "it's so good to see you. This winter has kept us in so much with its rawness I just haven't seen much of anyone. How are you and those fine children?"

"It's good to see you, too, Bessie, and you, Mary," Carrie responded. "We are all well. Eliza Thomas is with the children today and they love to stay with her. I hope your family is well."

They chatted for a few minutes and then Bessie and Mary took their leave. The store was fairly empty except for an older man and woman that Carrie didn't know.

"Good morning, Miss Carrie," said Mr. Faller. "It's good to see you out. This warm early spring weather seems to be bringing a lot of folks into town. Can I help you in any way?"

"Good morning, Mr. Faller," replied Carrie. "It is good to get out a little. Here is a list of some things I'll need you to fix up for me, and while you're doing that, I'll browse a little."

Carrie took her time, enjoying just looking at the merchandise without distractions. She found some needles she needed and some cloth for making a few more diapers. The ones left over from her other children were a bit worn and Clay could use some new ones. She also found some peppermint and licorice sticks for the children, and within thirty minutes she had her buys and Mr. Faller had the other items fixed up. She paid him and was ready to take her leave.

"I'll bet you enjoyed that new pink bedspread Tom bought for you the other day," declared Mr. Faller. "You are a lucky lady. It was the best we had and I had just gotten it in."

"Bedspread?" asked Carrie.

"Oh, no!" exclaimed Mr. Faller. "I hope I haven't spoiled a surprise. If I have, please forgive me, and don't tell Tom I spilled the beans."

"I won't, Mr. Faller," replied Carrie, trying to regain her voice. "Don't you worry about it. I'll just put on my surprised face."

Mr. Faller laughed as Carrie quickly took her leave. She was shaken, but tried to compose herself because she was determined to visit Lily and have a good sisterly time. As she neared Lily's, her thoughts were jumbling across her mind like clothes up and down a washboard. What had Mr. Faller meant about the bedspread? She didn't have a new bedspread, although she certainly could use one. Had he mixed Tom up with someone else? Besides, she didn't even like pink and Tom knew that. If Tom did buy a bedspread, who had he bought it for? His mother? Carrie didn't see him keeping that from her. Who, then, had he bought it for? As she neared Lily's yard, all of those thoughts just kept going around and around.

Carrie was just about to open the yard gate when she stopped cold. Something on the front porch caught her eye...something that was out of place there. It was Tom's dinner bucket! Carrie's heart went to her throat as did her hand. She was so weak in the knees she had to grab hold of the picket fence to keep from sitting down. Instead, she backed away, her eyes fixed the dinner bucket.

What is Tom's dinner bucket doing on Lily's porch? Carrie asked herself. *It's early afternoon and Tom should be at work.*

She looked again. Maybe it wasn't Tom's bucket. But it was. There was no doubt. There was a big splatter of red paint on the lid that Tom himself had spilled there when painting the little barn. Carrie backed further away, eyes still glued to the dinner bucket. Her head hurt from just trying to make sense of the whole thing. She went over to a nearby sycamore tree and just sat down. No one could see her there and she needed to figure out her thoughts. The answer that kept nagging at her was one Carrie didn't want to entertain. She finally decided to just stay put for awhile and see what transpired as it was only about one o'clock, and she had plenty of time before heading home.

At two o'clock nothing had changed and Carrie began to feel foolish sitting there spying on her own sister's house.

I'll just go ahead and visit Lily the way I had planned, decided Carrie. *There's probably a good reason for Tom's dinner bucket sitting there. Maybe he lost it and someone found it and brought it to Lily, knowing she is his sister-in-law.*

Just as she was ready to step out from her "hiding place", the door opened and Carrie heard laughter, then Lily's voice.

"Tom Swank, you always say the funniest things," she declared. "That's not all you do well either." With that she broke out into a boisterous laugh and Tom stepped out onto the porch.

"Lily, you're a live one, you are," laughed Tom. Laughing was something Carrie hadn't heard Tom do in a long, long time. Her heart began to shatter piece by piece.

As Tom bent down to pick up his lunch bucket, Lily said in her loud voice, "I'm already looking forward to your next stopping by, Tom. Dent's working every day, and a girl does get lonely, you know."

Responding only with laughter, Tom took his leave, heading back toward Haymaker instead of toward home. Carrie was so confused that her only thought at that moment was, *Is he going back to work?*

When he was out of sight, she arose to head home. Just as she stepped out she saw Peggy Tilton looking out her window from across the street. Peggy was the biggest gossip in Haymaker, so Carrie could just imagine the stories she would be telling. She headed home with a heavy heart and a confused mind. She had been worried about Loose Lizzie, when all the time Tom was carrying on with her own sister. How could they do this? Yes, Lily was wild, but how could she treat her own flesh and blood this way? Inside, a little voice whispered, *She gave her own children away. That's what flesh and blood means to her*. How could Tom do this? It was just beyond her comprehension.

Carrie walked on toward home slowly, her head and heart aching. She knew she had to pull herself together before she saw the children. As she neared the house, she pasted a smile to her face and tried to push all other thoughts from mind except the children. Just as she reached the bottom step, Ady Rose and Jessie came running out to meet her.

"Maw, your home!" cried Jessie. "We've had a hunky-dory time with Liza! Did you bring us anything, Maw?"

"Jessie, let her get up the steps," Ady Rose ordered in her big-sister voice.

"I'm so glad you had a good time," laughed Carrie. "I just hope Eliza can say the same."

"I most definitely had a good time," called Eliza, as she came out on the porch, carrying Clay. "These children would bring joy to anybody, Miss Carrie."

Apparently not to their Paw, came the thought unbidden to Carrie.

"Did you bring us anything, Maw?" asked Jessie again.

"I believe I might just have some peppermint and licorice sticks for anyone who has been extra good," offered Carrie.

"I been extra good!" replied Jessie. "Ain't I been good, Liza? Ady Rose has been extra good too. Right, Liza?"

At this everyone laughed and Carrie quickly fetched a licorice stick for each child. Eliza soon took her leave and, after hearing about everyone's day, Carrie began preparations for supper...probably another supper without Tom. To Carrie's way of thinking, that might be a good thing tonight. She would take care of her children today, and tonight would leave time for thinking. She was sure there would be little sleep for her.

CHAPTER 15

Tom actually did come home earlier that night, arriving about six o'clock in a better mood than Carrie had seen him for awhile. It was difficult to act as if she had not witnessed the scene at Lily's that day, and though she tried not to make the family time uncomfortable for the children, she could not look at Tom.

At the supper table he was in a talkative mood.

"Well, it's soon going to be time for a garden," he began. "Luke, you get your chores done as soon as you get home tomorrow and we'll start with the plowing. If we're going to feed this brood of young'uns we need a plentiful garden."

Luke made no reply except to nod. Tom frowned. The other children kept their silence.

That night held little sleep for Carrie. She pondered, wept and prayed. Her thoughts were still confused and her heart ached. What was her next step? What was she supposed to do?

Dear God, she prayed, *you know my thoughts. You know how my heart aches. This isn't the way marriage is supposed to be. I know it's not what you intended. What do I do, Lord? Show me the way. Touch Tom's heart, Lord...and yes, touch Lily's heart, too. Guard my sweet children, Father, and don't let them be hurt by all of this. It's not their doing, God, and I don't want them to feel unloved or unwanted. I don't want them to feel like they are the cause of any of this. Thank you, Lord. Amen.*

She arose the next morning at four thirty to fix Tom's breakfast and pack his lunch. As she picked up his dinner bucket the whole scene from yesterday came back to her...the dinner bucket sitting on Lily's doorstep. It was as if the dinner bucket had become her enemy. She knew that was silly, yet she could hardly stand to touch the awful thing. Carrie wiped away the tears as she heard Tom's footsteps. He sat down to eat as she poured his coffee.

"Come sit down and eat with me, Carrie," said Tom. "You don't seem yourself lately. Is something bothering you?"

"I'm not very hungry," replied Carrie, avoiding the question. "I'll just have a cup of coffee."

"I'll be home by five thirty this evening," he continued. "We'll get the garden ready, and there'll be corn to plant before you know it."

"You mean you won't be working late anymore?" questioned Carrie, looking into her coffee cup.

"Well, not every day," Tom responded. "I told the big man I needed some evenings to get the spring chores done. I'll probably work late a couple evenings a week. Gotta keep everyone happy."

Carrie turned away as the thought came racing into her head, *Just who are you keeping happy, Tom?*

In the ensuing weeks Tom settled into a routine. He worked late Tuesdays and Fridays, but the rest of the time he was home by five thirty. When he was home he was more like his old self, even nicer to the kids. Luke still kept his silent distance from his paw, and Jessie spoke to him only when he had to.

Carrie had settled upon a plan. First, she would still have that visit with her sister Lily that she had meant to have "the day of the dinner bucket." She would like to see Lily's reaction to her...and there was one more thing she had in mind.

Two weeks passed before she could put her plan into action. Eliza had once more agreed to stay with the children. The weather was warming even more and it had settled in to be a right nice day. She would visit the mercantile first and then stop back by Lily's house.

With her shopping finished and the items tucked under her arm, Carrie knocked on Lily's door. The door opened with a swoosh and there stood Lily with a flabbergasted look on her face.

"Well, as I do live and breathe," she declared with sarcasm, "it's my sister from years past come to pay this old heathen a visit. Come in, Carrie, and tell me what brought about this enormous pleasure."

Swallowing the feelings choking her, Carrie replied, "Yes, it has been a long time, Lily. I just decided it was time for a visit and some catching up. Sisters shouldn't go so long without good chats. Tell me all about yourself."

Caught a little off guard by Carrie's response, Lily seemed to feel more at ease. "Well, I guess you know me and Dent got married. He decided to make an honest woman out of me...or try anyway." With this she gave a booming laugh.

"I'm very happy for you, Lily," said Carrie. "I've always liked Dent. He seems like a pleasant sort. Is he working at the sawmill?"

"Yes, he is," replied Lily. "Thank God I don't have a man in the mines anymore. No more coal black washings and a man wheezing from the coal dust."

"Anything else new?" Carrie inquired quietly.

"As a matter of fact, there is," answered Lily. "I'm sure all the gossips will have a field day with this, but I don't care. Never did care about people's tongues. Me and Dent are going to have a baby!" With this she sat back in her chair and patted her already protruding stomach.

"A baby!" cried Carrie, as though this was total news to her. "That is really good news."

"Oh, I know what you're thinking," countered Lily. "Is she going to give this kid away? Well, to get rid of the curiosity, NO, I ain't going to give this one away. Dent's happy and I'm happy, and that's that."

Changing the subject, Carrie remarked, "You really have the house fixed up, Lily. It looks so warm and cozy. Have you decided you like housework?"

"No, I still don't like house chores," replied Lily, shaking her head adamantly. "My Dent knows I wasn't cut out for housework, so he pays

Sary Simmins to clean for me once a week. Now ain't that just the cat's pajamas?" This was accompanied by another booming laugh.

"Well, what do you do with all of that spare time?" asked Carrie, looking straight into Lily's eyes.

"Oh," laughed Lily, "I keep busy. Never doubt, Sister Dear. I keep busy."

"Lily," said Carrie, "I'm a mite thirsty. Could I trouble you for a glass of water?"

"Why, sure," responded Lily. "I could use a little something to drink myself. Are you sure you just want water?"

"Oh, yes," assured Carrie. "Just water."

Lily pushed up from the sofa and moved toward the kitchen. Carrie now had the chance to take the next step in her plan. She quickly arose and moved toward what she assumed was a bedroom. The door was open, so she peeked in. She did not see what she thought she might, and her hammering heart settled somewhat. There was another door that Carrie thought might also be a bedroom, so she moved toward it. As she looked in, the hammering began again. In fact, her heart felt like it would fly right out of her chest. For there on the double bed, was a pink bedspread...and Carrie could see that it was a NEW pink bedspread.

Just then, Lily came back into the living room. "What are you looking at?" she questioned.

Squelching the lump in her throat, Carrie replied, "Oh, just stretching my legs and looking at your cozy little home. You've done so much for this place. I love this pink bedspread. Is it new? Pink was always one of your favorite colors, wasn't it?"

"Yeah, I was always right partial to pink," answered Lily, with a dubious look on her face as she handed Carrie a glass of water.

"Thank you, Lily," said Carrie.

"What about you, Carrie?" asked Lily. "How's your life going these days? You have how many...five young'uns now?"

"Yes," replied Carrie. "Tom and I have Luke and Belinda who are in school, and Ady Rose, Jessie and Clay at home."

"That's a house full," said Lily. "Keeps you busy, I guess."

"They do, but I love every minute of it," responded Carrie. "Now I'd best be getting home to them. Eliza Thomas is keeping them, but supper time will be here before you know it and Tom will be home and hungry." She paused for a moment and then spoke, "Oh no, I forgot. This is Tuesday, and Tom always works late on Tuesdays."

The look on Lily's face spoke volumes.

In mid May, news came from Kentucky that Ellie's husband Henry had passed away. Carrie couldn't leave her family to go that far away for the funeral, but Papa, and three of her brothers made the trip. Charles chose not to leave Lucinda for both she and little Katie had come down with terrible colds. Carrie felt so sad for her sister Ellie. Henry was a good man and a good provider for his family.

It was about this time that Tom's brother, Nate, sent word that their mother was very ill. Tom left as soon as he found out, and returned in a forlorn mood.

"Maw won't be here much longer, Carrie," he said. "If she lasts another week it will fool me. They've had Doc Whitt over and he says it's her heart. Paw says she's been past going for several months now, but she didn't want to worry us."

Carrie wiped away a tear. She loved Maw Izzy very much. She was a good God-fearing woman and had always been good to Carrie.

"Do I need to go over and help, Tom?" she asked. "I'm sure Eliza would watch the children for me if I'm needed."

"No, I don't think so," replied Tom. "Nannie is staying with her, and Nate and his family are in and out all the time. I'll go back over tomorrow after work and check on her again. Thank you, Carrie, for caring."

Carrie put her arms around Tom as she saw his shoulders shaking. There was a time for anger later. This was a time for comforting.

Izabelle Swank lasted two more weeks, and then departed this world for the next. It was a sad time for all, but especially for Paw Charles. Carrie remembered Papa Silas when Mama Cynth passed away, and she felt an aching in her heart for Tom's dad. The funeral was held in Charles and Izzy's home with Brother Jonas from the Primitive Baptist church doing the preaching as he had done at Mama Cynth's funeral. Brother Jonas had been preaching for as long as Carrie could remember and was looking frail with age. Izzy was buried in the Swank Family cemetery atop the hill just out from their house. Most families had their own cemetery, and they seemed always to be located high on a hill. The cemeteries were well kept and visited often.

For weeks after Izzy's death Tom was home by five thirty, quiet and pensive, working until dark plowing, planting and fixing what needed to be fixed. He was even pleasant to the children and was teaching Luke things a boy ought to know about the farm. It was a quietly pleasant time in Carrie's life, but the scars wouldn't allow her to hope.

One day in early July, as she was sweeping the front porch, she heard peals of laughter coming from the little barn lot. She propped her broom against the door facing and went to see what was going on. Luke, Beanie, Ady Rose and Jessie were standing at the gate to the barn lot looking at Bossie as she cleaned her newborn calf. Each time the calf tried to stand, it fell back down and the children would laugh again.

"Look at it, Maw!" cried Jessie, his eyes sparkling with excitement. "Just look at Bossie's wobbly calf!"

"Ain't it pretty, Maw?" squealed Ady Rose. "When will it stand up?"

By this time Carrie was laughing, too. "Just give it a few minutes. It will be standing."

"Bossie's going to be a good mother," said Beanie. "Just look how she takes care of it. Why, she's just like you, Mama."

At this the other children broke into more peals of laughter. "Maw's not like a cow, Beanie," Jessie laughed.

"But she takes care of us just like Bossie is taking care of her baby," explained Luke. "That's what Beanie means."

Jessie just nodded. Whatever his big brother said was gospel to him.

"Can we name her, Maw?" asked Ady Rose.

"I don't see why not," replied Carrie. "Why don't all four of you think about it and see if you can agree on a good name. Now take your time. Names are important, you know."

That evening when Tom got home the children couldn't wait to tell him about the new calf. One sentence rolled into another as each tried to give his or her version.

"Maw said we could name it, Paw," said Beanie, "but we can't decide yet what we want its name to be."

"Well, have you picked out a boy's name or a girl's name?" asked Tom.

At this, the children stopped and just looked at each other. "I guess we didn't think about that," admitted Luke. "We don't know what it is."

"Tell you what," said Tom. "After supper I'll just go out and ask its mama whether she has a boy or girl." He winked at Carrie. "Then I'll come back and tell you, and then you can pick a name."

The children smiled at this and quietly ate their supper. No doubt, names were rolling around in their heads, leaving no time for talking. Carrie felt such a peace at that moment, wishing it could always be a happy home as it was this night.

Tom kept his word and informed the children the calf was a heifer.

"What's a heifer?" asked Ady Rose. "Is that a bad thing, Paw?"

With this, Tom laughed, "No, Ady Rose. A heifer is what you call a girl calf. She will be a heifer until she grows up and has a calf of her own. Then she'll just be called a cow."

"I guess it's sort of like people," inserted Luke. "I'll be a boy until I'm grown. Then I'll be a man."

"That's the gist of it," said Tom.

Summer wore on and Carrie was busy harvesting vegetables from the garden and canning and drying them for winter. Luke and Beanie picked blackberries, raspberries and then strawberries from which Carrie made jellies and preserves. As the apples came in, she dried some and canned some. Her whole family loved her fried apple pies. The folks of the Appalachians made the most of what God gave them to see that their families were well fed.

The children had named the calf Bluebell and visited her several times a day. At first, Bossie was a little particular with her baby but soon learned that the children meant no harm. Bluebell seemed to love the children's attention, but she especially took to Jessie. Once she could be turned out of the lot, when Jessie was outside she followed him around just like a puppy dog. Jessie's brother and sisters didn't seem to mind this and Jessie thrived on this new found friend.

Tom continued to come home by five thirty almost every day, spent time with the children and did the chores. About once a week he went over to see about his paw. Charles was living by himself, but Nate was there often and Nannie did his washing and cleaning.

It was after one of these visits in early October that Tom came home mad as a hornet. Carrie was in the kitchen cleaning up after supper when Tom slammed open the door, scaring her half to death. He strode over to the table and kicked a chair, causing it to topple.

"Whatever is the matter?" gasped Carrie, wiping her hands on her apron. "Sit down and tell me what has you so riled up."

He jerked out a chair, sat down and put his arms on the table. His face was blood red.

"He's gonna marry," declared Tom.

"Who's going to marry?" questioned Carrie.

"Paw is gonna marry," spat out Tom. "Maw's just been dead a few months and he's gonna marry. Of all the mean, disrespectful, uncaring, gol'darned hurtful..."

"Tom, please settle yourself," said Carrie. "You're going to have a stroke."

"I don't care what I have," yelled Tom, pounding his fist on the table. "I don't want to live to see a paw of mine act this way. Didn't Maw mean nothing to him?"

"Who told you he's getting married?" asked Carrie. "Are you sure about this?"

"He told me about it himself! Gol'darn fool!" shouted Tom. "Right there in front of Nannie. And do you know what? Nannie is alright with it! Now can you believe that? No respectful time of waiting; no 'What do you think, Tom?'; no nothing. It's a smear on Maw's good name, that's what it is. The whole bunch of them are gol'darn fools."

Sitting down beside Tom, Carrie asked, "Who is he marrying? I didn't know he was courting anybody."

"He's marrying Hala Forest and she's about half his age," he responded. "Can you beat that? The man has taken leave of his senses."

"Hala Forest..." said Carrie, trying to think. "Isn't she Wilber Forest's widow, the one who was killed about a year ago in a logging accident?"

"Yeah, that's her," snapped Tom. "Just looking for someone to put food on her table, I bet, and he don't have sense enough to know he's not sixteen anymore."

"Tom," said Carrie, soothingly, "I know this does seem awfully soon, and I wish he had waited a bit longer, but maybe he needs someone. A man just can't do for himself the way a woman does for him, and maybe she does need someone to support her. Try to look at it from their way of thinking. Besides, Paw Charles was good to your mother and was always faithful. That counts for a lot."

Tom pushed back from the table as his face reddened. "I'll bet you wouldn't be looking at it so calmly if it was your paw," he said. "What if Silas told you he was getting married again, even after all these years, Carrie? Then what would you be saying?"

"I don't know, Tom," she answered. "I think I'd be hurt, but then I think I'd want what's best for Papa. At least, I hope that's what I would feel."

Tom sat there for a moment, seeming to ponder what she had said. Then he got up and walked out to the porch and sat down. Carrie left him be, for she knew he needed time to think.

CHAPTER 16

Charles and Hala were married at Charles' home two weeks later by Brother Jonas. Hala moved in to Tom's old home place with her new husband. Tom had settled in to the idea by necessity but couldn't bring himself to attend the wedding. Carrie heard from Nora that Nate and Nannie were there.

Christmas was a happier time that year. Tom, though somewhat sullen, bought each of the children a gift on his own…a real rifle for Luke, a set of dishes and hair ribbons for Beanie, a doll and hair ribbons for Ady Rose, a wooden train set for Jessie, and even a rattle for baby Clay. They had all decorated the tree together much like it was done when Carrie was a child. Christmas day they piled into the old farm wagon and went to Papa Silas' house. Ellie and her three children had come over from Kentucky for a few days. Nora, Ben and their family were there along with Carrie's brothers and their families. The only ones missing were Dent and Lily. They had welcomed a little one into the world in November…Harlan Dent Tyler… and Lily preferred not to get out so soon. The house was filled with talk and laughter and more little ones than you could count. The only sad part for Carrie was when she thought of the children Lily gave away and wondered where they were spending Christmas this year.

While the others were engrossed in conversation, Nora and Carrie had some time to be off to themselves for some catching up.

"How are things with you and Tom, Carrie, if you don't mind my asking?" inquired Nora. "He seems more like his old self except for a quietness about him."

"I guess things are pretty good," replied Carrie. "Tom has been quiet lately. He just can't accept his paw marrying again. He was really riled at first; wouldn't even go to the wedding, but I think he's beginning to deal with it."

"I'm glad Lily didn't come today," said Nora. Carrie had told her sister the whole story.

"I'm sort of relieved myself," answered Carrie. "At least I can relax and not have to keep an eye out for any shenanigans."

"Let's go over and talk with Ellie," suggested Nora. "She looks so sad and forlorn, and she's lost a good bit of weight. I can't imagine how difficult this must be for her."

"Her little ones are certainly well-behaved," said Carrie, "but they seem sad, too, especially Jackson Henry. He and Henry were very close."

With this they made their way over to Ellie to spend time with her.

January came in fiercely with a blizzard that prevented Beanie and Luke from going to school for the entire month. Tom came home on time each day, but Carrie watched as he became more and more moody. They were cooped up in the house in the evenings, and he became increasingly short tempered with the children. Most evenings after supper the children played in the kitchen where it was warm and left Tom to his peace and quiet in the living room. It was only when their paw wasn't there that the children played and behaved like normal youngsters.

February was a carbon copy of January, but by early March changes were slowly coming about. Luke and Beanie were back in school each day and the others enjoyed playing at home. Some days they could even go outside for short periods of time. Unfortunately, Tom began coming home late again. This time Carrie didn't even question him about it. What was the use?

One warm day about mid March, Ady Rose and Jessie were sitting on the top step leading to the front porch eagerly watching for their brother and sister to get home. Carrie heard Jessie exclaim, "What happened to you?"

Carrie, sensing trouble, immediately went to the porch. There stood Luke and Beanie. Luke's face was bleeding, his hands were skinned and his shirt was torn.

"Luke, what happened?" cried Carrie, as she knelt down to touch him.

Luke just stood there, his head lowered, refusing to answer.

Carrie turned to Beanie. "Beanie, what happened to your brother?"

"He g-got into a f-fight with some older b-boys," answered Beanie, wiping her tears.

"Why on earth were you fighting, Luke?" Carrie questioned. "I've never known you to get into a fight before."

Luke did not raise his head nor answer. Instead, he walked past his mother toward the house, his shoulders bent with unseen weight.

"Some boys said some bad things about Paw," offered Beanie. "Luke tried not to pay them any mind, but they just kept on and on."

"What kind of things were they saying?" asked Carrie.

"I don't know exactly," answered Beanie. "Something about a woman named Loose Lizzie."

Carrie's hand went to her throat as her face became ashen.

"They said she has a little boy and he's our brother," continued Beanie. "Said he's the spittin' image of Jessie. That don't make any sense, Maw. Does it?"

Carrie sat down in the floor, struggling for air.

"Maw, are you okay?" cried Ady Rose. "Maw?"

Jessie began to cry. "What's wrong, Maw?"

Carrie managed to catch her breath and gather herself together. "I'm alright. I am just surprised by all of this. Now you children be good and let me go see about Luke. Don't worry about what those boys said. They are just being mean."

When she went to Luke, he was sitting on the side of his bed, head down and shoulders slumped. Carrie said nothing, but simply sat down beside him and took him in her arms. As she did that Luke gave in to his feelings and began to sob. She held him and rocked him in her arms until his crying finally subsided.

"Luke, you are a boy who loves," she began, as he calmed, "and I'm so proud of you for that. But not everyone loves. Some hate and some just like to cause trouble. If you can, just put their words out of your mind. Don't let them get by with hurting you."

"Maw, what did they mean?" he asked. "Do I have a brother? I don't even know anyone named Loose Lizzie."

"She is a woman who lives in Haymaker," answered Carrie. "I don't even know if she has children, Luke, so don't think anymore about it. Okay?"

Luke nodded his head. "Can I just stay in here for a few minutes, Maw? I'll do my chores in just a bit."

"Of course you can," replied Carrie. "Don't be in a hurry about the chores. When you feel better we'll get you cleaned up."

Carrie spent the remainder of the evening reassuring the children. Tom came home about seven o'clock and they avoided him as much as possible. The only one who looked at him was Jessie, and Carrie had never seen such a look of dislike on a face so little. It weighed heavy on her, and she resolved in her heart that night to get to the bottom of things. Did Tom have a child by another woman? She intended to find out.

The weather turned back nippy with snow as March days have a way of doing. Luke and Beanie were out of school for a few days, and Carrie had to postpone her plans to look into the "Loose Lizzie matter". Although Tom was on his better behavior, she was still determined to find out if what the boys had said to Luke was true. It was bad enough that Tom had hurt her, but it was unforgiveable for him to hurt her innocent babies. Ady Rose had just turned six and would start school in the fall and Carrie would have three that other children might pick on.

By the end of March the weather was still terrible, and Carrie had another worry eating at her. She was pretty sure that she was pregnant again...something she had promised herself would not happen. It wasn't that Carrie didn't want children; her children were her whole life. Yet, with Tom the way he was, she didn't want anyone else to be hurt by him. Still, if God saw fit to give her another baby, she would love it with everything in her.

The weather finally broke the second week in April, and as temperature warmed when the sun made its daily appearance, before long the hills and hollows were strewn with daffodils, hyacinths and blossoming trees. It was almost a time when one could forget all the troubles of the world... almost. By now Carrie's pregnancy was a certainty. She estimated that it would arrive sometime in late October, but so far she hadn't told Tom. She hadn't been sick at all this time, but then she doubted he would notice if she was.

In early May, while the two oldest were still in school, Carrie decided to go into town for some items and also to do a little "finding out". Eliza was more than willing to sit with her three favorite little ones.

First, Carrie went by Loose Lizzie's house. It was about ten o'clock and no one seemed to be out and about. Unable to conjure up the nerve to knock on the door, she proceeded on to Haymaker. At the mercantile she picked up the items she needed and then decided to treat herself to lunch at Lillian's Diner. She hadn't eaten there in ever so long. As she entered, who should she see but her sister Nora sitting at one of the little tables.

"Nora," she called, as she headed toward the table. "What a big surprise. Are you having lunch?"

"I've just now sat down," said Nora. "We can have lunch together and catch up on all the news. I never once thought I'd see you today."

They ordered their food and sat leisurely talking. It felt so good to relax and just be sisters. Carrie thought about telling Nora about the matter concerning Loose Lizzie, but for some reason she just couldn't ruin their good time with her troubles. They spent almost an hour eating and catching-up before Nora finally said she had to go. Carrie bid her farewell and headed back to the mercantile for some stick candy for the little ones. As she entered Berke's Mercantile, there was an elderly woman standing at the counter on which she had placed several items.

"Now, Matildy," said Mr. Faller, kindly but firmly, "I can't give you anymore credit. You haven't paid any on your bill for three months now."

"I'll pay some the first of the month," answered the woman. "I got a lot of mouths to feed and I don't have any money right now."

The small child beside of her began to whimper. "Granny, I'm hungry."

A look of pity came over Mr. Faller's face. "I'll let you take these things and I'll add them to your bill, but this is the last time, Matildy. Do you understand? Don't even come in here again unless you have some money."

Matildy eagerly agreed and turned to leave. As they passed Carrie, the little boy holding to the woman's dress tail looked up at her and Carrie caught her breath. The little boy, about four or five, looked just like Jessie.

Carrie placed her hand on the woman's arm to stop her. "May I ask your name?" Carrie said.

"I'm Matildy Willis," replied the woman, giving Carrie a withering look. "Most folks around here know me," she added, with a gleam in her eye.

"Is this your little boy?" inquired Carrie.

"He's my grandson," answered Matildy. "He's Lizzie's boy."

Carrie could make no reply, and Matildy and the little boy made their way around her. She stood and stared after them for the longest time before turning to get her purchases. As she turned she caught the look on Mr. Faller's face. He looked away quickly, but not before Carrie saw the pity in his eyes. She hurriedly finished her business and left the store. As she walked home, her thoughts were a jumble of anger and sadness. It was Tom's child; she had no doubt. He had fathered another woman's child and she would have to live with that knowledge, but worst of all, her children would have to grow up knowing this. There would be no getting around it. Everyone would know...probably already knew... and everyone would talk. From the look she had seen on Mr. Faller's face, she was probably the only person who didn't know.

That night Tom came home late again, but Carrie waited up for him, knowing she had to confront him. She had some food warm, but he wasn't hungry.

"What are you doing still up, woman?" he asked gruffly. "I'm tired and I need to get to bed."

"I'm tired, too, Tom," replied Carrie, in a determined voice, "but you and I need to talk."

"Talk about what?" asked Tom. Then he paused, "Is one of the kids sick?"

"No," she answered. "I think, Tom, that our marriage is sick."

"What in tarnation are you talking about, Carrie?" he stormed. "Have you lost your wits completely?"

"Don't wake the children, Tom," warned Carrie, in a calm whisper. "I need to ask you a question and you need to tell me the truth."

He said nothing as Carrie continued. "Luke and Beanie have been picked on by some children at school...children who seem to know a lot about Loose Lizzie."

At the mention of the name Tom blanched.

Carrie didn't hesitate. "They tell *your* children, Tom, that *they* have a brother who is Loose Lizzie's son. Is that right, Tom?"

"You don't know what you're talking about, Carrie," whispered Tom loudly. "Where on earth are you getting' all these ideas? Are you plumb adled?"

"I saw him, Tom," Carrie went on. "I saw him."

Tom sat down with a scowl on his face. "Saw who, Carrie? Saw who?"

"I saw the little boy with his grandmaw Matildy," she replied. "I saw *your* son."

With this Tom jumped up, knocking the chair over. "You shut your mouth, woman. Do you hear me? I don't never want to hear none of this nonsense again. Now I'm going to bed!"

"Are there more, Tom?" Carrie asked, showing no fear. "How many more children do you have that I don't know about?"

He stormed from the kitchen and stomped toward the bedroom. Carrie just sat there staring into space, drained beyond words. She knew without a doubt. Tom might never admit it, but Carrie knew...and it tore at her heart.

From the corner of her eye she caught a slight movement, and looking up she saw Jessie standing just inside his bedroom door staring at her.

"I hate him," he said, in a low, angry voice through gritted teeth. Then he turned and walked away.

"Oh, dear Jesus," whispered Carrie. "He's such a little boy to know all of this."

After that night, Carrie stopped wondering what Tom was doing and when he was coming home. He began coming home early again, but it didn't matter anymore. About a week later she told him she was pregnant, simply because she felt he should know. Tom just nodded his head and walked on out to do his chores and Carrie went on with her work. The days came and went as Carrie took care of her children, determined to give them enough love to make up for any hurts they might face, unable to admit to herself that it was an impossible task.

In June Luke turned nine and in July Beanie turned eight. They were both so much help, as were all of her children. They seemed to think if they just helped enough they could ease their mother's pain. She tried to keep a cheerful attitude for their sake, but they weren't deceived. Luke, Beanie and Ady Rose took such good care of Jessie and Clay that Carrie never had to worry about them. Luke was pulling a man-size load on the farm. Tom was still coming home on time and he and Luke worked until dark, but they seldom talked to each other more than necessity required. Tom could lose his temper with Luke quite easily, so Luke tried to avoid contact with him as much as the work would allow. Little Jessie worked much harder than most children his age, but he never wanted anything to do with his paw. Carrie kept busy, harvesting and canning, washing, ironing, and cleaning. The work was never done, but it was a blessed escape for her. Busy hands helped to occupy her thoughts.

In September, the three oldest went off to school. Carrie was getting quite large with child by now and her work was more cumbersome. Jessie became her little shadow, always at hand to make her chores easier. On washday, he handed the clothes up to her to hang on the line so she didn't have to bend so much. He learned to sweep and mop, and he was always ready to take care of Clay. He fetched firewood, gathered eggs, set the table...anything he could do to help. As he worked he jabbered and laughed, entertaining Carrie and Clay. It wasn't until Tom came home in the evening that a change came over him. Once Tom walked through the door, he never laughed or talked, just did his chores with somber eyes. His dislike for his paw often worried Carrie, but she didn't know how to remedy the matter.

It was the last day in October when Carrie went into labor. As she sent the three oldest off to school and washed the breakfast dishes, the pains began with a vengeance. Her back had hurt all night, and now she had no doubt that it was time.

Jessie looked up from playing on the floor with Clay. "Maw, are you alright?"

"Jessie," she answered, "I need you to do a big boy job for me."

"Okay, Maw. I can do it," he said, standing up.

"I need you to go down to Widow Thomases house and tell her and Eliza I need them," explained Carrie. "Tell them it's my time. They'll understand."

Jessie didn't hesitate, but left right away. Within minutes he was back with Eliza.

"Momma will be here in just a few minutes, Miss Carrie," said Eliza. "She's sending word to your sister Nora to see if she can come get Jessie and Clay. Now you just go rest and I'll finish up here in the kitchen and take care of my two favorite boys. Jessie will help me."

Carrie headed to the bedroom. She had no intention of lying down yet, but she needed to get things ready. In no time Widow Thomas was there. Just as she entered the bedroom, Carrie had a severe pain that caused her to double over and cry out.

Widow Thomas hurried to her. "Are they coming pretty fast now, Carrie?"

"Faster and harder," replied Carrie, through clenched teeth. "The pains are much harder than any I remember before. You don't think anything is wrong, do you?"

"No, I'm sure everything is fine," the widow assured her. "We have a tendency to forget just how bad the pain is."

Just then Eliza peeped around the door. "Nora has sent your Papa to take the children to her house, Miss Carrie and I have them all ready. Do you want to see them?"

Carrie smiled weakly, "Yes, let them come in."

Jessie and Clay walked meekly through the door, a mixture of fear and curiosity in their eyes.

"Now boys," smiled Carrie, "you be good for Aunt Nora. You will probably be staying with her just for tonight. When you get back home I just might have a surprise for you."

"You mean a new baby, don't you, Maw?" grinned Jessie.

"I can't ever fool you, can I?" laughed Carrie. "Yes, Jessie, my little man, a new baby. And if it's half as sweet as you, I'll be thankful for the rest of my life."

Papa Silas stuck his head in the door. "How are you doing, girlie?" he asked.

"I'm fine, Papa," laughed Carrie. "Are you ready for another grandchild? How many will this make?"

"Don't have enough fingers and toes to count them," he replied. "Just you take care, Carrie Tan."

With that, Papa and the two boys left, and none too soon. A terrible gripping pain overtook Carrie. By three, when the children came home from school, there was still no baby but horrendous pain. Eliza herded Luke, Beanie and Ady Rose outside to do the chores, then walked part way with them to Nora's house. Luke was old enough to take them the rest of the way.

"Eliza, are you sure Maw's gonna be okay?" questioned Luke. "Maybe we should stay just in case she needs us."

"Your Maw will be fine," assured Eliza. "She's done this five times before, you know."

"But we're big enough to stay," said Beanie. "I don't like leaving Maw."

"You'll be home first thing in the morning. I promise," answered Eliza. "Now just go along with you and don't fret. This is what your Maw wants."

By five there was still no baby. Tom arrived and assessed the situation quickly, then just as quickly headed back outside to do his chores.

"He didn't even talk to her," exclaimed Eliza. "What kind of man don't even want to say something to his wife when she's about to have his baby?"

Before Widow Thomas could respond, Carrie let out a piercing scream.

"Eliza, I think you had better go fetch Doc Whitt," her mother said. "Something just ain't right. I'm afraid this baby may be breech and I'm not sure I can handle it if there's more wrong than that."

Paling, Eliza hurried out to do as her mother said.

Dear Jesus, silently whispered Eliza as she hurried along, *I'm asking you to help Miss Carrie. Ain't no better woman living than she is, Lord, and she ain't had an easy life with old One-eyed Tom for a husband. Just help her and this baby to be alright. And, Lord, if you could just jerk a kink in old Tom's tail, I know it would mean a lot to her. But with him, Lord you got your work cut out for you.*

It was after six when Eliza returned with Doc Whitt, who quickly examined Carrie and confirmed Widow Thomases fear. The baby was breech.

"We're going to have to turn this baby, Carrie," the doctor explained calmly. "It's going to hurt a mite, but if we don't the baby won't make it. Are you up to it, girl?"

Carrie nodded weakly. "Just do what you have to, Doc. I want this baby to live."

The pain that followed was worse than any Carrie could have imagined. It seemed that it took hours for Doc and Widow Thomas to turn the baby. At five after eight Carrie gave birth to a baby girl. She was exhausted but could not believe her eyes when she held her daughter for the first time...she looked exactly like Mama Cynth. That was the last thought that came to her mind before she fell into an exhausted sleep with a smile on her face.

At four the next morning, Carrie awakened to the hungry cries of her baby. Eliza brought the baby to her.

"Looks like there's nothing wrong with her lungs...or her appetite!" laughed Eliza.

Carrie fed her daughter and immediately fell back asleep. The sun was shining through the bedroom window when she awoke later in the morning. Everything was peacefully quiet except for the birds singing happily in the trees. Carrie smiled to herself as she remembered the baby she had held...the spittin' image of Mama Cynth.

The door to the bedroom slowly opened and Tom came sheepishly into the room.

"Are you alright, Carrie Tan? They said you had a real bad time."

"I'm fine, Tom," she replied. "Have you seen your daughter?"

"I reckon I have," he grinned. "She's a little beauty."

"Can you bring her to me?" asked Carrie. "Or have Eliza bring her."

"I'll bring her," replied Tom, as he headed toward the cradle that had held all of their babies.

As he placed her in Carrie's arms, she looked into the little face, wondering if what she remembered was right.

"Look, Tom!" she exclaimed.

"What is it?" he asked with a worried catch to his voice.

"Look at her Tom!" she cried again. "She looks just like Mama Cynth!"

Tom bent to examine her closely. "Well, I believe she does."

"I'm going to name her after Mama," declared Carrie. "Cynthia Ellen. What do you think of that?"

"I think that's a mighty fine name," laughed Tom, "and she's named after a mighty fine woman, too."

Happiness enveloped Carrie at that moment. She hadn't felt such peace in a very long time, and she was still smiling when she heard a soft knock at the bedroom door.

"Miss Carrie, I have you and Mr. Tom some breakfast ready if you're hungry," said Eliza, just stepping inside the door. "I'll bring yours in here to you. Doc Whitt says you need at least two days in bed. That was a rough time you just had."

"Thank you, Eliza," said Tom. "You bring Carrie's on in. I'm going to eat a bite and then go fetch our children from Nora's. If you can stay until I get back, I'd be much obliged. I'm going to take the rest of the week off from work to help out around here."

Carrie could hardly believe her ears, and her surprise was mirrored in Eliza's face. Tom had never done this before.

"I'll be glad to stay," responded Eliza. "If it's okay I'd like to come check on her each day for awhile."

"Thank you," answered Tom. "We could use your help, Eliza, and Carrie always feels extra good with you around. I'll be out to eat in just a minute."

As Eliza turned to leave, Tom turned back to Carrie and sat down on the edge of the bed.

"Carrie, there's something I need to tell you."

"What is it?" questioned Carrie. "Is something wrong with the baby?"

"No, no," he replied quickly. "She's just fine. But, Carrie, you had a real hard time with her, and Doc says you need lots of rest. And...well, there's something else. Doc says you can't have no more babies, Carrie. Some damage was done. You're gonna be okay, but you just can't have no more little ones."

Carrie lay there for a moment, taking in what Tom had just said. Then she looked up at him.

"Well, Tom, God has given us six beautiful, healthy, well-behaved children, and I guess we can just be thanking Him for that. I remember Mama once said that God decides when we're to have babies and when we're to stop. If it's my time to stop, then I won't be questioning Him because I've been richly blessed."

Carrie ate breakfast, fed the baby and fell fast asleep again. She awoke to the voices of little ones outside her door.

"I'm awake!" she called. "Is that my sweet children I hear out there?"

With that, the door opened and all five came meekly into the room. Tom was right behind them.

Carrie's face lit up at the sight of them. "Come here and give your Mama a big hug. My, how I've missed you! "

The children came eagerly but carefully to her, each giving her a hug. Then their eyes wandered over to the little cradle.

"Can we see her, Maw?" whispered Ady Rose.

"Of course you can," answered Carrie. "She's a real beauty and so anxious to meet her big brothers and sisters."

The children went to the cradle and surrounded it, sitting in the floor and just gazing down at their new baby sister with big, wonder-filled eyes.

"What's her name, Maw?" whispered Jessie.

"I've decided to name her Cynthia, after my mother," replied Carrie. "She looks so much like her. Do you like the name?"

All five children nodded, and Jessie added, "I'm going to call her Baby Cindy. Okay, Maw?"

"I think that sounds just right, Jessie," laughed Carrie. "You'll be such a good big brother."

Tom shooed them out of the room and Carrie went back to sleep. She felt extremely tired, and in the next several days she slept a lot. Doc Whitt came back to see her three days after the birth and was pleased with her progress, but he still recommended plenty of rest.

"You can get up and sit for short periods of time, Carrie," he said, "but no work before next week. Tom says he will be here until then and Eliza and Widow Thomas will help for a week after that. By then you should be well mended and back to your old self. Taking care of a home and six children will take a lot of energy, so give yourself time to fully recuperate."

The next two weeks raced by quickly. Tom was good to his word and stayed home the rest of the week, doing chores both outside and inside. Eliza came once or twice a day and, with Beanie's help, did most of the cooking and house cleaning. On Monday, Tom went back to work and Eliza came to stay each day, washing, cooking, ironing and cleaning, as well as taking care of Jessie, Clay and Cindy. Carrie's life was bright once more.

By the time two weeks had passed, Carrie was up to par and ready to take over her home and her children. It was mid-November and Thanksgiving would be here before she could turn around. She reckoned she had about as much to be thankful for as any woman alive. Sure, her life had its problems, but what life didn't? Many times throughout the day she would stop and whisper, *Thank you, God, for all you have given me.*

It was decided they would all go to Papa Silas' house for Thanksgiving. Sile J. and Lula had stayed on with Papa, along with little Woody and Orin Tate. Lula never tired of having family over and was already planning for Thanksgiving. What a blessing she had been to their family. Carrie was still doing well, but Tom asked Eliza to come help prepare food to take to Papa's.

There was a nip in the air Thanksgiving morning, but they bundled up and rode the wagon across the hill to the hollow where Papa lived. As they arrived the yard was already filling up with little ones. Papa Silas always said he had more grandchildren "than you could shake a stick at." He loved them everyone and was out in the yard with them, pitching a ball as each one tried to hit it with a stick that Papa just happened to have around. Eb and Maggie were there with their four, Nora and Ben with their three, Will and Sally with their two, and Charles and Lucinda were just arriving with five-year-old Grace Katherine. Tom helped Carrie down from the wagon and carried Baby Cindy into the house where the aunts vied for the first holding of their new niece. Tom left to join the men.

Nora reached for Cindy first. "Oh, Carrie," she exclaimed. "I can see why you named her after Mama. Look girls! She looks just like her."

All of the women circled Nora and the baby and voiced their agreement.

"Where's Ellie and Lily?" asked Carrie. "Are they coming?"

Lula turned from the biscuits she was cutting and responded, "Ellie can't come, Carrie. Jackson Henry came down with the mumps and is in no condition to get out, plus she didn't want to spread them around."

"I'll miss her," said Nora, "but the mumps are very catching and dangerous, too."

"Lily is supposed to be here," added Lula. "She and Dent sent word that they planned to come. I haven't seen little Harlan and he's nigh on a year old now. Is that their wagon I see pulling in?"

Sure enough, it was Lily and her little family. Carrie went to look out the window. Tom was playing horseshoe with the men, but as Lily climbed down from the wagon she saw Tom look up and smile. Lily returned the smile with a wink and then looked away. *Well, some things never change, I guess*, thought Carrie. She immediately turned from the window and joined the others, determined to let nothing spoil her day.

Lily appeared in the doorway with little Harlan. "Hello, everyone!" she called. "The bell of the ball is here!" With this she gave her "Lily laugh" as the sisters called it, and Nora sneaked a glance at Carrie.

Harlan was a beautiful little boy and Lily seemed quite the devoted mother. Carrie couldn't help but think she should have been that kind of mother to the ones she gave away. Not a day went by that her heart didn't ache for those children.

Soon the meal was ready and everyone gathered around the table. An extra table was set nearby for the children to eat who could take care of themselves. Papa Silas lifted up the table grace.

"Our precious Heavenly Father, we are here today thanking you that we can spend another Thanksgiving together as a family. I thank you for my precious children and grandchildren and their good health. Just send me all the grandbabies you want to, Lord. They keep an old man going. Help all of my family to walk the straight and narrow. We ask you to be with Ellie and her children and help them to be better and let them know we miss them. We thank you for this bountiful table of food, Lord, and these dear hands that fixed it. And Lord, just keep taking care of my Cynthi, and when you're ready for me, just call me home, cause I miss her something terrible. We thank you again, Lord. Amen.

Carrie wiped the tears from her eyes and smiled as she noticed the other grownups doing the same. Even Tom was wiping his eyes with the back of his hand. Soon, however, everyone was talking and eating and the happiness at the table was what Mama Cynth would have wanted. Carrie felt her presence there with them.

The rest of the day was spent playing games and swapping stories. Even Lily seemed to enjoy being with her family. Carrie was somewhat amazed at the change in her. Maybe Dent had brought out the "better" in her. She saw no more looks between Tom and Lily and that relieved her, as she didn't want any troubles today.

They left Papa Silas' house about five o'clock, all of them seeming to find it hard to call an end to a wonderful day, yet needing to get home to their chores. Tom and Carrie talked about it on the way home the way they use to talk together, and the children listened quietly seeming to enjoy hearing their Maw and Paw talk in happy tones. This was a day that Carrie would hold on to in her storehouse of memories. By the time they arrived home Clay and Cindy were sound asleep and the others were battling heavy eyes. They unloaded, and after carrying Clay in, Tom and Luke went to do the milking and outside chores. Carrie put Cindy in her cradle, and with the help of Beanie and Ady Rose, went about her evening chores as Jessie carried in kindling and firewood. Tom had the rest of the week off, as did the school children, but there was still plenty to do before they called it a day.

On Sunday, they all loaded up again to go to Grandpa Charles' home. Tom was still not happy about his paw marrying Hala, but it had been a year now and he had made some sort of peace with it. Tom's sister Nannie and his brother Nate would be there and Carrie was glad Tom had wanted to go. As they pulled into the yard, Nannie's and Nate's children were already playing and Luke, Beanie, Ady Rose and Jessie ran to join them.

Tom carried Baby Cindy into the house as Carrie led Clay. Grandpa Charles met them at the door with a smile on his face.

"Good to see you! Good to see you!" he exclaimed, as he reached for Clay. "And just who is this fine looking young man? I believe he's grown a mile."

Clay gave a chuckle, enjoying the attention. Nannie came over and reached for the baby.

"I just couldn't wait to get my hands on this little one," she said. "Oh my, Carrie. She does look like your mama. You named her just right."

Hala came over to take a peek at Cindy. "She surely is beautiful," she added.

Tom, though nodding, walked on over to sit down by Nate, and Paw Charles, still holding Clay, joined them.

Things were going well until they sat down for the meal. Everyone was filling their plates when Paw Charles cleared his throat.

"Before we get started eating, I have something I want to tell everybody," he began.

Hands stopped reaching and bowls ceased their passing as everyone waited to hear what he had to say.

Charles cleared his throat again. Carrie turned her gaze to Hala and noticed a redness creeping up from her throat into her face.

"Well, I guess I might as well just come out with it," said Paw Charles. "Hala and me are going to have a baby."

A quietness covered the entire table. Everyone looked at everyone else. Hala's face was completely scarlet by now.

"Why, why, that's just wonderful news!" exclaimed Nannie, finally finding her voice.

"It surely is!" echoed Nate. "Why, it's just great news!"

With this, he picked up a bowl of mashed potatoes and handed it to Tom whose mouth was hanging open. Tom took the bowl automatically, seeming unaware of what he was doing. With mechanical movements he spooned some into his plate and handed the bowl to Carrie. She held her breath, not knowing what Tom might say, but thankfully, he said nothing. Conversation resumed around the table and everyone continued in a jovial mood...everyone except Tom, who ate in sullen silence.

About four o'clock Tom announced it was time they headed home. As they climbed into the wagon, Paw Charles stood beside it.

"Glad you and Carrie and the young'uns could come, Tom," he said. "Come back every chance you get."

Tom simply nodded and clicked to the horses. The disappointment was obvious in Paw Charles' eyes as Carrie and the children waved to him. They rode home in silence.

CHAPTER 17

Christmas that year was happy enough on the surface. Tom bought gifts for the children and a new winter coat for Carrie, but his mood had changed and Carrie sensed rough days ahead. It was a pattern she had come to recognize. January came in calmly, but by the first of February winter hit with a fierceness. On Groundhog Day it began to snow, and by the end of the next day the snow was a good three feet deep. There would be no school for quite some time, but Carrie enjoyed having her children home with her. She was teaching Beanie and Ady Rose to sew and Luke was teaching Jessie to write his name. Their days were filled with learning, playing games and doing chores.

After two weeks the snow was melted enough that school could resume, so off the three older children went. Carrie was thankful to have three at home and dreaded next year when Jessie would also go to school. It was a good time in her life, but Tom had settled back into his moodiness and at least one night a week he came home late. He talked very little and was extra gruff with Luke, yelling at him and belittling everything he did. No matter how hard he tried, Luke just couldn't please Tom.

In early March, Luke came home with a letter from his teacher. The letter was being sent out to all parents to let them know that there had been several cases of measles in the school. Carrie felt her heart skip a beat. Measles were dangerous and oftentimes fatal. *Protect my babies, Lord,* she whispered silently, and then added, *and the children of our neighbors, too, Father.*

By the end of the week another letter came home announcing that school was being dismissed for two weeks because of the outbreak. There were already twelve known cases among the children in the little one room schoolhouse and that was a third of the enrollment.

On Sunday Beanie awakened with a mild fever. Though a little anxious, Carrie hoped it was nothing more than a cold or sore throat. By Monday Ady Rose and Jessie both had a fever and runny noses. Carrie gave them as much liquid as they would take and kept them as quiet as possible. By Wednesday white spots appeared in Beanie's mouth and Carrie had no doubt that it was, indeed, measles. Her fever was also getting higher. The following day Ady Rose and Jessie had the spots in their mouth and raging fevers. It kept Carrie busy trying to get liquids in them, sponge them with lukewarm water, comfort their hurting bodies and still take care of Clay and Cindy. Luke was there every minute beside his mother taking care of his brothers and sisters, and Carrie could see the fatigue in his eyes. She was thankful that he had a mild case of the measles at a very early age. Now she didn't have to worry about him getting them. She did worry terribly about Clay and Cindy, though as the measles were especially dangerous for little ones. She tried as best she could to keep them away from the infected children.

Tom came home on time and helped each night. Carrie had to give him his just dues for that. But each morning he went off to work without an offer to stay home and help. It was as though he felt it his duty to help when he was there, but he couldn't wait to get away from all the sickness. *He has to make a living for us,* she reprimanded herself.

On Friday morning, as Carrie was battling fatigue and carrying another pan of water to sponge each child, there was a knock at the door. She set the pan down and went to see who it was and to warn them that the measles were present in her home.

It was Eliza. "Hello, Miss Carrie," she said. "I thought I'd better come check on everybody. Mr. Tom told Rollen that the children had the measles and I thought you might just need some help. Now don't worry, I've already had the measles years and years ago.

"Oh, Eliza, thank God for you," replied Carrie. "I'm going to have to rename you Saint Eliza because you are always there for us. Please come in, and yes, I could sure use your help."

Thank you, Lord, whispered Carrie.

As they worked, Carrie asked, "Have you heard how many others are down with the measles, Eliza?"

"I don't know all, but it seems to be about everywhere. I know two of Nora's and Ben's children have them, but I don't know which ones."

Carrie sent Luke to take a good nap as he seemed ready to fall over any minute. Looking in about five minutes later, she found him sound asleep.

Eliza stayed until Tom came home then took her leave with a promise to return the next morning. By nightfall red spots began popping out on all three children, beginning on their faces and moving down their little bodies. Their fevers continued to rage and Carrie got no sleep that night. By morning Beanie even had the spots on her feet and seemed completely lifeless, reminding Carrie of the time before when she was ill.

Eliza arrived, as she had promised, right after Tom left. She brought with her a can with orange juice in it.

"Rollen brought home some oranges and Mama squeezed them into some juice for the children. She says it's supposed to be good for them."

They managed to get some of the juice into the children, but each seemed too weak to drink. Ady Rose had a terrible cough along with her other symptoms which tired her even more. Neither of them could stand light in their eyes, so Carrie kept the curtains pulled and only lit the kerosene lamp when necessary. It made the room seem dreary, but she knew it was what the children needed.

About midday there was a knock on the door and Carrie sent Luke to see who it was. He returned with Ben following behind.

"How is everyone?" Ben asked with concern.

"Well, I guess you can see we're not all well, Ben," replied Carrie, with a weak smile. "How about your bunch?"

"Carl Joseph has them, but so far, no one else. We thought Leona had them, but it turned out just to be a sore throat, thank the Good Lord."

"I'm so glad," said Carrie. "Do you know about anyone else?"

"Yes, It seems little Woody and Orin Tate have them, two of Eb's, both of Will's, and little Grace Katherine."

"Oh, my goodness," gasped Carrie. "This is just awful!"

"It seems to be in every home around," sighed Ben. "I have to go to the mercantile to get some things and Nora wanted me to check on all of you. Is there anything I can bring you from town?"

"Oh yes, Ben," answered Carrie. "You could bring me a few oranges if they have them, and some barley if they have it. I've heard that barley water can be good for this and later barley baths will give some relief. Just have Mr. Faller put it on our bill. Oh, and Ben, bring a few licorice sticks just so I can see if they might try some. They aren't eating at all."

Ben nodded. "I'll be glad to, and I just might get some of that barley for Nora to try, too. Maybe I could even take some to the others."

In a few hours Ben returned with the items and headed on toward home. He promised to come back by with more news as soon as he could. Carrie and Eliza continued to take care of the sick ones, and Luke spent most of the day doing chores and entertaining Clay and Cindy. That was a great help and Carrie was so thankful for him. Cindy had lived up to her name. She was such a happy little girl and so easy to take care of. Clay was always well-behaved, but right now he missed his brother Jessie. They had been close since the day Clay was born, and Clay couldn't understand why Jessie couldn't play with him.

The next few days were much the same...pouring as much liquids into the children as they could take, giving sponge baths, trying to get food into their ailing bodies, trying to take their minds off their sickness, as well as tending to the healthy children. Carrie was so fatigued by the end of the day that she could hardly talk. Tom continued to help out and showed a gentleness with the children she had never seen before.

Finally the fevers began to break...first with Ady Rose and then Jessie. Beanie's fever was not quite as high, but still a cause for concern. It was hard to tell who was happier, the children or Carrie and Eliza. Soon Ady

Rose and Jessie were eating in small amounts and trying to brave the discomfort of the itching, but Beanie was another matter. She ate nothing, took in only small amounts of liquids and showed little response to her surroundings. The only time she responded to anyone was when Luke sat beside her bed, holding her hand and talking to her. She did not speak, but squeezed his hand and turned her head toward him. That gave them all hope.

As Tom was getting ready to leave for work one morning, a knock came at the door and he went to answer it. Instead of inviting the caller into the house, he stepped out on the porch. In a moment, he opened the door just a crack and called, "Carrie, I'll be back in just a minute."

Carrie started to the door but heard Beanie moan and hurried to see about her. She gave her a sip of water and placed a cool cloth on her forehead, and as she returned to the kitchen Tom was entering followed by Eliza and Widow Thomas. Immediate foreboding engulfed Carrie.

"What is it, Tom?" she asked. "What's happened?"

Tom came to her. "Carrie, we need to go to your Papa's house. "He's sick."

"Papa?" said Carrie, as in a fog. "What's wrong with Papa?"

"He has the measles, Carrie. It seems he's had them for several days but no one could let us know because they're all tending the sick."

"But why do we need to go just because he has the measles," asked Carrie. "If he's had them several days, shouldn't he be getting better?"

Tom looked at Eliza and Widow Thomas, as if begging for help.

Widow Thomas came over and put her hand on Carrie's shoulder. "Carrie, it seems that with your Papa the measles have turned into pneumonia. That happens sometimes, especially in the elderly."

Carrie just couldn't seem to put it all together. The fatigue in her just couldn't grasp what was being said.

"Carrie," continued Widow Thomas, "you need to get your coat and go to your father. Eliza and I will be right here with the children, and we'll take the very best care of them. Now go on, honey. Get your coat and go."

As Carrie still stood as though unable to move, Eliza went into the bedroom, got her coat and brought it to her.

"I have the wagon ready, Carrie," said Tom gently. "Now let's be going. The children will be alright."

They rode in silence to Papa Silas' house as Carrie tried to get her mind around what was going on. Just as the sun began to peek through the trees, they arrived to a quiet dark home that bespoke none of its usual happiness. With Tom's knock, Sile J. came to the door. He looked at Carrie, threw both arms around her and began to sob uncontrollably.

"Papa's bad, Carrie and I don't think he's gonna make it. Woody's bad, too. We had Doc Whitt over and he don't hold out much hope for either one of them."

With this, he began to sob again. When he finally let go, Carrie moved into the house and toward Papa Silas' bedroom. She walked to his bed and sat down on the edge, taking his withered and calloused old hand in hers.

"Papa? Papa?" she whispered. "Papa, it's me...Carrie. Can you hear me, Papa?"

It appeared that she would get no response, and then Papa turned his head toward her.

"Papa," she said softly, "I want you to hurry and get better. I need you, Papa. We all need you."

Papa's hand slowly moved as it faintly squeezed Carrie's.

"My Carrie girl," he whispered, his words barely audible, and Carrie could hear the terrible wheeze from his chest. "Gonna see my Cynthi."

Tears raced down Carrie's face as she looked up to see Nora standing beside her. She put her arm around Carrie and knelt beside the bed, placing her other hand on Papa's and Carrie's.

"Papa," said Carrie. "Nora is here with me. We've come to make sure you get better. We love you, Papa."

"Love you, too," rasped Papa. It seemed to take all of his strength to say a few words. "Gonna see my Cynthi. Been too long."

Carrie realized from somewhere within her that what Papa was saying was true. An inexplicable peace suddenly covered her. She bent down close to his ear and said, "Tell Mama hello for me, Papa. Tell her we will all see her again before too long, and tell her we miss her every day."

Papa Silas nodded his head almost imperceptibly and there was just the hint of a smile on his tired and aged face. Carrie placed her hand on his face, bent down and kissed his check, tears falling from her face to his. Then she moved back just a little so Nora could do the same. At that moment Papa gave a little gasp, his hand went limp, and he departed to go meet his Cynthi.

Carrie didn't know that her heart could hurt so badly. Her arms went around Nora and they cried together, each one knowing the other's pain.

At that moment, Lula let out a terrible piercing scream followed by wailing. Carrie and Nora hurried from the room to see what was wrong. They ran to Woody's bedroom where Sile J. knelt with one arm around Lula and the other holding Orin Tate. All were sobbing loudly. Carrie and Nora stood with their arms wrapped around each other as if neither had the strength to stand on her own.

Within a minute of each other, Papa and his little Woody had passed from this life. Tom and Ben came and each took his wife by the hand, leading them to a chair by the table, and each sat, unable to speak, so great was their sadness. The door opened and Doc Whitt stepped inside, his look telling them that he knew. He went to each bedroom and then returned.

"Girls," he said to Carrie and Nora. "I know how you must be hurting right now, but Sile and Lula need your help. Can you help them?"

Each looked up through her tears and nodded.

"I'll spread the word and get what help I can," said Doc, "but there's so much sickness it's going to be hard to get much. There's hardly a house within miles that's not affected by the sickness. I've lost three more besides these two."

Carrie immediately pulled herself together and arose from her chair as Nora did the same.

"I'll take care of Papa, Carrie," Nora said, "if you'll see what you can do for Lula and Sile. Ben, can you and Tom go tell the others?"

Both men nodded and took their leave. Carrie went in to Lula and Sile.

"Lula," she said. "Lula, let's go in to the living room. Let me fix you a cup of coffee."

"No!" screamed Lula. "I can't leave my boy. He needs me."

With this Orin Tate began crying more loudly.

"Lula?" Darling?" begged Sile J. "Come with Carrie and me. Lula, Woody's gone with Papa to be with Jesus. Let's let him be now. Come on. Please."

It took Sile J. and Carrie both to pry her from the bed. Finally they were able to get her to the living room and lay her back on the sofa where she lay whimpering like a hurt animal. Sile J. sat in a chair next to her, holding her hand, trying to give her strength yet immersed in his own pain. Carrie took Orin Tate from him and held him close, comforting him as best she could.

In less than an hour, Myrtle Shortt and her daughter arrived to prepare the bodies. Myrtle had prepared Mama Cynth's body some years before, and Carrie so appreciated her being there for them again. Myrtle's husband and three other men were heading up the hill to dig the graves. The next to show up was Eb. He looked so tired and sad.

"How are your sick ones, Eb?" inquired Carrie.

"They're not over the measles completely, but they're surely on the mend. We're thankful for that. It's been rough and Maggie is just plumb worn out. How are all of your young'uns?"

"Just our Carl is all that had them," replied Nora, "and he's almost better. We were spared I reckon."

"Ady Rose and Jessie are doing better," said Carrie, "but Beanie is still pretty sick. She just lies in her bed and moans. Things always seem harder on her and I'm really worried.

Just then Will and Sally arrived with news that their two were not completely better but were definitely on the mend. Sally's mother was tending them. Both boys went in to have a few minutes alone with Papa Silas before the women began their work. Sally reached for Orin, and as she rocked him in Mama Cynth's old rocking chair, he fell asleep.

Soon Tom and Ben returned with Papa's coffin and a little coffin for Woody. They brought the news that Charles and Lucinda couldn't come because Grace Katherine was extremely ill.

"Oh, I pray nothing happens to little Katie," cried Nora. "She's all they have. They've wanted more children so badly, but with two miscarriages it just hasn't happened. I pray Grace Katherine won't be taken from them."

Word arrived that Lily would not be able to come. Harlan didn't have the measles, but Lily was expecting again and didn't want to take a chance of getting them. Since there was enough men to dig the grave, Tom decided to go back home, do the chores, and check on the children. Carrie was still concerned about Beanie.

While Myrtle and Pearl prepared the bodies, Carrie, Nora and Sally prepared the house so that the bodies could be laid out. They also began to prepare food, although they doubted that many would be able to come for the funeral. There was just too much sickness for people to leave their homes.

Tom arrived back at Papa's house about four o'clock with the news that Ady Rose and Jessie were now out of bed and happily listening to Eliza's stories. Clay and Cindy were still healthy as could be. Only Beanie remained the same. She had taken some liquids but had not responded in any other way. Luke was keeping vigil at her bedside and Widow Thomas and Eliza sent word that they would stay just as long as they were needed.

A few neighbors dropped by to pay their respects and see what they could do to help. Some brought food; others who couldn't get out, sent food by those who could. At five o'clock, Lula's sister Cora arrived with plans to spend the next few days and nights, allowing Carrie and Nora to return to their families.

CHAPTER 18

Tom and Carrie returned home to find Ady Rose and Jessie much improved and Clay and Cindy active and well. Only Beanie remained ill. Widow Thomas did report, however, that her temperature was down more and she had taken liquids a little better throughout the day. *Thank you, Heavenly Father*, whispered Carrie. Eliza wanted to stay the night, but Carrie insisted she go home and get some rest.

"I'll need you tomorrow if you can come," said Carrie. "We're going to bury Papa and little Woody. There's no need to wait because I doubt that many can come anyway."

Widow Thomas and Eliza both assured her that they would return early and would help every day as long as they were needed. Then they headed home, aware of Carrie's fatigue.

The next morning Carrie awoke with a start. She could not believe she had fallen asleep. What if Beanie had needed her? As she looked over at Beanie's bed, there was Luke sitting beside her, holding her hand, and he smiled as his eyes met Carrie's.

"She's okay, Maw. Her fever is gone and she slept all night."

Carrie smiled. "Thank you so much, Luke. Beanie is blessed to have a big brother like you."

Just then Beanie moaned and Carrie went to her side. Slowly her daughter's eyes opened. "Thirsty," she whispered hoarsely.

"I'll get her some water, Maw," said Luke, as he hurried off to the kitchen.

"How are you feeling, sweet girl?" asked Carrie.

"Tired," responded Beanie, "and thirsty."

Luke returned with a glass of water and Beanie, unable to hold the glass on her own, drank thirstily.

"Do you feel like eating anything?" asked Carrie.

"Not just yet," replied Beanie, as she closed her eyes and drifted to sleep again.

Carrie knelt by her bed. "Dear Lord, thank you," she prayed. "Sometimes my faith gives out, but you are always there for me. You are my constant strength, and I do thank you. You've made Ady Rose and Jessie well, and now you're making Beanie well. You've kept Clay and Cindy from the measles, and you've given me this fine young son to help me. Now, Lord, I ask one more thing. Please help me get through this time of loss. I thank you for the fine Papa you have given me and for the years I've had him with me, but oh, Lord, it is so hard to give him up. I know you'll take good care of him, though, and he'll be so happy to see Mama again. Just give me strength, Father, and keep me trusting in your word. You said you would never leave me or forsake me, and I know you will be true to that. Please be with Sile J. and Lula, too. Papa had a good full life, but I don't know how you go on after losing a child. Help them, Lord. I don't know how, but you do. I thank you and I do praise you. Amen."

As Carrie opened her eyes she was surprised to see Luke kneeling beside her, his hand in hers. She didn't even know when he had taken her hand. She put her arm around him and kissed his cheek, wet with tears. As she rose and turned, she was even more surprised to see Tom standing in the doorway, head bowed, hat in hand. He slowly turned and walked back into the kitchen, but not before Carrie saw the tears streaming down his cheeks.

The funeral for Papa Silas and Woody was one of the saddest Carrie had ever experienced. Papa was loved by people far and wide, yet only a handful was able to attend his funeral. Even some of his children couldn't be there. Ellie didn't want to bring her children over from Kentucky into a measles outbreak, and Lily was afraid because of her pregnancy to expose herself and the child to the measles. Charles and Lucinda could not leave Grace Katherine as she remained extremely ill. Nora and Ben, Will and Sally, and Carrie and Tom were there. Sile J. and Lula followed little Woody's coffin up the hill...Lula so weak from mourning that she could hardly walk and Sile J. was not much stronger. Brother Jonas, old and feeble, was there once more for them. The day was chilly, but not cold, and the sun brightened the sky, but there was no sunshine in the hearts of the mourners. Jonas spoke only a few words and then Sally sang again Mama Cynth's favorite, *Rock of Ages*. As those present turned to walk back down the hill, Lula threw herself across her little boy's coffin, begging them not to put him in the ground. Will and Sile J. pulled her away and half carried, half pulled her down the hill. Sile J. was sobbing almost as loudly as Lula, and Carrie's heart ached for them.

When they reached the house they took Lula to her bed and Sile J. remained by her side. Cora, Lula's sister, laid Orin Tate on his bed, worn out and fast asleep from the rigors of the last few days and recuperating from his own case of measles. The friends and neighbors who had been able to attend the funeral chose not to stay, out of respect for the grief-stricken parents, who needed no company right now. Will and Sally left for their home, planning to stop on the way to see how Grace Katherine was doing. Nora and Carrie helped Cora straighten the house and fix a light meal, then they, too, departed. Carrie looked back as they rode away, knowing the home would never be the same again.

As they pulled into their yard, Luke came running out to meet them.

"She's sitting up, Maw!" he called. "She's sitting up!"

"Who's sitting up?" asked Carrie.

"Beanie's sitting up, and she drank some orange juice...and now Eliza's fixing her some toast. Ain't it good, Maw? Ain't it good? God must have heard you, Maw!"

"Praise God!" cried Carrie. "I reckon it is more than good, son. I reckon it's wonderful!"

Tom laughed, tears on his cheeks. "I reckon it is at that."

It had been a difficult, sad day, but God had turned it into something good.

Beanie made a slow but complete recovery, as did Charles' and Lucinda's daughter. Although there was much sorrow and sadness in the little Appalachian hills and hollows, there was also reason to rejoice. The measles outbreak was over. Life, though, for some would never be the same, yet it had to go on. For Sile J. and Lula the hurt would never completely go away, for they had lost their precious little boy and Papa Silas at almost the same moment. Lula took to her bed and remained there for almost a month until she realized that Orin Tate still needed her. Lula's sister Cora had stayed on with them, and according to her, Orin Tate just climbed in bed with his mother one day and said, "Get up, Mommy. I'm still your little boy." With this, Lula arose from the bed, went to work in the house, played with Orin and welcomed her husband home from work that evening.

Carrie's little family returned to its normal routine. The children were so happy just being together. School resumed, and although Beanie didn't go back right away, by the middle of April she was back and doing well. Unfortunately, Tom returned to "normal", too. Within a few weeks he was coming home late two or three nights a week, sometimes more. While it bothered Carrie, she was busy taking care of her children and praising God for their health.

The year passed slowly by. There was no Thanksgiving get-together at Papa Silas' house that year, but Lula assured them they would get back to it next year. Nor was there a gathering at Tom's father's home, as Hala had given birth to a little girl in June and Tom refused to acknowledge her existence. Christmas was a "solemnly happy" occasion. Tom managed to buy each child and Carrie a gift, and Carrie did everything she could to make it a memorable for all of them.

Lily had given birth to another son in November, and about a week before Christmas, Ellie sent word that she was getting married again. She had met a man who had lost his wife to consumption, the same disease that took Henry. He had no children and loved her three dearly, and according to Ellie, even Jackson Henry liked the man. Carrie was happy for her sister and immediately dispatched a letter to Ellie telling her as much. She also invited them to come for a visit.

The best news of all came from Charles and Lucinda. God had answered yet another prayer. Not only had he spared Grace Katherine, but Lucinda was going to have another baby. They had prayed for another one for five years, and the entire family was happy for them. Carrie was sure Papa Silas was smiling down from heaven, and she could just hear him saying, *Carrie girl, I don't have enough fingers and toes to count them all.*

God, whispered Carrie, *if you could just see your way clear, could you send Sile J. and Lula another child? I know it can't take the place of little Woody, but God, it might help fill up that big empty space in Lula's heart and put a smile back on Sile J.'s face.*

The year 1915 came in white and cold. For two days they experienced almost blizzard-like weather and temperatures far below zero. It was a chore just to keep the little homes in the area warm, and smoke constantly poured from the chimneys. Luke and Jessie kept busy each day just carrying in coal and firewood. There was no school for several weeks.

The bad weather didn't bring Tom home any earlier each night. It seemed he was always late on Tuesdays and Fridays. Some Friday nights he didn't get home until midnight or later. When Carrie asked him about it, he got in a huff and started ranting about bringing home a good paycheck and it wouldn't hurt if his wife was a little more grateful. Eventually Carrie just let the matter go.

March and April provided a thaw for the little area. People ventured out of their homes and into life again. Flowers began to bloom, trees began to bud, and gardens were prepared for planting. Tom came home, ate his supper, and, with the help of Luke and Jessie, set to plowing and getting ready for the planting. Still, Tuesdays and Fridays were his. He gave the boys orders for those days and he stayed out as late as he pleased.

One Sunday in early May, Tom's brother Nate came to see them. It was the first time they had seen him in almost a year. Tom and Carrie were sitting on the front porch while the children played in the yard.

"Howdy, Tom. Howdy, Carrie," called Nate, as he neared the yard gate.

"Why, hello, Nate!" called Carrie. "It's so good to see you."

Tom nodded and said. "Have a seat, Nate. What brings you over this way?"

"Well, two reasons, I reckon," responded Nate. "I just got to wanting to see you all. It's been a long time and these young'uns are half grown."

"They grow so fast, don't they?" returned Carrie. "I'm just glad they're all healthy again. That measles outbreak was a terrible thing."

"I'm real sorry about your paw, Carrie," said Nate. "He was a mighty fine man. Never heard nary a bad word about him in all my life, and that can't be said about too many folks."

"Yes," said Carrie, "Papa was the best, but he's with Mama Cynth now, and though I miss him, I'm happy for him."

"What's the second?" asked Tom, a little gruffly.

"I beg your pardon," replied Nate.

"You said you came for two reasons. What's the second one?"

Nate sort of twisted in his chair uncomfortably. "Well, the second reason is Paw," he said.

"What about him?" questioned Tom. "Him and his new family got problems?"

"No. No problems like that," responded Nate. "Paw seems right happy, and little Mary Belle is the light of his life."

"I'll just bet she is," huffed Tom.

"How are all of them, Nate?" asked Carrie, rather quickly.

"Paw is the happiest I've seen him since Maw died," answered Nate. "Hala and that little gal of theirs have put the joy back in his life."

"Did you come all the way over here just to tell us Paw is feeling like a young man again?" asked Tom. "I guess he's just kicking up his heels to beat the band."

"No," said Nate. "Paw is happy, but right now he's not kicking up his heels."

"What's wrong, Nate?" asked Carrie. "Has something happened to Paw Charles?"

This seemed to get Tom's attention.

"Ain't nothing terribly wrong," replied Nate. "Paw had a fall the other day and broke his leg. He can't get around none too well."

"How did he fall?" questioned Tom.

"Well," explained Nate, "he went down to the spring house to bring up some butter and slipped on some loose rock. His leg went up under another rock and he couldn't get it out. It was about an hour before Hala found him. She had to leave him and come get me to pull him out. I knew it was broken the minute I saw it. Me and old Taze Hurd got him back to the house and Taze went and fetched Doc Whitt. It's a pretty bad break and he won't be walking too easy for quite some time. I thought you'd want to know, Tom, and I was hoping you might go see him. He's pretty bruised up and sore."

Tom just sat there for a few minutes, seeming to digest Nate's news.

"Carrie," he said finally, rising up from his chair. "I guess I'd best go back over with Nate and see what the old fool's done to himself. I'll be back in time to get the milking done, but the boys can go ahead and feed."

Carrie's heart suddenly felt so joyful. "Don't you worry. We'll take care of things here. You just go see about your Paw."

With that the two men took their leave, talking together as they walked down the hill. The sight made Carrie smile. *You sure do work in mysterious ways, Lord, and I thank you.*

Tom returned later that evening with a lightness of heart that Carrie had not witnessed in a long time. He seemed to have made some sort of peace with his paw.

"Paw's really messed up his leg," he said to Carrie. "It's gonna be a long time before he can do much around the farm."

"Are Nate and Nannie helping with the chores?" inquired Carrie. "I don't imagine Hala can do too much outside the house with little Mary Belle to look after."

"Nate's been feeding and milking," said Tom, "and he and Nannie's husband Joe are working up a garden. I think Nannie goes over and helps Hala as much as she can, but the doctor told Nannie she has a bad heart and she just can't do as much as she used to."

"Why don't I fix up some food and you take it over one day," offered Carrie. "It's the least we can do to help."

"That would be right fine. I've been thinking that I might try to go over on Saturday afternoons and help out a little...chop some wood and stuff like that."

Carrie smiled. "You most certainly could. You could even take Luke with you to help some."

Tom frowned. "We'll see about that." At the supper table he had more to say about his Paw and Hala.

"I guess I've been wrong about Hala," he said. "She's really got that place fixed up and she treats Paw like some sort of king. She's a good mother, too. Pretty little girl, that Mary Belle. Why, she sat on my knee and started talking away like she had known me forever. Of course, most of it was gibberish, but to her it was talking."

The thought came unbidden to Carrie, *He never holds his own children on his knee.*

True to his word, Tom went over every Saturday afternoon to help out at his Paw's. However, he never wanted to take Luke with him. Each Saturday evening he returned in a jolly mood, full of praise for Hala. Carrie suggested a few times that they all go over one Sunday afternoon, but Tom said the children would just be too much for his Paw right now.

By June, Paw Charles had improved greatly and was no longer using crutches or a cane to get around. He could do some farm work as long as he took it slow and easy. Tom still insisted on going to help on Saturdays, although he had plenty of work to do at home. Carrie said nothing because she wanted Tom to have a good relationship with Paw Charles and his family. Her only concern was that it was putting so much extra work on Luke and Jessie. Even Beanie and Ady Rose had started helping with some of the farm work, hoeing corn and taking care of the garden and they carried in fire wood as Luke cut it. At least it was summer and school was out. Carrie was glad her children were good workers, but she hated seeing them do chores that were far above their age for doing. They needed time to be carefree and enjoy their childhood.

Tom still worked late two or three evenings a week, but his mood was more jovial than it had been. He was still short tempered with Luke quite often, and lately Carrie had noticed his irritability even aimed at Jessie. One Saturday morning as Tom and the two boys were hoeing the corn, she heard Tom yelling.

"We ain't gonna have no corn, boy, if you keep hacking down the plants."

"I didn't mean to, Paw," said Luke. "Sometimes it just happens."

"I'll show you what just happens," yelled Tom. "You worthless piece of trash! Mama's boy! What good are you if you can't even hoe corn right!"

As Carrie reached the doorway she saw Tom raise his hoe to hit Luke.

"Tom, stop!" she called.

"Don't you tell me to stop, woman!" yelled Tom. "You get in that house where you belong. It's your fault he can't do anything right!"

With this Tom whacked Luke across the back with his hoe. Luke fell to the ground and while he was down Tom hit him again.

As Carrie ran toward Luke, Jessie lunged at his father.

"You let Luke be!" he screamed. "You let Luke be right now!"

With this he began hitting Tom with his fists as hard as he could hit. Stunned, Tom just backed away. Then, as he gathered his wits, he yelled, "Do you want me to take this hoe to you, too, boy?"

Jessie pulled himself up to his full six-year height and gritted his teeth. "You just try it," he said. "One of these days I'm gonna kill you." He turned and ran to the house as Tom stood with his mouth wide open.

"Leave him be, Tom," said Carrie. "I think we've had enough hitting and yelling today. I'm going to take Luke inside and make sure you didn't break anything. You just go on over to your Paw's."

She led Luke away toward the back porch as Tom stood there, hoe in his hand, just watching. He couldn't seem to grasp the idea that Jessie, and now Carrie, stood up to him.

CHAPTER 19

Luckily, nothing physical was broken in Luke from Tom's beating with the hoe. Sadly, the brokenness was in his spirit. Always a quiet child, he became more withdrawn, even when Tom was not around. He was good to his brothers and sisters and always found time to play with them, but it was like a dark cloud engulfed his soul, and it broke Carrie's heart. He had just turned eleven, and yet he was an old man.

Jessie, on the other hand, became a child full of hate. He, too, was good with his brothers and sisters, and he adored Carrie, but there was a terrible anger in him that bore down on Carrie to the point that she feared for him. She couldn't explain it; she just felt an ominous foreboding.

In September, her four oldest went off to school. Carrie was thankful to still have Clay, almost four, and Cindy, almost two, at home with her. *What will I do when they all leave me*, she thought to herself. *They're all I have.*

Jessie took to school like a fish to water. It was all he talked about. He learned to read almost without effort, and was entirely fascinated by arithmetic. His teachers loved him and he got along well with the other children. Somehow, it seemed to ease the hate in him just a little, for which Carrie was thankful.

Luke, on the other hand, hated school. He did his homework only to please his mother. His teachers worried about him because of his lack of interest and his withdrawal from his classmates. At lunch and recess Luke kept to himself. He answered his teachers respectfully when spoken to but spoke not a word otherwise.

Both girls were good students and seemed to love school. Beanie had been asked to be in a Thanksgiving play and was so excited. With the help of Ady Rose, she worked on her lines every single night.

Tom continued to go to his Paw's on Saturday afternoons, and even after work from time to time. Carrie couldn't understand this because Paw Charles seemed to be fully recovered and could handle the work on his own. She kept her silence, though, glad that Tom and his Paw were getting along again and Tom no longer harbored ill feelings toward Hala. She should have known something was up. One evening in October Tom had come home a little late from his Paw's and had gone straight to the barn to do some work. Carrie took some mending and went out to the back porch while the children did their homework. As she was sewing, she looked up to see Paw Charles coming up the hill, and was surprised to see him walking so briskly on his newly healed leg.

"Hello, Paw Charles," called Carrie. "Looks like your leg is all mended."

Charles didn't even smile. "Where's Tom?" he asked brusquely.

"He's out in the barn working," answered Carrie. "Is something wrong?"

Just then Tom came out of the barn. When he saw his Paw he stopped short. Charles headed straight toward him, grabbed him by the shirt collar, and threw him to the ground.

"You've gone too far this time, boy!" he yelled. "I've watched you treat Carrie like dirt for years and I didn't say anything because I thought it wasn't any of my business. But now it is by business!"

Tom started to get up from the ground when Charles kicked him back down.

"It would be in your best interest just to stay where you are," he said. "That's where you belong anyway...right there in the dirt. You're nothing but filth and you are no son of mine. Right now it's all I can do just to keep from killing you."

Carrie, who had been watching, suddenly gathered herself and hurried toward the two men.

"Paw Charles, what's wrong? Why are you so mad at Tom?"

Charles turned to look sadly at her. "I'm sorry you have to know about this, Carrie. You've been through enough because of my lowdown son. I don't know how me and Izzy went so wrong in raising him. He just must have come into this world with the devil in him."

"Paw," said Tom, still on the ground. "Let's don't bring this to Carrie. Let's me and you just go to the barn and talk about this."

"There ain't no talking to do!" yelled Charles. "You stay away from my home and my wife. Somehow Hala and me will work this out, though I don't know how, but I don't ever want to see you again. Do you hear what I'm saying, boy? Don't you ever come about my home or my wife or my daughter ever again. When I die, don't you even come to my funeral, and I sure won't be coming to yours."

He turned to Carrie. "If you ever want to leave this pile of dirt, I'll be glad to provide you and the young'uns a home. You're always welcome, Carrie. I'm sorry I've set by all these years and done nothing. I've heard about the other women, but I guess I didn't want to believe it. Heard about other young'uns he's fathered. Didn't want to believe that either. But today I came home and caught him with my own wife, and I know it's all true. I thought he was coming over so often just to help me, but I should have known better. He ain't never cared about anybody but himself. I don't even know how long this has been going on between him and Hala. God help you Carrie. You don't deserve this."

"Oh, Paw Charles," gasped Carrie. "Surely not Tom and Hala." She felt as if her heart was being pierced by a red hot poker.

"Saw it with my own eyes," said Charles. "I don't know how I'm going to forgive her, Carrie, but for little Mary Belle's sake I've got to try. Won't nothing ever be the same anymore."

With this, he turned and slowly walked back down the hill, shoulders drooping like the weight of ten men was riding on them. Carrie stood watching him go, her hand clutching the collar of her worn old house dress. She turned to look at Tom, still lying on the ground.

"How could you, Tom?" she asked, in a voice void of all emotion. "I've known for years you didn't care about me...but your own Paw's wife?" Then she turned and walked away. At that moment, any love she had left for her husband was left lying there in the dirt, and she shed not a tear. He wasn't worth it.

As Carrie neared the door she saw a movement. The person was gone before she could tell who it was, but her heart told her who had witnessed the whole sickening episode. It had to be Jessie.

Looking back later, Carrie could hardly remember the rest of that year. It was like a sad, lonely smothering fog had taken over. The world was out there continuing on its normal path, but she just couldn't quite see it for the fog. For the sake of the children, she carried on as she must, but her life changed that day. She saw no way out of her marriage. With six children she had nowhere to go and she had no way to support them. Tom came home when he took a notion, ate in silence, did his chores in silence and went to bed. Carrie moved into a bedroom of her own with little Cindy, glad to be away from this man she had never really known.

The next year or so continued this way. Carrie's children were her life. She kept a neat home, the clothes washed, good meals and plenty of time for her children. She was always there for them. When they were sick, she nursed them. When they got hurt, she doctored their cuts and kissed their bruises. When there was something at school she was always there. On Sundays she and the six children walked to the little Primitive Baptist church, and she read the Bible to them each and every night before bed and knelt by their beds to pray. She tried to be both mother and father to them, knowing inside that it was impossible. Luke, Jessie and even Clay worked with their father, but they seldom spoke a word to him. As Tom spent more time away from home, more chores were left to Carrie and the children. She hoed corn until her fingers bled, but it had to be done and she couldn't add more to Luke and Jessie's load.

Yet, through all of this, Carrie spoke not a bad word to the children about Tom. She knew they heard enough at school, although they never told her what was said. Carrie also continued to pray for Tom because she knew only God could change him.

CHAPTER 20

It was the summer of 1917 and Luke had just turned thirteen. In the fall he would begin his last year of school, as the little one-room school in Haymaker went only to the eighth grade. He had grown into a handsome young man, looking much like Carrie's Papa Silas, but taller, standing at almost five feet ten inches already. He had gone to town for Carrie to pick up a few needed things at Berke's Mercantile. She was sitting on the front porch stringing and breaking green beans as he came up the hill walking a little faster than usual, a walk that looked like it had a purpose in mind.

"Hi, Maw!" he called as he neared the gate. "I got all the things you sent for."

"That's good," replied Carrie, with a smile. "I'm going to need those can lids tomorrow and I was afraid they might be out of them."

Luke came up, set the bag down on the porch and then sat down beside it. "Maw, do you know Troy Ashton, the sheriff of Haymaker?"

"Why, yes, Luke. I do. Is there some kind of trouble?"

"No. No trouble at all," said Luke. "Maw, he wants me to come work for him at his house two days a week and then two afternoons a week once school starts, if he likes my work. He wants me to chop wood and do other odd jobs for him and run errands for Mrs. Ashton. I told him I'd ask you and then let him know. Do you think I could, Maw?"

"Well, I don't know," answered Carrie. "How late would you be working? Your Paw won't like it if you don't get your chores done around here."

"Mr. Ashton said he wouldn't keep me more than five hours a day this summer, and when school starts back, no more than two hours in the afternoon," replied Luke. "He said most of the time it would be up to me."

"I don't know, Luke," said Carrie, hesitantly. "You're awfully young to have a job."

"Maw, I'd really like to try it," said Luke. "Just let me give it a try, and if it don't work out then I'll tell Mr. Ashton I can't do it anymore. I promise I'll keep up my chores here. And, Maw, I was thinking Jessie might start milking Bossie in my place and I could pay him so's he would have a little extra money. What do you think?"

Carrie looked at her son's eager face. "I'll tell you what, Luke, we'll try it this summer. Then we'll talk it over again when school starts. How's that?"

"That's grand, Maw," said Luke eagerly. "That's just grand." With this he gave her such a big hug that Carrie just couldn't regret her decision.

"I'm going to go talk to Jessie about the milking," he said, racing on into the house.

This was the happiest Carrie had seen her oldest son in a long time. *Please let it work out for him, Lord,* she thought. *He deserves some happiness in his life.*

Carrie wasn't sure just how she would tell Tom about this, but one thing was for sure...she would not back down. Her son deserved some joy. Besides, when he finished school, he would be looking for a job anyway.

When Tom did come home on time, it was his habit to sit on the front porch after chores were done and supper was over. It wasn't that he liked to relax with his family. He mainly enjoyed spying on his neighbors. Tom had a mean streak in him that way. He loved to think up every bad thing possible on people, something Carrie never understood. It was while they were sitting on the front porch that Carrie decided to tell Tom about Luke's new adventure.

"What in tarnation has put that in the boy's head?" Tom asked gruffly.

Carrie kept rocking. "You know, Tom, Luke only has one more year of school and then he'll be getting a full-time job, so this will be good training for him."

"I can give him all the training he needs right here on the farm. There's plenty to keep him busy," vowed Tom, rearing back in his chair. "I don't like that Troy Ashton. He thinks he's the cock of the walk."

"I've never heard anything bad about Sheriff Ashton," replied Carrie. "Besides, I've already told Luke he can try it this summer and we'll see after that. He'll keep his chores up here."

Tom paused a minute as though he wanted to put his foot down on the matter. His mouth was open to say something when he saw the determination on Carrie's face. "He just better see to it that he don't lag behind on his chores," puffed Tom. "I ain't putting up with no dilly-dallying and I ain't coming home and doing his chores for him."

Carrie said no more. She considered the matter settled.

Luke began his job the next day. He did his morning chores at home and left about nine to go to Sheriff Ashton's. He was usually back home by two or three, giving him plenty of time for his chores at home, which, in the summer, included hoeing a large field of corn. Jessie was now doing the milking and seemed to thrive on the fact that he, too, had a "paying job". He also helped his brother hoe the garden and the corn, and Clay now took on the job of carrying in wood and kindling and sweeping the outhouse. Beanie and Ady Rose helped with the inside work and both were becoming quite adept at sewing. Beanie could mend almost as well as her mother. Even little Cindy was old enough to help set the table and dust. Everyone had chores and everyone did them with a happy attitude.

Luke was like a new person. From the time he returned from work until Tom came home, he regaled them with stories about his work, Mr. and Mrs. Ashton and people who were constantly stopping by their home. "Mrs. Ashton cooks a big meal right in the middle of the day, Maw," he said. "Mr. Ashton comes home to eat and then goes back out to work. You should see what they have to eat...ham, chicken, cakes, pies. They must surely be rich, Maw. Half the time Mr. Ashton brings someone home with him and Mrs. Ashton just sets another place like she don't mind at all. Can you believe that, Maw?"

Unable to restrain herself, Carrie burst into laughter.

"What's so funny, Maw?" Luke asked, a perplexed look on his face.

"It just does my heart good to see you so excited, Luke," she replied.

"She can't cook as good as you, Maw, but she always stuffs me full before the meal is over," he said. "She says it sure is good to have a young person around the table."

"I don't believe they have children, do they, Luke?" asked Carrie.

"Well," answered Luke, "it's kind of a sad thing, Maw. One day when I was carrying in wood, she gave me a glass of lemonade and a cookie, and while I was eating she got to talking. It seems they had some little ones...I believe three...but each one died while just a baby. Mrs. Ashton's eyes got all sad and misty when she talked about it. We sure are lucky to have all the kids in this family, I reckon."

Carrie's eyes were misty, too, but full of pride as she looked at Luke. "Yes," she said. "Right now I feel very lucky."

By the end of summer, Luke was a changed person. He was even looking forward to going back to school, mainly because it was his last year. The only time he reverted to the old Luke was when Tom came home, speaking hardly a word. He worked no more than two hours for Mr. Ashton each afternoon, then came home and did his evening chores. Tom had no reason to find fault, although he continued to criticize most of the work Luke did.

Tom came home late two or three evenings a week. What he was doing, Carrie didn't know. His mood seemed to swing from sullen to talkative. However, when he was talkative it was usually to growl at his family or find fault with the neighbors. The children steered clear of him as much as possible, retreating to their rooms after supper to do homework or play games while Tom sat on the porch and passed judgment on the neighborhood.

Nora and Carrie tried to get together as often as possible, but both were busy with their families. Eliza still "popped her head in" now and then, but Carrie saw little of her neighbors. Ellie wrote about once a month, seeming to be happy with her new husband and new life, and

Carrie knew she deserved the happiness. Lily was busy with her two sons, Harlan and Raymond. It was rumored that she and Dent were having problems but Carrie didn't know whether or not the rumors were true. Nothing surprised her with Lily. Her brothers were all busy with their homes and families. Charles and Lucinda now had a little brother for Grace Katherine, but the best news of all was that Lula was expecting again. Carrie's prayer had been answered. *Now, God,* she whispered, *if you could just turn Tom around.*

In September, the four oldest children returned to school. Next year, as Luke ended his schooling, Clay would begin, and then Carrie would have only Cindy at home. These were her thoughts one day when there was a knock at the door. Eliza stood on the porch with a bright smile on her face.

"Why, Eliza," exclaimed Carrie, "what a wonderful surprise! It seems ages since I saw you. Come in and let's do some catching up."

"It has been awhile, Miss Carrie," laughed Eliza.

"Eliza, you look simply radiant, said Carrie. Has something happened to make you all aglow?"

"That's why I'm here," replied Eliza. "I'm getting married, Miss Carrie!"

"Married!" shrieked Carrie. "You're getting married? Just who is this lucky man?"

"Do you know Turner Ashton, Miss Carrie?" asked Eliza. "He's Sheriff Ashton's brother."

"I can't say I know him," returned Carrie, "but I have heard his name."

"He's been coming to see me for quite some time now," said Eliza. "He's right much older than me...about fifteen years...but he's so good to me. His wife died in childbirth several years ago and he never married again. I do love him, Miss Carrie."

"Then I wish you much happiness," said Carrie, giving her a big hug. "He's a lucky man to get someone as loving and giving as you. I'm so glad you came by to tell me."

"Well," said Eliza, somewhat timidly, "there's another reason I came by. Miss Carrie, you are so good with the needle. I was hoping you might make my wedding dress."

"Oh, Eliza!" exclaimed Carrie. "I would be honored to make your wedding dress. Just what did you have in mind?"

They spent the next thirty minutes talking about the design for Eliza's dress, both filled with excitement.

"Now you have to name your fee for this, Miss Carrie," declared Eliza. "Turner is paying for everything."

"That's very nice of him, Eliza," said Carrie, "but there will be no charge. This will be my wedding gift to the best friend I've ever had."

"There's one more thing," ventured Eliza. "It's somewhat exciting but also sad. You see, Turner wants Mama, Rollen and me to come live with him in Haymaker. He has a large house and it would be plenty big enough for all of us, but I just hate to move away from you."

"I will miss you, too," Carrie assured her, "but I think it's a wonderful thing he is doing. I'm so happy for all of you, and besides, we can still visit."

Carrie didn't know it at the time, but that day opened up a whole new venture for her. Eliza and Turner were married just before Thanksgiving, and within two weeks Carrie was getting orders from all over the area for dresses, suits and other items people wanted her to make.

Thanksgiving was spent with Lula and Sile J. and the rest of Carrie's siblings. Even Ellie, her new husband and her children came. Lula, though still mourning Woody, was radiant with expectancy of their new baby in April. Tom was on his "better" behavior, and the day was a happy one.

Carrie, Tom and their children returned home about five o'clock, but Tom's mood had changed on the way home and he was growling at everyone, including Carrie. "Luke, you need to feed and clean out the barn you've been letting go," demanded Tom. "Seems your job with Ole Ashton takes first place over your obligations at home anymore."

"I cleaned out the barn just Monday," replied Luke.

"Don't lie to me, boy!" Tom yelled.

"He ain't lying," inserted Jessie. "I helped him clean it."

"When I want any sass out of you, I'll ask for it. And that would be never," said Tom, pointing his finger at Jessie.

Carrie could see the anger in Jessie's eyes.

"Boys, go finish your chores," she said, placing her hand on Jessie's shoulder. "I just might have an apple pie warmed up by then."

Luke nudged Jessie and they walked away toward the barn. Tom stalked away toward the house, but the evening went from bad to worse. Tom had a crow to pick with someone and his family received the brunt of his anger. It was a cool evening but his foul mood took him to the front porch to sit and brood. When the pie was ready, Carrie called to him. "Tom, we're fixing to eat a piece of pie if you want to join us."

He resentfully arose from his chair and came to the kitchen. "Is this all you can fix for a man's supper, woman?" he growled.

Carrie looked at him. "I figured we were all just full from the Thanksgiving meal. What would you like to eat?"

"Just forget it," he answered, plopping down in his chair. "I'll make do."

The children ate their pie in silence. When Tom's pie was gone, he looked at Luke. "Boy, if you can't keep your chores up around here, you can just quit that job of yours."

"Paw, I've kept my chores up and more," replied Luke, looking Tom square in the eye.

Before any of them knew what was happening, Tom backhanded Luke, knocking him out of his chair.

"Tom!" cried Carrie, rising from her chair.

As Tom stood, he raised his hand as if to hit Carrie also.

"Don't you do it!" yelled Jessie.

Everyone stopped to look at him, including Tom. Then Tom backhanded Jessie, knocking him backwards. Jessie rose from the floor, fists clenched and Carrie stepped between them.

"That's enough," she said. "This will stop now. Tom, Luke has kept his chores up. We are all working as hard as we can work around here and Luke *will* keep his job with Sheriff Ashton. Children, get ready for bed."

Tom stood for a moment looking at her, then stalked away.

In late April, Lula gave birth to a beautiful baby girl. She brought more joy back into their family than they could ever have imagined and, as much as Sile J. and Lula loved her, Orin Tate loved her even more.

The last of April a new neighbor moved into the home vacated by Widow Thomas, Eliza and Rollen. His name was Henry Hankins and he had recently been widowed. The neighbors seemed to like him...all except Tom, who took an instant and unreasonable disliking for him. He would sit on the front porch thinking up one negative comment after another to say about Henry. It was as if he wanted to take out all of his frustrations on this new neighbor that he hardly knew.

In May, Luke finished up his schooling and went to work full-time for Troy Ashton, and in July, Sheriff Ashton came to see Carrie.

"Mrs. Swank," he began, "I don't mean to be so frank with you, but Luke has told me about his trouble with Tom."

Carrie hung her head. "I don't know why Tom is so mean to Luke, Sheriff. He is a hard-working boy and has always tried so hard to please his Paw."

"Luke is a fine boy, Mrs. Swank," agreed Sheriff Ashton. "That's why I'm here. I would like for Luke to come live with Mrs. Ashton and me."

Carrie's head jerked up. "Move away from home?" she gasped.

"Mrs. Swank," he continued, "I've seen this sort of thing so many times. It will only get worse and eventually someone will get hurt. I want to prevent that. We really care about Luke and we would treat him as well as we would treat a child of our own. I will pay him a good wage, and when he's a little older, I will see that he gets training for a better job."

"I don't know that Tom will ever agree to it," said Carrie, shaking her head.

"You just let me handle Tom," assured Sheriff Ashton.

Carrie slowly nodded her head. "If you can get Tom to agree to it, then I guess I will agree also."

Three days later Luke moved out. Carrie didn't know what Sheriff Ashton had said to Tom, but he raised no objections. She felt like her heart was splintering into a million lonely pieces. Her firstborn was leaving the nest...never an easy event, but even more difficult because of the reason.

Luke squeezed her as though he could not let go. "Maw, I love you more than anyone on this earth and you've been the best Maw in the world. I'll come back when Paw's not here and help Jessie and Clay do the work. I don't want it all to fall to you and them. And, Maw, I'm going to save my money so's I can get you out of all this. I promise, Maw."

Though Carrie's cheeks were wet with tears, she could make no response other than to nod her head.

It was a lonely time for all of them with Luke gone. He had always been their rock, spurring them on no matter what trouble reared its ugly head. True to his word, he slipped over sometimes in the afternoons and helped hoe the corn and do other chores, but it wasn't the same as having him live there. What troubled Carrie even more than the loss of Luke, was the hatred growing in Jessie. She knew the hate was an unhealthy thing for him, but she had no clue as to how she could stop it. In fact, she understood his feelings.

In the fall, Beanie began her last year of school along with Ady Rose, Jessie and Clay. Only little Cindy was left at home. Thankfully, between caring for the home and sewing for people, Carrie kept busy. She was grateful for the sewing jobs she had because Tom gave her less and less money for the running of the household, and sometimes it was hard to make ends meet. When she tried to talk to him about it, he flew into a rage and accused her of wasting money.

It was a school day in early October and Carrie was sitting on the front porch basting a dress sleeve as Cindy played beside her with her dolls. As she looked up, Carrie saw Tom's brother Nate coming up the hill. He had not been there since the episode between Tom and Charles, and Carrie felt a sense of uneasiness as she lay her sewing to the side.

"Hello, Nate," she called, as he entered the yard.

"How are you, Carrie?" Nate asked, puffing as he climbed the steps.

"I'm well. Come have a seat. How is Paw Charles? Is anything wrong?"

"I'm afraid Paw's not doing too well, Carrie," answered Nate. "That's why I'm here."

"Tom's not here, I'm afraid," said Carrie. "I don't have any idea what time to expect him as he works late most days."

"Yeah, *works late*," spat out Nate. Then catching himself he added, "Sorry, Carrie, you don't deserve my sarcasm."

"It's okay." she replied. "I understand how you feel. Now what's wrong with Paw Charles?"

"Paw had a heart attack about two months ago," related Nate. "He wouldn't let any of us say anything for fear Tom would try to come around. Since the attack he's just not done well at all, and Doc Whitt ain't offering us too much hope. Paw wants to see you, Carrie...not Tom...just you."

"Of course I'll go see him," said Carrie, her voice trembling. "Paw Charles has always been good to me. What about Hala? How is she doing?"

"I'll let Paw tell you everything, Carrie," replied Nate. "Do you think you can come soon?"

"Yes," she assured him. "I'll take Cindy by Nora's tomorrow and she can visit with her a spell. You tell Paw Charles I'll be there."

After swapping more news about family and friends, Nate took his leave.

The next morning, as soon as Carrie finished her chores, she headed toward Nora's with Cindy. Nora was overjoyed to have her little niece for a few hours, and after sitting and talking a few minutes, Carrie left for her father-in-law's house.

The change in Paw Charles was so obvious that Carrie's breath left her at the first sight of him. He was as white as the sheets on her bed as he sat in his old rocking chair near the fireplace. There was a fire burning despite the warm weather.

"Paw Charles, it is so good to see you," said Carrie. "I'm sorry to hear that you've not been well. Can I get you a glass of water?"

"I'm alright, Carrie," he replied weakly. "Let me just catch my breath a jiffy."

She pulled a straight backed chair over beside of Charles and took his hand, saying nothing until he was ready to talk.

"Carrie," he said, after a minute, "I just had to talk to you and get some things said before the Maker calls me home to be with Izzy. I do miss her, you know...never should have married again. There's worse things than being alone, but I guess I couldn't see that at the time."

"Paw Charles, I know Maw Izzy would have wanted you to be happy," said Carrie.

"And I was for a while," responded Charles, his eyes clouding. "But it just lasted for a little while 'til my own son took it away from me."

"Are you saying things are not good between you and Hala?" questioned Carrie.

"No," he answered. "No, things never quite got back to being like it was. We both tried...but sometimes the hurt is just too much. Hala left two days ago to live with her mother. Her maw is getting up in years and needs someone, so we decided it would be for the best. I miss my little Mary Belle something terrible, but I know that Hala will take care of her, and I don't want her here to see me die."

"Paw Charles, don't talk that way," begged Carrie. "We're not ready to see you go."

"But I'm ready," he answered softly. "I'm more than ready. Ain't nothing to hold me here and Izzy's waitin' for me. But there's some things I want to say to you, Carrie." He settled back in his chair and closed his eyes for a moment as Carrie rubbed his wrinkled old hand and waited patiently. Then he roused and began to speak again.

"I don't know where we went wrong with Tom. He's got good brothers and Nannie is a good God-fearing woman. There's just something in Tom... The devil just got hold of him at an early age. He never liked his family...thought we was all mean to him. The only thing he liked was the attention of women, and it was like he just lived for that attention. Don't know what made him that way, but it sorely pains me. Carrie, I don't know how you've put up with it all these years. You're a good Christian woman, but you don't have to put up with it, and he don't deserve a woman like you. The Good Book don't require a woman to put up with an unfaithful husband. I just had to say that to you. I will understand and even rejoice if you choose to leave him. Think about your children. Pray about it, Carrie, and then do what the Lord tells you to do. I won't be here much longer and I had to get that off my chest. You don't have to put up with that sister of yours, either. She's no good, just like Tom, and they've hurt you more than you even know."

"What do you mean, Paw?" asked Carrie.

"That part is not for me to say," answered Charles. "That is a part that has to be answered by Tom and Lily."

After staying a little while longer, Carrie took her leave with a sad heart full of pain and questions. What had Paw Charles meant about Tom and Lily?

Charles Swank lingered on until the beginning of another year, and then left this world joyfully to go meet his Izzy. Tom refused to go to the funeral and forbade Carrie to go, but she went anyway.

"Carrie, if I'm not at my Paw's funeral I don't think my wife ought to be there either," Tom said.

She straightened her shoulders and looked Tom square in the eye. "I'm going to the funeral, Tom, and I'm going to the cemetery. Paw Charles was good to me and I loved him, and I will pay my respects in every way I can." With this she turned and walked away leaving Tom staring after her, his face like a thundercloud.

That May Beanie finished her schooling, and shortly after that, Sheriff Ashton came to see Carrie again. After a brief, but friendly, hello, he immediately got down to business. "Mrs. Swank," he began, "Luke's been talking to me about his sister and I've been doing some talking around. How would she like a job at the hotel in Haymaker, do you think?"

"A job?" asked Carrie. She had just never thought about Beanie getting a job.

"I talked with Martha Faller," continued Sheriff Ashton. "She needs a girl to do maid chores at the hotel. She also has a little dress shop in the hotel and could use someone to do alterations and even make some dresses and such. She would pay her a fair wage and give her a room of her own. I know Martha well, Mrs. Swank, and I know she would be good to Belinda and treat her well. Luke thinks it's a wonderful idea. What about you?"

Carrie sat for just a moment, trying to absorb all that Sheriff Ashton had said. Beanie, a job...leaving home...a room of her own? Finally, she found her voice. "I-I don't know what to say," she stammered. "I'm losing my children too fast."

"I don't want to tell you what to do, Mrs. Swank," said Sheriff Ashton. "Like I said, Luke has talked to me about it. He wants his sister to have a good life, and he's hoping that someday you can have a good life, too. He sees this as one more step toward that goal."

"I guess the decision will really be up to my daughter, Sheriff," said Carrie finally. "I'll talk to her about it tonight and get back to you with her answer."

That night, as Carrie reiterated to Beanie all that Sheriff Ashton had said, she saw the uncertainty and then the excitement in her daughter's eyes.

"A real job, Maw?" gasped Beanie. "I have wondered what I could do with my life, but I just didn't see anything out there for me. I love you,

Maw, and I will miss you terribly, but I want to make something of my life that is worthwhile. I think I want to take the job, if it's agreeable to you."

Two days later, with a heavy heart, Carrie helped Beanie pack her meager belongings and ride away with Sheriff Ashton to the hotel where she would live and work. She tried to feel the excitement for her daughter, but all she could feel was her heart breaking like pieces of fine china onto a roughly hewn floor...pieces that could never be put back together.

CHAPTER 21

The next two years settled into a routine. Luke continued to live with and work for Sheriff Ashton and his wife and seemed happy and content. He came by at least twice a week to help with the chores, and on many of these occasions, gave Carrie money. She hated taking his money but Tom gave her less and less to meet the needs of her family. Beanie, who now liked to be called Belinda, usually came once a week on her day off. She was blossoming in her new world with her job and new friends, and this made Carrie happy for her although her absence, like that of Luke, left an emptiness in her heart that only a mother could understand. Their absence also left much more work for Carrie and the four remaining children. The daily toil never seemed to end, and most nights she fell into bed exhausted. Tom rarely came home before eight o'clock, leaving all of the daily chores to his family. The children were Carrie's only joy in life, yet there was very little time to dwell on her sorrows. Trouble and sorrows have a way of getting one's attention, however, no matter how little the time.

It was a beautiful sunny day in late June as Carrie and Ady Rose sat on the front porch stringing and breaking green beans. Ady Rose had finished her schooling in May, but seemed quite content to stay at home and help on the farm. She had a beau who came to visit on Saturday evenings and Carrie was pretty sure that Ady Rose was going to choose the role of wife and mother for her life. She just didn't want her to make that choice any too soon. Jessie and Clay had gone to Sheriff Ashton's to help Luke with some chores and make some extra money. It wasn't something they did often, and definitely nothing Tom would approve of if he knew, as he thought they should spend every waking moment slaving on the farm. As Carrie and Ady Rose worked they kept up a happy conversation, and today Luke was their main topic. Ady Rose had learned from some friends that Luke had a girlfriend, though he had never mentioned it to his family. He had confided to his mother just last week that he was thinking of going to work at the sawmill in Haymaker and Carrie wondered if the two things were connected. As the conversation ebbed, Ady Rose lapsed into an old hymn, and Carrie smiled contentedly, loving to hear Ady's smooth soprano voice. As she listened, movement caught her attention on the hill below and she saw Beanie and another young lady coming toward the house.

"Oh my!" she exclaimed. "What a wonderful surprise!"

Ady Rose looked toward the hill, and then jumped to her feet. "Beanie!" she called, waving her hand joyfully.

"That must be one of her friends," said Carrie, looking at Beanie's companion. She looked about Beanie's age, maybe a little older. She was tall and thin with beautiful long, wavy dark hair.

They climbed the steps and Beanie gave first Carrie and then Ady Rose a hug. "This is my day off," she said, "and I wanted to come visit my two favorite people. Maw, Ady Rose, I want you to meet my friend Alice."

"It's so nice to meet you Alice," said Carrie. Something about the girl just looked so familiar, and Carrie was taken by her beautiful eyes and flawless complexion.

Alice gave a little laugh. "You don't know me do you, Aunt Carrie?"

Carrie's breath caught all of a sudden. "Alice?" she gasped. "Are you Lily's Tiny Alice?"

Alice laughed. "Yes, that's me. Although I guess I've never thought of myself in that way, and I began calling myself by my middle name as soon as I left the orphanage."

"Oh, Tiny," cried Carrie, pulling her into a tight embrace. "How often I've thought about you and grieved over you and wondered where you were and how you were. How did you come to know Belinda? What about your brothers and sisters? Where are they? Oh, I have so many questions."

"Let's sit down, Aunt Carrie," said Alice, "and I'll tell you everything and answer all of your questions. It is so good to see you. I remember when we were taken away, how hard you and Aunt Nora cried and begged my mother to let you take us. I've never forgotten that. It kept me going through some terrible times, knowing that somewhere there was someone who loved me. I haven't experienced too much love in my life…until lately."

"I'm so sorry, Tiny, or I mean Alice," said Carrie. "I wish I could have made life better for you. Now tell me everything, especially about James and Belle and Homer."

"Well," began Alice, "Belle and Homer were adopted within just a few months…not by the same people…but at least they were adopted. Little ones are much more adoptable than older children, although we weren't that old. I don't know the names of the families, but I'm searching for them. I WILL see my little brother and sister again someday."

"And you and James?" questioned Carrie.

"We were never adopted," Alice answered quietly, a sadness suddenly appearing in her eyes. "I've been at the orphanage all this time until just six months ago. I'll tell you more about that in a bit."

"What about James?" asked Ady Rose. "Is he living with you?"

"No. I'm afraid not," replied Alice, her eyes misting. "James died eight years ago."

"Oh, no!" cried Carrie and Ady Rose simultaneously.

"You see," continued Alice, "life at the orphanage was not easy. They kept James and me separated most of the time. We had to work hard and Mrs. Waller didn't like any of us. For some reason she especially disliked James. He cried a lot and she couldn't stand his "sniveling" as she put it. She would often send him to bed without supper, and soon James became quite malnourished. Then there was an outbreak of the flux in the orphanage. Hardly anyone escaped it, but most survived….all except James. He was just too weak to fight the illness. They didn't even have a real funeral for him, Aunt Carrie. He was just buried in the orphanage cemetery."

Carrie sat listening, tears making paths down her cheeks. "Poor little one. How alone and unloved he must have felt."

"I grieve for him still," said Alice. "But I know that he is so much better off, and that gives me solace."

"What about you, Alice?" questioned Ady Rose. "How did you get away?"

"After James died," Alice said, "Mrs. Waller disliked me even more. She made me begin work before dawn and it continued until all were in bed at night. She constantly found fault with my work and punished me for the least of reasons. It was on one of those occasions that my whole life changed. I was down on my hands and knees scrubbing the kitchen floor for the second time that morning. She stood over me pointing out places I had missed. As she pointed out one place for the second time, she kicked me in the ribs."

"Oh, Alice," gasped Carrie. "How could she?"

"Well, as it turned out," Alice went on, "it was a good thing. God can use bad things for good. You see, just at that moment Sheriff Ashton walked into the kitchen. He always came by about once a month, as he and Mrs. Ashton are benefactors of the orphanage. He usually calls ahead and Mrs. Waller is on her best behavior, but this time he just dropped in. He saw it all and he was furious. He had me pack my bags immediately, and took me to his home where I've been since that day. He also had Mrs. Waller dismissed and the situation at the orphanage is being looked into."

"So you are now living with the Ashtons?" questioned Carrie.

"Yes. They have filled out papers to become my legal guardians. I'm also working at the hotel and that's how I met Belinda."

"Then you must know Luke, too," said Carrie.

At this, Alice's cheeks turned a rosy pink. "Yes, I know Luke," she answered.

Sensing Alice's discomfort, Beanie spoke up. "She and Luke are quite good friends, Maw. He has helped her a lot since she came to live with the Ashtons, but then, Luke always helps people. He's a loving caring soul. Alice and I have become good friends, also. She's so good at everything she does and has such an abundance of joy in her heart for one who has been through sad and trying times."

Carrie sat quietly, in deep thought. It was almost more than she could absorb. Then she looked up at Alice. "Have you been to see your mother?"

Alice shook her head. "I mean no disrespect to you, Aunt Carrie, but I have no mother. That ended for her and for me the day I boarded that train. Actually, I don't think motherhood ever really began for her. I'm sorry if that sounds cruel, but I want to be honest with you."

Carrie smiled as she patted Alice's arm. "You are not being disrespectful, dear. I understand completely how you feel. I have never understood my sister."

"Lily doesn't know I'm living here," continued Alice. "Even if she saw me, which she hasn't, she would not recognize me or my name. When the time is right I will see her, but only as God leads me. Right now, nothing can be gained from a meeting. I am happy with my life today, knowing Belinda, the Ashtons, and Luke. I can't tell you the difference they have made in my life...and now to see you again, and Ady Rose...I feel for the first time in my life like I have a family, and that's a wonderful feeling."

"You are a part of our family, Alice," Carrie said fervently. "Lily will never hear anything about you from any of us. It is a loss she will never understand."

After becoming reacquainted, Alice took her leave with Beanie. They both promised to return on their next day off together. Carrie and Ady Rose continued stringing and breaking beans with a new joy and lightness of heart.

It became a habit for Beanie and Alice to come visit when they had a day off at the same time, and that happened about every other week. With these visits, Carrie also became aware that each of them had a beau, but they wouldn't tell her who these beaus were. She would often catch them in conversation with Ady Rose, talking about marriage and families. One day as she was fixing all of them a snack, she overheard Alice, "I really think we are in love," she was saying, "but I don't want to get in a hurry. I want to be absolutely sure that I will always love him and be a good wife, and I want to be the best mother that anyone can imagine. I don't ever want to bring hurt or sorrow to my family."

Please, God, thought Carrie, *help her to overcome the sorrows she has gone through, and to know that she will be a fine wife and mother.*

CHAPTER 22

The spring of 1922 brought many changes to the little town of Haymaker, as well as to the lives of Carrie and her family. Appalachian folk always pray for and cherish the good fortunes that come their way, at the same time girding themselves to battle the hard times that inevitably follow.

Eliza came by to see Carrie frequently, bringing her three-year-old daughter with her. She seemed quite happy in her marriage to Turner Ashton and was grateful to have her mother and brother living with them. She paid Carrie a visit in late April with some special news.

"Miss Carrie," she began after the usual greetings, "I have some wonderful news and I wanted you to be the first to know after Turner, Maw and Rollen."

"I always love to hear wonderful news, Eliza," laughed Carrie, "especially from my very best friend. Now tell me before you burst."

"I'm going to have another baby!" squealed Eliza. "Ain't it just glorious, Miss Carrie?"

Carrie immediately drew Eliza to her in a crushing hug. "It is definitely glorious, Eliza. I'm so happy for you because no one could be a better wife and mother than you."

"Oh yes, they could, Miss Carrie," countered Eliza. "You are the best mother in the whole wide world and you are the one I most want to be like."

Tears moistened Carrie's eyes. "Thank you, for those kind words. Now tell me, what does Turner have to say about all this?"

"Oh," laughed Eliza, "you should just see him. He's strutting around like a big old happy peacock."

"That's just grand," said Carrie, laughing. "You are very blessed, Eliza."

In June, Eb's and Maggie's son Eb Jr. married his longtime sweetheart and two weeks later their daughter Molly wed. While Eb Jr. would remain near his folks, Molly and Nathan moved to Kentucky where Nathan had a job running a mill and feed store. On July 4, Nora's and Ben's daughter Leona married. It seemed wedding bells were ringing up and down all of the little Appalachian hollows. Where had the years gone? Wasn't it just yesterday they were all visiting Papa Silas and Mama Cynth with their babies?

With the happiness, as usual, sorrow always lays claim to its own space. Tom's sister Nannie passed away in late July, succumbing to the heart failure she had dealt with for several years. Though Tom had had nothing to do with any of his family for several years, he had always been somewhat close to Nannie so he attended the funeral with Carrie, keeping a distance between himself and Nate. On the way home he was melancholy and he immediately headed to his perch on the front porch where Jessie and Clay were seated playing a game of mumbly peg with their pocket knives. Each looked up with disdain as Tom sat down.

"Well, boys," he said, "looks like you two don't have enough work to do...or you're just not doing it. Guess I'll just have to go checking."

The boys looked at each other and rolled their eyes. Tom soon turned his attention to the little house across Lacy Creek where Henry Hankins lived.

"Well," he drawled, "wonder where old Short Legs is today. Probably out showing off in that fancy car of his. I'm surprised he can even drive it with them short legs of his."

Jessie and Clay ignored him.

A few minutes later Henry's car pulled into the little space beside his house.

"Well, speak of the devil!" bellowed Tom. "I do believe that is him right now."

Henry emerged from his car, but instead of going toward the house he walked around to the passenger side. As he opened the door, a woman stepped out. Her hair was a glaring red and Tom's eyes widened like saucers. Jessie immediately recognized her and a big smile spread across his face.

"Look, Clay," he said loudly. "Why, it looks like Henry Hankins has him a lady friend. Can you tell who it is? Why, it sort of looks to me like that Lizzie Willis. Can you tell, Clay?"

Clay, picking up on Jessie's fun, responded in a serious tone, "It sure looks like her, Jessie. I didn't know they were seeing each other. That Henry sure is a lady's man."

By this time, Tom's face was a stormy blood red, but he said nothing.

Jessie just couldn't let it pass.

"Paw," he said, "do you know who that is? It sure looks like Lizzie Willis to me. I think most people call her Loose Lizzie. Can you tell if that's her?"

"You just mind your own business, boy!" stormed Tom. "It's hard to tell who that woman is. Probably somebody who took pity on old Short Legs. Now don't be spying on the neighbors!"

As they watched, Henry took her hand and they walked toward the house. He said something to her and she gave a laugh that could be heard all over the neighborhood.

"That don't sound like a laugh of pity to me," said Jessie. "Sounds like she's reeaaalll smitten with ole Henry. Why, he may have a new wife in no time."

With this, Tom arose from his chair so fast that it toppled over.

"I've got better things to do than sit here and watch that fool," he said, "and you boys have, too. Now get to your chores."

As he made his way inside, Jessie and Clay were shaking with silent laughter.

Tom's mood, never anything to brag about, became even more putrid as the days and weeks wore on. He began spending more of his spare time on the front porch watching the neighbors, but especially Henry Hankins. Clay made the comment many times to Jessie that their paw was "sick in the head", to which Jessie replied, "He ain't sick. He's too mean to be sick. He could even give the devil a run for his money."

Carrie overheard the boys talking about Tom many times, but she offered no defense. He had hurt them all too much to be defended. The hurt Tom caused, however, was far from over.

It was nearing Thanksgiving and Carrie decided she wanted all of her children home for a Thanksgiving dinner. Beanie and Luke had promised to be there as had Alice, now very much a part of their family. Tom had been at home a few times when Alice had visited and, although polite, he showed little interest in her. Carrie had never mentioned that she was Lily's daughter, keeping her promise to Alice. He did ask why she called Carrie "Aunt Carrie."

"It just makes her feel more like a part of our family," she explained.

One day as Beanie and Alice were visiting and they, along with Carrie and Ady Rose, were making plans for Thanksgiving, Carrie said, "Girls, I want you to bring your beaus for our Thanksgiving celebration. I've met Ady Rose's Willy, but I have yet to meet two others that I keep hearing about and I think it's time we remedied that. You girls tell Luke I want to meet his secret girlfriend, too."

Beanie and Alice exchanged glances, but promised to see what they could do.

That night Carrie told Tom about her Thanksgiving plans. She was geared up and ready for his complaints, but he gave none. "I guess it's time we met these people who sound like they will be a part of our family. Never figured Luke would find a girl the way he's been molly-coddled all of his life. She's got her work cut out for her."

Carrie's temper flared. "Luke is a fine hard-working young man and a girl will be mighty blessed to marry him."

"Pshaw!" replied Tom, making his way out to the front porch.

Thanksgiving Day dawned cold and crisp with snowflakes floating lazily in the air. Carrie was busy in her kitchen where she had spent a large portion of her time for the past several days. She was excited at having all of her children under her roof again and anxious to meet the "mystery" people in her older children's life. The turkey, which she had purchased from Paul and Hildy Turner, just over the hill, was in the oven, sending wonderful aromas throughout the house. Her apple and rhubarb pies were cooling and her chocolate cake was iced and ready, not to mention the molasses stack cake she had made the day before. She was determined that everyone would have their fill of food. This was the happiest Carrie had felt in a long, long time. Ady Rose had worked diligently beside her but was now readying herself for Willy's arrival, and just as she appeared from her bedroom, there was a knock at the door.

"Hi, Ady Rose," said Willy, as she opened the door.

Willy was a nice young man with a good reputation and a willingness for hard work, and Carrie had no qualms about the fine husband he would make for Ady Rose. He was eighteen and had a good job at the sawmill, along with farming alongside his paw. She had no doubts either about the way he and Ady Rose felt toward each other.

"Hello, Mrs. Swank," he said, as Ady Rose brought him in to the kitchen. "I know you have plenty to eat, but Maw insisted I bring this pumpkin pie to you. We had an abundance of pumpkins this year and Maw's made pumpkin everything lately."

Carrie laughed. "You tell your Maw I appreciate it very much. We all love *pumpkin everything* around here."

"Hey, Willy," called Jessie from the living room. "Come on in. I need someone new to take on for checkers since I've already beat the britches off Clay and he won't play no more."

Willy headed in for a checker game while Ady Rose stayed to help her mother. Tom was in the living room and, thankfully, seemed to be on decent behavior today.

About twenty minutes after Willy's arrival, there was another knock at the door.

"I'll get it," announced Ady Rose cheerfully.

In a moment she reappeared with Beanie, Alice and Luke, as well as a nice-looking young man Carrie didn't recognize.

"Mama," began Beanie. "I would like you to meet Joseph Bells. Joseph this is my very special mother."

Joseph shook Carrie's hand, smiling. "I'm very pleased to meet you, Mrs. Swank. Belinda talks about you all the time."

Carrie turned her attention to Luke. "And where is your special girl, Luke. Couldn't she come?"

"Yes, she could," responded Luke, a nervous catch to his voice. "Maw, I want you to meet Alice, my very special girlfriend."

Carrie's mouth fell open. She could think of nothing to say.

Luke looked at Alice and Alice looked at Luke. Finally Alice spoke. "I'm sorry to spring it on you like this, Aunt Carrie, but we just couldn't seem to find a way to tell you. Luke and I have been dating for quite some time. I hope you don't disapprove."

Carrie still stood there, her mouth frozen.

"Maw," said Luke anxiously. "Say something. Please don't be mad. I really care for Alice."

Finally finding her voice, Carrie spoke, "I-I'm just so flabbergasted, Luke. I had no clue. Of course I'm happy about this. Just give me a moment to get my head around it. You mean, all this time you were Alice's beau and she was your girl?"

"That's about it," answered Luke. "From the moment I first saw her, I knew she was the one for me. I know we're kin, Maw, but being kin don't stop love."

Everyone stood there looking expectantly at Carrie. Gathering herself, she reached out and pulled Alice into her arms. "One thing is for certain," she said, laughing nervously. "There's no doubt that I already love your girlfriend as a daughter." With this the awkwardness ended and the relief was easy to see.

Before the day was over, Willy had taken Tom and Carrie aside to ask for Ady Rose's hand in marriage. Tom gave his consent without even questioning Willy, as if he really didn't care. Carrie hugged Willy and told him she would be happy to have him for her very first son-in-law. She had hoped they might wait until Ady Rose was a little older, but she knew they were unquestionably in love, and Willy treated Ady Rose with the utmost respect, as Carrie could see the adoration in his eyes. The rest of the day was spent talking about their wedding, and Valentine's Day of the following year was set for the big day.

Carrie observed Alice and Luke throughout the afternoon, and it was obvious how much they cared for each other. Alice was such a wonderful girl, and Carrie knew no one could ask for more in a daughter-in-law. But why did she have this uneasy feeling in the pit of her stomach? Luke's eyes bespoke his happiness, and he deserved to be happy more than anyone Carrie knew, as did Alice. Carrie was frustrated and angry at this doubt she had.

Dear God, she prayed, *please don't let anything bad happen to these two dear ones. They deserve to be happy. There has been so much tragedy in their lives, especially Alice. She needs to be loved, Father. She needs a family. Please hear my prayer. Amen.*

The rest of the year was a busy, chaotic time for Carrie's family. After Thanksgiving, plans began for Christmas. They were all determined that it would be the happiest Christmas ever, and it was. Carrie had never seen her children so excited. There were secrets hiding everywhere, giving rise to curious eyes and hush-hush mouths. No one dared poke around in another's belongings for fear of spoiling a surprise.

Christmas day dawned sunny, cold and brisk...a glorious day. Carrie had baked and cooked for days and loved every single moment of it. She was determined to have everyone's favorites. Even Tom seemed to give in to the excitement. There were many presents under the tree, but all had agreed that none would be opened until the entire family was gathered. The one exception was Cindy. At the age of nine, Carrie knew it would be difficult for her to wait so long, so she arranged for Cindy to open one gift when she woke up. Everyone watched with excitement as though she was opening a gift for all of them.

"Oh my!" she exclaimed when the wrappings fell away. "It is the most beautiful dress I have ever seen!"

Carrie had made the dress for Cindy. It was solid blue with white lace and pink ribbons and an abundance of skirting.

"I thought it would make you a nice dress for Ady Rose's wedding," said Carrie. "What do you think?"

"Absolutely," replied Cindy. "Oh, Maw, I can't wait to try it on!"

At that moment Tom pulled another package from under the tree. "Well, if you're doing some trying on, you might just want to open this."

Cindy took the gift, eyes wide with surprise and opened it to find a new pair of black shoes. Immediately she threw her arms around Tom in the unrestrained way that only a child can exhibit. "Thank you, thank you, Paw!" she cried. "I truly love them."

With this she hurried to try them on, and as she returned, everyone declared her the most beautiful sight they had ever seen.

If only Mama Cynth could see her namesake right now, thought Carrie, tears in her eyes and joy in her heart.

As Cindy put away her gifts, everyone got to their chores, for the festivities would begin before they could turn around. Tom, accompanied by Jessie and Clay, went outside to do the milking and feeding. Carrie, Ady Rose and Cindy set about fixing the Christmas meal, and the girls chattered away as they worked.

"What is Willy getting you for Christmas, Sis?" questioned Cindy.

"I don't have any idea," answered Ady Rose. "He won't even give me a hint."

"I bet he'll like the new suit coat you got him," said Cindy. "Do you think he'll wear it for the wedding?"

"I imagine he will," laughed Ady Rose. "He doesn't have one that I know of."

Before long the food was ready and the others were arriving. Luke and Alice, Beanie and Joe arrived together, and Carrie could see the happiness in each face. It wouldn't be long, she ventured, until there would be other wedding announcements, but that was for another day. Today was Christmas and a time for celebration. After greetings and hugs, they all settled down at the dining room table.

"Luke," said Carrie, "would you be so good as to say the blessing over our food?"

Luke looked a little surprised but replied, "I would be most glad to, Maw."

"Dear Lord," he began, "we do thank you for this Christmas day. But most of all we thank you for that special day many years ago when you sent your Son as a babe in a manger. You must surely love us, Lord. I thank you for my family as we gather around this most bountiful table. I thank you for the best Maw in the world, not to mention her good cooking. I thank you that Ady Rose and Willy love each other and will soon be married, and I thank you, Lord, for the new happiness you have brought into my life. I thank you for all of my brothers and sisters and for Mr. and Mrs. Ashton. Help us to always remember what you sacrificed for us, Lord. Amen."

"Amen," chimed in the others. "Now let's dig in," added Jessie. And that's just what they did.

After everyone had eaten their fill and then some, they gathered around the tree as Carrie read the Christmas story from the Bible. Then they swapped gifts as they laughed, joked, nudged each other good-naturedly, and ooed and aahed over the gifts. Willy loved his new suit coat, and he gave Ady Rose a beautiful gold heart-shaped locket that opened.

"I thought you could put our wedding picture inside," he said. "That's why I left it empty."

Luke, Alice, Beanie and Joe had gone together and bought Willy and Ady Rose a complete set of white dishes with blue flowers on them. Tom, with Carrie's help, had bought them a set of silverware, but the most beautiful gift of all was the double wedding ring quilt that Carrie had made for them. Everyone declared it the absolute loveliest quilt they had ever seen. The others opened their gifts with joy and thanks. Beanie had received a beautiful pair of gloves from Joe and Luke had bought Alice a diary. Carrie knew it was a special gift for Alice, for she had told Carrie that she had begun keeping a diary when she was still in the orphanage. As they all settled back to relax from the meal and the gift opening, Luke turned to Willy.

"Where will you and Ady Rose live after the wedding, Willy?"

Willy and Ady Rose looked at each other and she nodded to him.

"Well," began Willy, "Paw has a little log cabin on the farm. It ain't much but it can be fixed up. He wants to deed us the cabin and six acres of land as a wedding present."

"That sounds good," said Luke. "Are you going to take him up on the offer?"

"Yes," answered Willy. "We've talked it over. The cabin only has three rooms, but Paw said he will help us add on to it. It's built soundly and won't be hard to heat, and it will certainly help us financially. The sawmill pays pretty well and I've saved up enough to fix it up. I'd like to buy us a cow or two for milk and for raising calves to sell for some extra money. The six acres should be enough for that."

"It sounds quite cozy," said Carrie. "I'm sure the two of you will have it looking like a special home in no time."

Tom sat in silence, offering no opinion. Then out of the blue he said, "You know, Bossie is about ready to wean her heifer calf. How about if I give you that for a wedding present and that will be a start for you."

Everyone sat in silent surprise.

"Why, Tom," said Carrie, finding her voice, "that's a wonderful idea!"

"We would be most grateful, Mr. Swank," said Willy. "Thank you very much."

"Yes," added Ady Rose. "Thank you, Paw. That will be a big help to us, and I always love Bossie's calves. Remember Bluebell and how she used to follow Jessie everywhere he went?"

"Yeah," laughed Clay, nudging Jessie with his elbow. "That's the only female he could ever get to follow him."

With this they all laughed and shared memories of Bluebell and other calves that Bossie had supplied. Carrie sat watching with happiness and pride, and as she looked at Tom she saw a twinkle in his eye that had not been there in a long, long time.

Thank you, God, she said, *for this special day.*

CHAPTER 23

January of 1923 was ushered in with snow, cold temperatures, excitement and activity, as everyone was preparing for Willy's and Ady Rose's wedding. Invitations had been sent out, by word of mouth, to all the family and a few friends. Even Ellie and her family were planning to come. Carrie was exhausted but happy, and Tom actually seemed to have joined the merriment, actually coming home on time each day. How long that would last, Carrie didn't know, but she was learning to accept the joys of each day one at a time, without the worry of tomorrow.

She, Ady Rose and Cindy had cleaned every nook and cranny of their house where the wedding would take place, and as they cleaned, they had shared giggles and stories as never before. Cindy had regaled them with her description of the man she would someday marry. Each day she would add a new requirement for that "someday man". He must, of course, be handsome and he would lavish her with gifts and take her to faraway places. Carrie and Ady Rose listened with amusement, sharing a wink every now and then.

Valentine's Day and Ady Rose's wedding day dawned cold but sunny...a just right day for a wedding. The baking had been completed the day before and had only to be put out on the serving dishes. Ellie and her family had arrived the night before and would be staying a few days with Tom and Carrie, to Carrie's delight. All of her siblings would be there, and even Nate and his wife had sent word that they would come. Eliza, Turner, Widow Thomas and Rollen would also be in attendance, as would Sheriff Ashton and Mrs. Ashton. Sally, Will's wife would be singing at the wedding, and Ady Rose would also sing a special song to her new groom.

Ellie was up early helping Carrie with the finishing touches as they shared some special sister time. The first to arrive were Luke and Alice. Carrie was careful not to reveal to Ellie that Alice was Lily's daughter. She wondered what the reaction would be when Lily arrived and Alice saw her for the first time in years. Would Lily have any recognition of Alice?

No sooner had Luke and Alice hung their coats than Beanie and Joe arrived followed quickly by Nora and Ben, Will and Sally and then all the others. Tom was friendly with Nate when he arrived, relieving Carrie's worry. Eliza, Turner, Widow Thomas and Rollen arrived with an obvious surprise of their own. Eliza was again expecting, she whispered to Carrie. This would make them three and the mother-to-be was radiant. Lily and Dent arrived with their two sons. She saw Alice looking at the two little boys with tears in her eyes and Carrie could only imagine what she was thinking. Lily showed no sign of recognition for the daughter she had given away. Soon all of the guests were present and the wedding began with a song by Sally. Ady Rose absolutely glowed as Willy repeated his vows, his eyes adoringly fixed on her. It was a beautiful wedding...one to put in Carrie's book of special memories. Before she knew it, though, it was all over and one more of her children had left the nest. She was glad she would have Ellie for a few days, to help delay the emptiness. Tom actually seemed to take to Ellie's husband, and they enjoyed working outside together and playing checkers and talking in the evenings. All too soon their visit was over.

Carrie kept busy in the days and months ahead. Three of her children were now gone and the other three were growing too fast. What would she do when they were all gone? Yes, she wanted her children to be happy, but oh, how she would miss them. Would she and Tom have anything left?

They hadn't had much of a marriage for years. Would Tom settle down and be content with his life with her? He was coming home on time each day, and Carrie wondered what had brought about this change, yet she dared not hope.

It was a lovely warm day in May and the three youngest children were still in school. Carrie took her sewing out to the front porch to enjoy the warmth of the sun as she worked. She had three new dress orders to be finished by the first of July, so she had plenty to keep her busy. As she sat sewing she looked up to see Luke and Alice coming up the hill. Joy immediately filled her heart as she waved to them.

"Hi, Maw," called Luke, as he unfastened the gate to the yard.

"Hi, Aunt Carrie," called Alice.

Carrie arose from her chair as she put her sewing aside. "What a wonderful surprise!" she called. "I get to see two of my favorite people. Come up and sit with me on this bright, sunny day."

"Alice had the day off, so I took the day off, too," said Luke. "Bet you're missing Ady Rose something awful, aren't you, Maw?"

"I surely am," answered Carrie. "But mothers want their children to be happy, and I know that Ady Rose is."

"Well, I guess happiness is why we wanted to come see you today," said Luke, looking mischievously at Alice.

"Why do I feel that you have something on your mind?" asked Carrie, curiosity in her voice.

"You always could read me like a book," laughed Luke.

"We do have something to talk to you about, Aunt Carrie," said Alice. "We wanted to come when we could talk to you alone."

Luke fidgeted in his chair nervously.

"What's on your mind, Luke?" questioned Carrie. "You know you can talk to me about anything."

"I know, Maw," said Luke warmly. "You've always been there for me and I love you. You see, Maw, it's like this...I've asked Alice to marry me." With that he let out a deep breath.

Carrie sat in silence for a moment. "I guess this comes as no surprise for me," she said. "I've known for quite some time that you both love each other. It's easy to see when you are together."

"Well, how do you feel about it, Maw?" asked Luke, wringing his hands.

Carrie placed her hand lovingly on her son's shoulder. "I think you are two very lucky people, and I couldn't be happier for you. Alice is already my daughter, and I don't know of two people anywhere who deserve happiness more than you do. You most definitely have my blessing."

"Whew!" gasped Luke, collapsing back in his chair like a weight had been lifted from him. "I feel like a big old elephant just got up off of my chest."

Alice arose from her chair and went over to Carrie, knelt down in front of her chair and grasped her hands. "Aunt Carrie," she said, "I have thought long and deeply about this. I wouldn't say "yes" to Luke if I wasn't sure. I've always been afraid that I might have too much of my birth mother's blood in my veins, if you understand what I mean. But I know that I love Luke, and I know that I will be faithful to him and will love, with all my heart, any children God sees fit to give us. I won't ever let him or you down, Aunt Carrie."

With tears in her eyes, Carrie pulled Alice into her arms. "I know you will make a fine wife and mother. You are nothing like Lily. There is nothing but good and love and truth in you."

Luke came to Carrie's chair and put his arms around both of the women he loved. Then he and Alice sat down on the porch at Carrie's feet.

"Maw, there's one more reason we wanted to talk to you," said Luke. "I'll let Alice tell you."

Alice took a deep breath. "Aunt Carrie," she began, "there's something I must do before beginning my life with Luke, and it's a very difficult thing for me. You see, I can't begin a marriage of honesty and truth with him as long as there is dishonesty in my life. I have to go see Lily and tell her who I am. I don't want a relationship with her. I just want the truth to be known."

"You are a very wise young woman, Alice" said Carrie. "I know it won't be easy for you, but I think you are doing the right thing. Maybe by getting this out in the open, you can begin to forgive Lily. She doesn't deserve it, but forgiveness will help you. You are not the type of person who can carry bitterness inside of her."

"Aunt Carrie," continued Alice, "I know this is asking a lot of you, but do you think you could go with me to see Lily? I don't think I can do it on my own. Luke says he will go, but I don't think that would be the right thing just yet. I know I'm asking much of you and I'll understand if you can't do it."

"Of course, I'll go with you," Carrie assured her. "It won't be easy for either of us, but with God's help, we can do it."

"Oh, thank you!" cried Alice, rising to hug Carrie again.

"When do you want to go?" asked Carrie.

"Well, I have Thursday of next week off. Would that be good for you?"

"It will be fine for me," nodded Carrie. "The children will still be in school, although they are old enough to be by themselves. I'll just walk to Haymaker to meet you and we will go to Lily's. Would ten o'clock be good?"

"It will be perfect," replied Alice. "Oh, Aunt Carrie, you have taken a burden from me."

They left a short time later, and as Carrie watched them go hand-in-hand, she felt love and happiness, but as they began to get farther away a feeling of uneasiness came over her. The feeling frightened her but she couldn't shake it.

The next week was a busy one. Carrie sewed every spare moment she had from chores. Cindy was to be in a spelling bee at school, so each night she gave out spelling words to her, promising to be there the day of the competition. Cindy was a good student and Carrie was proud of her and her willingness for hard work. This was Jessie's last year of school and he would graduate at the head of his class. Each night he practiced the speech he would give at the graduation ceremony. Clay had moved ahead a year in his classes and he would graduate next year. Her children were just growing too fast for Carrie. Luke was now a foreman at the sawmill full time and Sheriff Ashton had already asked Jessie to come work for him after he finished school. During the summer Clay would also work for him a few hours each day.

Thursday morning Carrie got the children off to school, finished her morning chores, and set out for Haymaker to meet Alice. It was a sunny morning and the birds were singing happily, but Carrie had butterflies in her stomach. She just couldn't shake the feeling of foreboding.

Please, God, she whispered as she walked along, *don't let Alice be hurt more today*.

Alice met her in front of the hotel and they walked to Lily's house.

"Are you nervous, dear?" asked Carrie.

"A little, I guess," replied Alice. "But not as much as I thought I might be. She can't hurt me more than she already has. I expect nothing from her."

As they arrived at the house, Carrie thought of other times she had been there...the day of the dinner bucket...the day of the pink bedspread. With a heavy heart, she knocked at the door. On the second knock, Lily opened the door with a look of surprise.

"Well, if it isn't my sister," she said. "Come in, Carrie."

"Thank you, Lily," replied Carrie. "How have you been?"

"Oh, I can't complain I guess. Of course, I do. It keeps Dent on his toes." With this she gave her "Lily laugh."

They followed her into the living room and took a seat on the sofa. "Who is your young friend, Sister?" she asked.

"Lily," began Carrie, "this is Alice. You met her at Ady Rose's wedding."

"I believe I do remember," said Lily, eyeing her curiously, "For some reason you look familiar to me. Are you from around here?"

"Yes," replied Alice. "I was born here, but I lived away for several years. I've been back here for awhile. Actually, Alice is my middle name. My full name is Tiny Alice."

With this, Lily's mouth gaped open and a pallor shadowed her face. All she could do was stare, for once at a loss for words.

"I thought you might remember the name at least," said Alice. "It's been a long time, Lily."

"How-how did you get up with Carrie?" stammered Lily. "Carrie, how long have you known?"

"I came here to live and work last year," said Alice, without giving Carrie a chance to speak. "I have a job at the hotel and dress shop where Belinda works and it was through her that I met Aunt Carrie. I live with Sheriff Ashton and Mrs. Ashton, who have become my legal guardians."

"But-but, how did that come about?" Lily was quite flustered. "Didn't you get adopted?"

"No," answered Alice emphatically. "I was never adopted."

"B-But, why not?" asked Lily. "They assured me that all of you would be adopted."

At this point Carrie stood. "Why don't I get all of us a glass of water, Lily? This has been a shock for you, I know." When Lily didn't respond, Carrie walked into the kitchen to get the water, and returning, she handed a glass to each.

"Wh-what about the others?" asked Lily. "Were they adopted?"

"Belle and Homer were adopted the second month we were there," replied Alice, lips pressed tightly, "but James and I were never adopted. They prefer to adopt babies, and Mrs. Waller preferred to keep the older ones for slave labor."

Lily almost dropped her glass. "What do you mean, slave labor? That wasn't what she told me would happen. She assured me people would be standing in line to adopt all of you."

"Mrs. Waller said a lot of things to a lot of people," said Alice. "Most of what she said was never the truth."

Lily squirmed in her chair, looking like an animal caught in a trap with little hope of freedom. "Do you know who adopted Belle and Homer?"

"No," Alice answered, shaking her head. "But, I assure you, I *will* find them some day."

"Is James with you?" questioned Lily. "Is he coming to see me?" She almost sounded hopeful.

"No, Lily," answered Alice. "James won't be coming to see you."

"Does he hate me that much?" Carrie was surprised to hear the sadness in Lily's voice. Did she have a heart after all?

"James had no hate in his heart," replied Alice. "He was the most loving, kind-hearted boy I ever knew."

"Was?" whispered Lily.

"James died several years ago due to mistreatment, malnourishment and illness," said Alice. "James cried a lot, missing home and his...mother. Mrs. Waller hated him for that and often starved him as punishment. When he got the flux, he just couldn't fight it. He died and was buried in the orphanage cemetery without even a funeral, and they wouldn't even let me see him or visit his grave."

As she finished her story, tears rolled down Alice's cheeks, and as Carrie looked at Lily, she saw the wetness of her face. She looked at Carrie with tormented eyes. "You tried to stop me, Carrie, and I wouldn't listen," she said. "Why wouldn't I listen?"

"I remember Aunt Carrie and Aunt Nora begging you to let them have us," continued Alice. "Why wouldn't you let them have us, Lily? The love I saw in them that day was the only love I ever knew until I came back here to live with Mr. and Mrs. Ashton."

Lily sat, head hung down, shaking it back and forth as she rung her hands. "They told me you would each get a family and that most likely you would all end up with the same family. I thought you would be better off. I wasn't a good mother and Reed and I didn't love each other. When he left, I just couldn't face raising you by myself. I've been selfish all my life, Alice. I have no excuses."

"I've seen you with your two little boys," said Alice. "You seem to love them. How can you love them, but not us?"

"I don't know how to answer that," returned Lily weakly. "Truth be told, I'm still not a good mother like my sisters are. Dent pays someone to clean our house and he pays for babysitters so we can go out some. I guess that keeps me happier and better able to tend to my boys, but I'm still selfish. I was just not cut from the same cloth as Carrie, Nora and Ellie. I wish I was, but I won't lie to you. I'm not a good wife either. Settling down has never been easy for me."

"At least you are honest about it," said Alice sadly. "I guess that's something."

Lily looked at Alice. "How did you come to leave the orphanage? Did they send you out at a certain age?"

Sadness permeated Alice's eyes. "No, we weren't sent out. The older you were the harder you could work."

Lily hung her head once more, her shoulders shaking at Alice's words.

Alice continued, "Mr. and Mrs. Ashton have always given money to the orphanage. They have no children of their own after losing three babies, and they have a special love for children. Mr. Ashton came at least once a month to visit the orphanage and sometimes Mrs. Ashton came with him. They usually let the orphanage know ahead of time and Mrs. Waller would make us clean until everything was spotless. On the day he was to arrive, we were in our best clothing and were admonished to use our best manners. Mrs. Waller pasted a smile on her face that appeared only when visitors came. However, on this particular day, Mr. Ashton had not called ahead. I think he had some business over that way, so he just decided to drop in. I was cleaning the kitchen floor and Mrs. Waller was standing over me yelling at me to do a better job. Then she kicked me in the ribs as she had done many times before. At that moment, though, Mr. Ashton stepped through the door. His face was red with rage. Mrs. Waller's face was as white as a January snow.

In a very controlled and calm voice, Mr. Ashton said, "Alice, dear, go pack your belongings. You are going home with me."

Mrs. Waller, regaining her composure somewhat, began to sputter. "W-Where are you taking her? You can't just t-take a child from here without proper papers."

"Just watch me," returned Mr. Ashton, as I slipped away to follow his orders.

I heard him say to Mrs. Waller as I left the room, "It won't be long, I assure you, Madam, until you will be packing your bags. I am ordering a full investigation of this place and you will be lucky if you don't end up in prison."

"I didn't hear Mrs. Waller's response," added Alice, "but I left that day with Mr. Ashton, and it was the best day of my life. He and Mrs. Ashton have shown me what a family is all about and I love them dearly. They got me a job at the hotel and I work part time in the little dress shop where I met Belinda, and she's become the sister I never was allowed to enjoy. Make no mistake, though, I do still have a sister somewhere as well as a brother, and I will never rest until I find Belle and Homer."

For a moment, there was silence. Then Carrie spoke, "Lily, we didn't come here to cast blame or hate. Alice is getting ready to begin a new journey in her life and she didn't want to do it with anything hidden. She is an honest and loving young woman, and I do not believe it is in her to hate."

Lily looked at Carrie and then at Alice. "How can you not hate me?"

"I cannot hate, because God tells us we are not to hate," responded Alice. "I can never view you as my mother, but neither do I want to view you as my enemy. All I want is for there to be truth between us. I have told you the truth today, and I believe you have spoken truthfully to me. That's all I want."

As though pondering her words, Lily sat again in silence. Then, as if jogged by a memory, she spoke, "Carrie said you are beginning a new journey. Does that mean you are leaving Haymaker?"

At this, Alice smiled a smile of happiness. "No, I'm not leaving; just the opposite. I'm getting married to a wonderful man and we plan to live here in Haymaker."

"Getting married?" asked Lily. "Who are you marrying?"

Alice smiled serenely. "I'm marrying Carrie's son, Luke. When I came to live with Mr. and Mrs. Ashton, he was living with them also. He was good to me and we became close friends. Then we fell in love. I have taken it slow and easy, though, because I wanted to make sure I truly loved him and that I could be a faithful and loving wife and a good mother to our children."

As she spoke, Alice hadn't noticed the stricken look that came over Lily's face, but Carrie noticed. "What's wrong, Lily?" she asked. "Luke is a wonderful man, even if he is mine, and they are very much in love."

"Sh-she can't marry Luke," gasped Lily.

"Why on earth not?" asked Carrie.

"Th-they're close kin," Lily answered. "They're too closely related."

"Close kin marry all the time," admonished Alice. "You know that, Lily."

"I guess so," Lily acquiesced rather dubiously. "When do you plan to marry?"

"We haven't set a date yet," replied Alice. "We have talked about the end of summer...maybe September. Luke has been saving his money for quite some time, and I've saved a little myself. We hope to buy a little house in or near Haymaker and have it ready when we marry." Alice paused for a moment, picking at an invisible spot on her dress. Then she looked at Lily. "W-would you tell me a little bit about my father?" she asked.

Lily was taken aback, but after some thought, she replied, "I guess I would have to say Reed was a good man. It wasn't his fault the marriage didn't work; it was mine. I just never could settle down to being a wife and mother. I wanted to have fun. Still do, I guess. Reed was a hard worker and he had a good Maw and Paw. He was proud of you kids. He use to get right down on the floor and play with you when he had time, but he worked long hours in the mines and his health wasn't good. I didn't give him much of a chance, and when he walked out, he just never came back. He did send money each month for his children, although I spent most of it on booze and partying. I'm not making any excuses for myself, Alice. I'm just telling you the truth. He was a far better person than I could ever be."

"Thank you for your honesty," said Alice. "I kept remembering a man playing in the floor with me and riding me horsey. I just wondered if it was real."

They sat quietly for a minute. Then Alice stood. "I guess we had better be going, Aunt Carrie. Thank you for your time, Lily, and for being truthful with me. I hope to see you again."

Carrie stood also. "Lily, it is good to see you. Sisters should keep in touch better than we have."

Lily walked with them to the door. "You are both welcome to come back anytime," she said. "Alice, I would say I'm sorry, but that wouldn't change anything. I'm just glad you have found some happiness...and I hope it will last."

Carrie and Alice took their leave. Alice fairly bounced along the road, her face wreathed in smiles. "Oh, Aunt Carrie," she cried, "I feel like such a weight has been lifted from me. Thank you for going with me. You know, I almost feel sorry for Lily. She doesn't realize how much she has wasted of her life and all the love she has missed out on. Do you think she even knows what love is?

Carrie smiled without answering, happy to see Alice's elation. Yet, something bothered her...something she couldn't quite put her finger on. That veil of gloom was back...and what had Lily meant when she said, "I hope it will last."

CHAPTER 24

The summer was a burdensome one for Carrie. There was so much work to do and fewer workers to do it. Jessie worked each day for Sheriff Ashton and then came home and worked more. Clay was working part time for the Sheriff, so it was difficult to get all of the chores done. Cindy helped diligently in the house and was even quite good at milking, but it was hard to keep up with the feeding, gardening and the big field of corn that seemed to constantly need hoeing. Carrie was trying to fill several sewing orders for women in the community and still keep up all the other chores. Most days she worked way into the night to get a dress or coat or shirt finished. She was only thirty-eight years old, but felt like an old woman, tired and worn from the troubles and hardships of life. Yet, at the same time, Carrie knew she had much for which to be thankful, and she was; she truly was. Her children were the happiest she had ever seen them, and when her children were happy, that gave her joy. Tom was coming home on time more than he had in the past months, but he, too, was busy just trying to keep everything caught up. He talked very little, but was less cranky, seeming to know that he couldn't yell at Jessie and Clay as he had Luke. They had already shown that they would stand up to him.

It was a hazy Sunday in July and Carrie was preparing a big lunch, as all of her children would be joining them. The little kitchen was hot and the open windows helped little because no breeze was stirring outside. She wiped the perspiration from her face as she heard the front door open.

"Hi, Maw, Paw!" called someone as they entered the house.

Carrie immediately recognized Ady Rose's voice, and, sure enough, there she and Willy stood in the kitchen doorway. Ady rushed to give Carrie a hug, followed by Willy. Both were wreathed in smiles, making it obvious just how happy they were.

"It's so good to see the two of you," exclaimed Carrie, returning the hugs.

"Do you know what today is Maw?" asked Ady Rose.

"Why, other than Sunday, I haven't a clue," responded Carrie.

"It's our five-month anniversary!" laughed Ady Rose.

"Well, I do declare. How could I forget that!" cried Carrie, feigning surprise.

"You have to keep on your toes with Ady Rose," warned Willy. "Tomorrow will be our five-month and one-day anniversary. The day after that our five-month and two-day anniversary, and I am in deep trouble if I forget." At this they all laughed.

"It is wonderful to see the two of you so happy," sighed Carrie. "It does a mother's heart good."

More voices sounded in the living room. "Smells good around this place," called Luke. "I believe I smell the best apple pie in the world! Is that also chicken and dumplings that are tickling my nose?"

"Your nose is too nosey," laughed Alice, punching him on the arm.

"I believe I smell fresh baked bread," chimed in Beanie, as she and Joe joined the others. "Did you make it for your favorite daughter?"

"Are you talking about me?" teased Ady Rose, hugging her big sister.

After more good-natured kidding, the men all withdrew to the living room while the girls helped Carrie ready the meal for the table. She smiled to herself. There was just nothing like family.

The meal went well, with everyone talking and laughing. Even Tom joined in the fun, and he actually seemed happy to have his children home. He and Willy talked about farming while the others filled them in on news from Haymaker, the hotel and the sawmill. Carrie did notice that Tom and

Luke talked little to each other, but there was plenty of talking with the others so that no one else seemed aware. After the meal, they all moved to the front porch to talk and try to get a breath of air. Willy and Jessie began a game of checkers with a set Willy had brought over, and Clay and Joe began a game with the home set. As the conversation began to ebb, Luke cleared his throat.

"Well, folks," he began with a manner of importance, "Alice and I have set the date. She just won't let me be until I marry her." At this, everyone laughed.

"I have an idea it's the other way around," said Beanie.

"That it is, Sis. That it is," vowed Luke. "I'm the luckiest man in the whole United States of America. No. No. I'm the luckiest man in the whole wide world, including the sky and the ocean."

"Well, just when is this special event to be?" asked Ady Rose.

Luke reared back and puffed out his chest. "We have set this monumental event for Saturday, September 4, at three o'clock in the afternoon."

"And where will this *monumental event* take place?" asked Ady Rose.

"That, my dear little sister, is what we must talk about today," returned Luke.

"Okay, Luke," admonished Alice. "Let's get serious now."

"Not even married and she is already giving me my come-uppance," declared Luke, a forlorn look on his face. "Okay, serious it is."

"We wanted to talk to all of you about the place for the wedding," said Alice. "You see, Mrs. Faller has offered to let us use the gathering room and the dining room of the hotel for the wedding at no cost. It would be her wedding gift to us. Aunt Carrie, would you be hurt if we have the wedding there instead of here? I know Ady Rose had hers here and it was beautiful. It's just that Beanie and I both work there and Mrs. Faller has been so good to us..."

"Oh, Alice," admonished Carrie. "Of course I won't be hurt. A wedding should be where the bride wants it to be, and I think the hotel will be a beautiful place."

"Thanks, Maw," said Luke, blowing her a kiss. "I told Alice you wouldn't mind. Mrs. Faller has been good to Alice, and she has also offered to have the wedding cake made."

"That is exceptionally nice of her," said Carrie. "Alice do you plan to work there after you are married?"

Alice looked at Luke and smiled. "Luke and I have talked about it, and I think I will for awhile. We have found a little house just outside of Haymaker, and I can walk to the hotel in fifteen minutes. I could at least work for part of the day and still be home to fix supper before Luke gets home. He says it's alright with him."

"I think that's an excellent idea," injected Beanie. "The hotel and dress shop are wonderful places to work, and the extra money will also come in handy for a couple just starting out, not to mention I'll get to see you every day."

"There's something else..." began Alice, somewhat hesitantly.

"What is it, Alice?" asked Carrie, a worried look on her face.

"I have an enormous favor to ask of you, Aunt Carrie. Would you... could you make my wedding dress?"

Tears flooded Carrie's eyes. "I would absolutely be delighted to make your wedding dress, my dear daughter-to-be."

"Well, there's something else..." continued Alice.

"And what would that be?" laughed Carrie.

Alice looked around at the others sheepishly. "I want Belinda to be my maid of honor and Ady Rose and Cindy to be my bridesmaids. Could you make their dresses, too? Luke and I will be paying for all the material," she added hastily.

"I'm sure I can handle that," answered Carrie. "Wow, I will need to start right away."

"It's Sunday, Carrie Tan," said Tom, joining in the fun. "Maybe you could wait until tomorrow." At this, everyone joined in with laughter, all talking at once, as plans were made for the wedding, and Carrie was smiling both inside and out.

After the others had taken their leave, Carrie, Tom, Jessie, Clay and Cindy sat on the porch enjoying the weather and thinking on all that had taken place.

Tom looked over at Carrie. "Whatcha thinking about, Carrie?"

She pulled herself from her reverie. "Oh, just thinking how happy they all seem. I guess I'm a little bit worried about how I'm going to get all of that sewing done, although I'm also looking forward to it."

Clay looked over at his Maw. "I think I'll tell Sheriff Ashton that I'm needed at home until after the wedding. I can do a lot more of the chores that way, and I know he'll let me work again when I'm able. He's an understanding man, especially where family is concerned."

"I believe he would let me off one day a week to come help," added Jessie. "I could get a lot of the chores done in one day, plus evenings when I could come over."

"How about if I cook supper all by myself one day a week?" asked Cindy. "I'm old enough, don't you think, Maw?"

"Of course, you are," answered Carrie, "and I think that would be a splendid idea. I thank all of you, and I can use all of the help I can get."

After a few moments of quiet, Tom spoke, "Bunn Wilkins was telling me the other day that his two oldest boys have been trying to find some work to help out at home. I think maybe I could hire them to hoe that old cornfield. That should help out some."

Carrie could hardly believe her ears. "Why, that would be a big help, Tom," she said. "Well, it looks like I'll have plenty of time for those dresses, and I'll be ready to start just as soon as Alice gets the material to me. Oh my, I'm looking forward to this."

On Tuesday of the following week Alice came by with the material for her wedding dress. She had a picture of the design she wanted and Carrie assured her it would be no problem to make. As she was taking measurements, Carrie asked, "Alice, are you going to invite Lily to the wedding?"

Alice paused a moment. "I suppose I will. It wouldn't be right to leave her out since we're inviting all of Luke's other aunts and uncles. If she comes, okay, and if she doesn't, okay."

After some further discussion of the wedding plans and the dresses for Beanie, Ady Rose and Cindy, Alice took her leave and Carrie began work on the dress. She was certainly happy about the wedding coming up and the love she saw between Luke and Alice, yet for some reason she just could not explain, this feeling of gloom kept returning, clutching at her heart, almost taking her breath away.

That afternoon Jessie came over to help Clay with the chores. He was smiling from ear to ear as he kissed his maw. "Guess what, Maw," he exclaimed.

"You won a million dollars," laughed Carrie.

"Nope," responded Jessie.

"You have found a girl and you want to have a double wedding with Luke and Alice," ventured Carrie, a twinkle in her eye.

"Not even a possibility within the next fifty years," he groaned. "No women for me!"

"Then I give up," said Carrie, throwing her hands in the air.

"Well," he began. "You know we men are going to need suits for the wedding, and I've been trying to figure out how we can afford them or where to have them made. Well, guess what! Mr. and Mrs. Ashton just told me this morning that they want to buy a store-bought suit for Luke, Jessie, and me. Now, ain't that just the best thing you've ever heard, Maw?"

Carrie's eyes widened with surprise. "I think that is absolutely wonderful of them, Jessie. We can never repay them for all they have done for this family. Yet, love and generosity like that doesn't want repayment. It is freely given and that's what makes them such special people."

Everyone stayed true to their word in helping with the chores, and by mid-August Carrie was finished with the dresses for the wedding except for hemming those for Ady Rose and Cindy. The last Sunday in the month they all came for their final fittings, accompanied by the menfolk who were not allowed to even glimpse the dresses.

Lunch was over, the dresses had been tried on and the entire family was gathered on the front porch to relax and talk about the wedding the following Saturday.

"It's going to be the most beautiful wedding Haymaker has ever seen," declared Ady Rose. "Just you wait and see."

"I will definitely have the most beautiful bride Haymaker has ever seen," avowed Luke.

Just then Alice sat up straighter in her chair. "Who is that coming up the hill?" she asked. "It looks like Lily."

Carrie shaded her eyes with her hand. "Why, it surely is, and she seems in a hurry. I hope nothing is wrong."

As Lily opened the yard gate, Carrie arose from her chair. "It's good to see you, Lily."

Lily made no response, but closed the gate and ascended the steps. When she reached the top, she paused. "I'm sorry to interrupt your family gathering," she said, her voice trembling, "but this couldn't wait any longer."

"Sit down, Sister," said Carrie, a worried look on her face. "Is something wrong with Dent or the boys?"

Lily shook her head. "No, they're all okay. I got something to say and I just might as well up and say it. Alice can't marry Luke."

For a moment everyone on the porch sat in stunned silence. Then Luke spoke.

"Lily, what on earth are you talking about? I don't see as you have any say in the matter. You gave up your rights a long time ago. I love Alice and we are going to get married."

"This hurts me more than you will ever know," continued Lily, "but I just can't keep silent. The two of you can't marry."

"Is this about us being cousins?" asked Alice. "I've already told you that doesn't matter to us, Lily."

Lily shook her head again. "No, it ain't because you're cousins."

"Then what on earth would make you so against them getting married, Lily?" asked Carrie, bewildered.

Lily paused as though trying to make her mouth say the words she needed to say. "It ain't because I'm against it, and it ain't because they're cousins...it's because they're brother and sister!"

Carrie and Alice let out a gasp simultaneously.

"What are you talking about, Lily?" cried Alice. "Are you just trying to cause trouble for me? Haven't you ruined my life enough? Is it so hard for you to see me happy?"

Carrie tried to rouse herself from a daze. As she heard Lily's words reverberate in her head, a realization of what she had said came to her. She looked over at Tom who was as white as a sheet.

"No, Alice," answered Lily, pleadingly. "I don't want to cause you any more hurt, but I couldn't let you go ahead with this wedding without telling you the truth. It pains me more than you will ever know to destroy your happiness. I reckon it's true what the Good Book says about "the sins of the parents being visited on the children". It's my sin you are going to pay for and I'm so terribly sorry."

"I still don't understand," whispered Alice, in a distraught voice. "Explain to me why you are saying this awful thing."

Carrie looked first at Tom and then at Lily. "Yes," she said, "explain to all of us, Lily."

Lily wiped tears from her face with her dress tail. "I'm so sorry for all of this, Carrie. If I could erase it I would, but I can't. Reed was not Alice's real father."

"Not my real father?" questioned Alice. "That makes no sense, Lily."

"Reed wasn't your true father," said Lily. "I was pregnant when I married Reed, but he wasn't the father. He didn't even know I was pregnant. When he found out, it destroyed what he felt for me and he left for several days, but then came back. I would never tell him who the father was, though. He never knew, but he did love you, Alice."

"And who was the real father, Lily?" asked Carrie, in a voice filled with trepidation.

Lily wiped her eyes again. "I'm sorry, Carrie, but Tom is Alice's father. That's why they can't marry. They are half brother and sister."

With that, everyone gasped, and Jessie slammed his fist down on the porch banister. Tom looked as if he would pass out.

"Before you get any wrong ideas," went on Lily, "Tom didn't know this either."

"How can you be sure who the father is?" questioned Luke.

"I'm sure because Tom was the only one I was ever with like that before I was married. Reed had this thing about not being with me until our wedding night...although I tried to persuade him otherwise when I knew I was pregnant. Tom was the only one it could possibly have been, no matter how loose you think I was."

"Tom?" said Carrie, hoping he would say something to contradict the things Lily had just said.

"I-I swear I didn't know, Carrie Tan," he half cried. "I swear I didn't know." With this he bent, with his head in his hands in utter defeat.

Carrie shook her head, as though trying to make some sense of it all. "So, you were unfaithful to me even before we were married?"

Tom did not raise his head.

Lily reached for Alice's hand, but Alice drew away from her. "Don't you ever touch me!" she cried. "Everything you have ever done has destroyed my life. You gave me away to a life of loneliness and pain, and now when I have finally found love and a place to belong, you are taking that away from me. I hate you, Lily! I hate you with a hate I never knew I could feel!"

With that, she ran in to the house and Luke followed.

Lily rose from her chair. "Carrie, I didn't want to do this today, but I couldn't let a brother and sister marry. You see that, don't you?"

Carrie sat in her chair, too sad to even look up. "Just go on home, Lily. Just go on home."

With that, Lily left, slowly descending the hill. There was absolute silence on the porch. Finally, Beanie stood up and reached her hand to Joe, then nodded to Ady Rose and Willy. "Let's go see about Alice," she said.

As they went into the house, Cindy followed them and Jessie and Clay headed toward the barn, the rage obvious in their faces.

After several silent minutes had passed, Carrie found her voice. "I never knew before what it was like to hate, but I think I know now. Your paw knew all of this, and he tried to warn me, and even Reed's maw and paw knew, but I was just too blind to see. I remember the day Lily gave her children away, Reed's paw said something to me about having more reason than anyone to dislike Lily. When I told Lily you and I would take two of the children she said something about wondering which one you would want. I was just too stupid and blind to realize what they were all talking about because I was so sure that you loved me then. Later, when I had to face the truth, I still believed in my marriage vows and so I tried to hold it all together. I even let you hurt my children and drive them away. What kind of mother does that make me?"

"You are a wonderful mother," said Tom, finally finding his voice. "Never doubt that, Carrie. It's all me. I'm the one who has done the wrong. Please believe me when I tell you I never knew Alice was mine. I never loved Lily. She just always seemed to have some sort of hold over me. I'm just no good, Carrie, and I'm as sorry as can be about all of this."

"At least you have said one thing truthfully," said Carrie. "You are no good." As she arose from her chair, she turned back to face Tom. "How many women have there been, Tom, and how many other children have you fathered? No, don't answer that. I don't even want to know, because I don't care anymore."

With that, she went to see about her children. She found them all in the living room, trying as best they could to console Alice and Luke.

"It doesn't matter, what she said," Luke was saying. "We'll go away from here and get married. We don't ever have to come back here."

Sobbing, Alice shook her head, "But don't you see, Luke? No matter where we go, we'll still be brother and sister. We can't marry. Not ever." With this, she began to sob uncontrollably as she fell into Beanie's arms. Cindy began to cry because Alice was crying and came running to Carrie's outstretched arms. Willy held Ady Rose as she cried.

After a while, Alice stood, with a semblance of control. "I need to go home, now, if Beanie and Joe will walk with me. Luke, you and I can talk in a few days after I have digested all of this. Right now I'm in no frame of mind to think or talk."

Luke reached out for her, then dropped his arms. "Okay," he said, nodding in defeat.

They took their leave, and Luke headed out toward the barn. Carrie knew he needed to be alone. She consoled Cindy and finally talked her in to lying down for a nap. Carrie walked to the kitchen table and sat down, head in hands, too sad even to cry. After a few moments, she heard someone come into the kitchen, and she could tell by the footsteps that it was Jessie. He sat down beside her and put his arms around her.

"Maw," he said. "Are you okay?"

She patted his hand. "I'll be okay. Don't worry about your Maw, sweet boy."

He reached his hand out and turned Carrie's face toward him. "Maw, I want you to listen to me. Look at my face and listen to my words, Maw. HE WILL NEVER HURT YOU AGAIN. Do you understand me, Maw?"

Carrie reached her hand to his face. "I know you mean, well, Jessie. But don't worry. Your Paw can't hurt me any worse than this. Just try not to have vengeance in your heart, boy. It will only hurt you."

"Just remember what I said," reasserted Jessie. "NEVER AGAIN, Maw."

Luke returned from the barn a few minutes later, said goodbye to Carrie and took his leave. When Carrie and the children went to bed that night, Tom was still sitting on the front porch, staring into the darkness. Carrie felt no pity for him.

CHAPTER 25

The following week was a wretched one for Carrie, but she realized that the real pain was felt by Alice and Luke. On Thursday she went into town to see Alice. When she arrived at the hotel, Mrs. Faller met her with misty eyes and open arms.

"Alice and Belinda told me everything, Carrie. I can't tell you how my heart breaks for all of you. I've never met two finer young ladies than those two, and Luke is everything a man should be."

"Thank you," replied Carrie, returning the embrace. "I am beholden to you for the kindness you have shown them."

"Oh, I love them as if they were my own," answered Mrs. Faller. "That's why all of this pains me so. I just wish I could do something to help."

"Is Alice here today?" asked Carrie. "I was hoping to talk to her."

Mrs. Faller nodded. "Yes, she's in the dress shop right now with Belinda. Let me call her in here so the two of you can talk privately. Go on in to the sitting room and I won't let anyone disturb you."

Carrie was astounded by Alice's appearance as she came into the room. She couldn't have eaten a bite or slept at all this week. Her eyes were dark, sunken orbs of misery as she came immediately to Carrie's waiting arms. They stood in silence for awhile, then sat on the sofa.

"I won't ask how you are doing," said Carrie. "I can see you are in a terrible way. Can I help you, my darling girl?"

"Just your being here helps, Aunt Carrie," answered Alice. "But no one can really help."

"Have you and Luke talked?"

"Yes," replied Alice, wiping a tear. "We talked last night."

"That's good," replied Carrie, patting her hand.

"I'm going away, Aunt Carrie," said Alice.

Carrie sat upright with a jolt. "Going away? Oh, no, Alice. I've just found you. Please don't go away again."

"I have to, don't you see? I just can't stay here after all that's happened," she explained. "I won't be going so far that I will never see you again. Mrs. Faller has helped me to get a job at another hotel over in Lawrenceville that her cousin owns. It's only about two hours from here. We can visit from time to time...after a while. I just need to get away and find some sort of peace with all of this. Please understand, Aunt Carrie."

"I do understand, dear," Carrie answered reassuringly. "I just don't want to lose you."

Alice hugged her again. "You will never lose me. You have shown me a love that I have longed for all my life. I promise to write to you every week and let you know about my life, and I want you to write to me, too."

"I will most certainly write to you...and we will visit," affirmed Carrie.

After saying goodbye to Alice and then Beanie, Carrie took her leave and headed for Sheriff Ashton's home. By now it was late in the afternoon and she knew Luke should be home. When Mrs. Ashton answered the door, she immediately drew Carrie into her arms. "I'm so sorry for all of this, Carrie," she said. "Those two young people do not deserve such hurt...and neither do you."

"Thank you, Martha," answered Carrie. "I was hoping to talk to Luke. Is he home yet?"

"I'm sorry, but he isn't," replied Mrs. Ashton. "He's been working some overtime. I think it helps him to keep busy, and I don't know what time to expect him."

Carrie sighed. "Will you just tell him I was here and that I would like to talk to him?"

After Mrs. Ashton assured Carrie that she would deliver the message, Carrie took her leave. As she walked back by the hotel, the thought came to her, *Day after tomorrow would have been their wedding day, if not for Tom and Lily.*

She returned home and went through the motions of living, although she was dead inside. The children seemed to tiptoe around the house, not knowing just what to say. Jessie returned to full time work for Sheriff Ashton, and Clay began his last year of school. Two weeks after school began, Clay came home one day with the announcement that when he finished school in the spring he planned to go to Kentucky.

"There are some horse ranches up there," he explained, "and Sheriff Ashton is helping me get on at one of them to help train race horses. Well, it will be a while before I can actually *train* them. I will start out working in the barns, cleaning stalls and such, but eventually I can start training them. You know how I've always loved horses, Maw."

"I know how you love all animals, Jessie," laughed Carrie.

He hugged his Maw. "It's like a dream come true for me. I'll be doing the thing I love most."

I'm losing one more child, thought Carrie.

Tom was a shadow around the house, seldom speaking a word to any of them and none of them had anything to say to him. In early September Henry Hankins married Lizzie Willis and moved her into his house across the road. Tom said not a word, but stopped sitting on the front porch.

It was mid-September before Luke came to the house. It was noon and Carrie was alone, and she was sure that was why Luke chose this time. He had lost weight and his face was the epitome of sadness. Without a word, he put his arms around his mother and just stood holding her for a minute.

"I can see you are in much pain, my sweet darling boy," said Carrie. "I wish I could make the pain go away, but I know it's not in my power."

"I don't think it will ever go away, Mama," declared Luke in a voice void of hope.

Just hearing the term "Mama" told Carrie much about Luke's feelings.

"I hope you know that I had no idea about all that Lily told that day, Luke," said Carrie. "Maybe I should have had some clue, but I just didn't know. I knew your Paw was unfaithful to me. We all knew that. But I didn't know he was unfaithful even before we were married. He just has the devil in him. That's the way Paw Charles said it, and he was right. He has the devil in him, and everyone else has to suffer because of it. I never wanted you children to suffer, and I should have left him the first time he ever hit you, but I didn't know where to go. Still, I should have gone somewhere."

Taking her by the shoulders, Luke shook his head. "No, Maw. This is not your fault. No one ever had a better mother than you and I won't let you blame yourself. Like you said, Paw just has the devil in him. I've tried not to hate him, Maw, but I do."

"I know," said Carrie, patting his arm, "but we must try not to hate him. Hate only hurts us and it won't change what's done. It will eat you up inside."

"Maw," said Luke, pulling her down on the sofa beside him. "Maw, I came here today to tell you I'm going away."

Carrie could almost feel the splintering of her already tattered heart. "No, Luke. Please don't tell me that. Am I going to lose everyone I love? Luke, you just can't go!"

He reached for her hand. "I have to go, Maw. Please understand. I just can't stay here anymore. Everywhere I look there are reminders of Alice and I just can't live like that."

"Where will you go?" asked Carrie, trying to still her shaking body.

Luke quickly continued. "The people who own the sawmill at Haymaker also own a big one in Pennsylvania."

"Pennsylvania!" exclaimed Carrie, her body shaking harder than ever.

"Now, Maw, listen," begged Luke. "It's not the end of the world. They're going to give me a job up there as a superintendent and I'll make good money. I can ride the train down for a visit now and then...and we can write, Maw. Please tell me you understand. I need you to support me in this."

Although Carrie's heart was breaking, she knew what she must do, so she placed her hand on his arm and said, "Of course, I'm for you, Luke. It does sound like a wonderful opportunity, and I suppose a change would do you good. You have my blessing, sweet boy."

Throwing both arms around her, Luke cried, "I knew you would understand and be here for me, Maw. You always have."

"Have you told your brothers?" asked Carrie.

"No," he answered. "I wanted to tell you first, and now I'm going by to tell them while they're still at the Ashton house. I haven't told Mrs. Ashton either, although Sheriff Ashton has been in on all of this. He's been so helpful to me, Maw. Don't know what I would have done without him. Did you know that when I went to live with them Paw threw a fit? Sheriff told him it was either that or he would have him thrown in jail for the way he beat me. That simmered Paw's ranting right quickly."

Soon Luke left to go tell his brothers the news. Carrie had never felt such utter abandonment as when Luke walked down the hill and out of sight. *I'm losing them so quickly*, she thought. *What will I have left? Oh, Tom, what have you and Lily done to our lives?*

Alice moved away the following week and two weeks later Luke boarded the train for Pennsylvania. In the spring Clay would be leaving. It was a sad time...a time of loss.

Thanksgiving and Christmas were somber occasions that year, although the children did everything they could to make things lively. Carrie decorated, sewed and baked, but her heart was miles away, and she just wanted the holidays to be over. A letter came from Alice every week and she made every attempt to sound happy, but Carrie could read between the lines. She knew how badly the girl must be hurting even as she talked about Mrs. Sneadville, the hotel owner, and how much she was like Mrs. Faller. Luke, too, wrote often, and she kept all of his letters in the dresser drawer with her Bible. His job was going well and he was staying extremely busy as well as making good money. He couldn't hide the fact that he was hurting, though. Carrie kept one of his letters in her apron pocket and took it out daily to read it.

Dear Maw,

It's late here and I couldn't go to sleep, so I thought I'd write a few lines to my favorite lady. I sure would like to sit down at your table and eat a piece of your apple pie and talk like we use to. I sure miss those talks, Maw. You always took time to really listen. You never passed judgment and you never offered advice unless I asked for it. Everyone is good to me here, but it's so lonely. I wrote a letter to Alice yesterday. I don't know if it was the right thing to do or not, but I just couldn't help myself. I know we can't ever be together like we wanted, but I hope somehow we can keep in touch. I hope you write to her, Maw. I know she needs you.

Maw, I try not to have bad feelings toward Paw, but it sure is hard sometimes. Seems like he has hurt everyone and he had no reason. He has a good family and the love of a good woman. Maw, I pray that I won't turn out like him. I wouldn't want to live and turn out like that, hurting people and all. Sometimes I worry about Jessie and the feelings he has toward Paw. He hates him with all of his being. I pray each night that God will help all of us not to have hate in our hearts, but especially Jessie.

I'm saving my money, Maw. I know you won't leave there as long as Cindy's in school, but maybe once she's finished, maybe you and her might want to come here to live with me. Will you at least think about it?

Guess I'd better get some sleep now. Tomorrow will be here before I know it, and sawmill work is not easy. I don't mean to sound so down, Maw. It's just that some days are worse than others. Write real soon. I love to get your letters. Tell all of my brothers and sisters hello for me. I love you, Maw.

Your loving son, Luke

Carrie had read that particular letter so many times she could recite it by heart. She could feel Luke's pain and sadness in every line and every word, and she prayed that someday Luke and Alice would find someone to love and that they would be happy once more, yet she knew that it would take a long time.

Don't worry, my darling boy, she whispered, *you are nothing like your father*.

No matter how severe the storm, though, sooner or later those clouds have to move on to make room for the sunshine. The new year ushered in a little bit of sunshine, much needed by the Swank family. One Sunday in March, when Beanie and Joe came for lunch, they announced nonchalantly that they had gotten married the day before.

"Married!" gasped Carrie. "You just went out and got married?"

"That's just what we did!" laughed Beanie, looking lovingly into Joe's eyes.

"And didn't say squat to your family?" gasped Ady Rose. "I am hurt to the bone, Sister!"

With this she stuck out her lower lip in the biggest fake pout she could muster.

"Now, Ady Rose, I know you're not angry with your dear sister," laughed Beanie again.

"No, I'm not angry," confessed Ady Rose, "but why didn't you have a family wedding?"

Joe placed his arm protectively around Beanie's shoulders. "With all that's gone on in the past months, we just didn't think anyone would be up to celebrating. We thought this was the best way to do it, and we are very happy, so we just want everyone to be happy for us."

Carrie gave her daughter and her new son-in-law each a big hug. "We are overjoyed for you."

"Where are you going to live?" asked the practical Jessie.

"Well," began Beanie, "the house Alice and Luke were buying was still for sale, so we bought it. Do you think that's a mistake, Maw?"

"Of course it's not a mistake," answered Carrie. "There was no need for it to just sit there. A house needs to be filled with love."

"Do you think Alice will feel hurt?" asked Ady Rose.

"As a matter of fact, it was her idea," replied Beanie. "She suggested it in a letter just after she moved away. Then she reaffirmed her idea when I told her we were going to get married in secret."

"We're happy for you, Sis," inserted Clay, giving his sister a hug.

"Now let's sit down and eat before the food gets cold," said Carrie. "Joe, would you say grace over our food today?"

With this, grace was said and everyone began eating and talking... everyone except Tom, who ate and listened in silence. He wasn't in one of his bad moods, but the life had gone out of him lately. He seldom talked anymore, nor even fussed at his family. Jessie and Clay chose to ignore him totally, even when they had to work with him on the farm.

As dessert was passed around, Ady Rose sat up straight in her chair, reached for Willy's hand and cleared her throat. "I do not want to distract from Beanie and Joe's wonderful announcement, but Willy and I have an announcement of our own." With this she gave a noticeable pause as everyone stopped to listen.

"Well....?" said Jessie, putting his hands out, palms up. "Are you going to tell us or not?"

Willy and Ady Rose looked at each other and then said in unison, "We're going to have a baby!"

Everyone sat in stunned silence for just a moment. Then Carrie's hands went to her face in a mixture of joy and disbelief.

"A baby!" she whispered. Then as the realization permeated her brain, she yelled loudly, "A baby!"

Beanie arose from her chair to go hug her sister.

Clay clapped his hands. "I'm going to be an uncle," he said. "We're going to be uncles, Jessie. How about that! Uncle Clay and Uncle Jessie. Of course, Uncle Clay will be the little fellow's favorite uncle, but he'll like you too, Jessie."

Jessie punched him on the shoulder. "And just what makes you think you will be his favorite...and how do you know it will be a boy, Mr. Know-It-All?"

As if she had not heard the good-natured bantering of her sons, Carrie gasped again. "My first grandchild!" she cried. "Tom, we're going to be grandparents!"

Tom said nothing, but smiled as a tear came to his eye.

Cindy had been listening quietly, but suddenly looked at Carrie. "Does that mean I'll be an aunt, Maw?

Carrie had to laugh. "You certainly will, my sweet girl...or should I say *Aunt Cindy.*"

The rest of the afternoon was spent with plans and merriment. It was decided that Carrie would go the following week to help Beanie get her new house all fixed up, and she was as excited as Beanie. Then the talk turned to baby clothes and how much Ady Rose would need help with that.

"I know," offered Beanie. "We can both come to Maws on my days off and make baby clothes. Then, after the baby comes, we can come to Maws and we can piece quilts together. Won't it be such fun?"

"Who will birth your baby," asked Carrie, remembering Mama Cynth and all the babies she had birthed.

"Well," began Ady Rose, "Dr. Green has replaced Dr. Whitt in town since he retired, and Willy and I both like him. I want him to birth the baby if he is available at the time, but if not Willy's mother can catch it, or even help Doc Green. She's birthed several, you know."

Carrie wiped a tear from her eye. "You know, I use to get so upset when Mama Cynth was away from our home birthing a baby, but when I was having my own babies I had a new appreciation for her and her ability. Being a midwife is a special gift."

Her heart was far from mended, but Carrie awoke on Monday morning without the usual dread of facing another day, and there was a lightness to her step as she fixed Tom's breakfast and got him off to work. She had new purpose in her life. *She was going to be a grandmother!*

I wonder what it will be? she thought to herself. *I know Willy would like a little boy so he could teach him all about farming. Yet, a little girl would be wonderful also. Oh well, we will love whichever God chooses to send us. Maybe he'll send us one of each!* With this she had to laugh to herself. New grandmothers could certainly be silly.

Next, she began thinking about all the things she would need to take to Beanie's. There was much work to do in the new house and she couldn't wait to get started. She had already agreed to make some new curtains for it.

No sooner had Tom left for work than she began fixing Clay and Cindy's breakfast to get them off to school. After they had departed, she began the Monday wash, thankful that the skies were previewing a sunny day for drying laundry. Her day was filled with chores, but not so many that she couldn't take time to think some more about Beanie's new marriage and Ady Rose's new announcement. *She was going to be a grandmother! Oh, Mama Cynth,* she whispered silently, *I wish you could be here right now because you would understand the joy I feel.*

Cindy came home alone that afternoon as Clay went to Sheriff Ashton's to work. She helped her mother in the kitchen after finishing her homework. By four thirty Clay was home and doing his chores. By five thirty Carrie had supper prepared and ready to go on the table, but Tom was not home. This was unusual of late because Tom had been coming home right on time.

Is he up to his old tricks? Carrie wondered.

By six o'clock he still hadn't made it home, so Carrie and the children went ahead and ate as Clay needed to finish his outside chores. By eight o'clock Tom still had not appeared and Carrie began to feel just a tat uneasy. At nine o'clock she shooed Clay and Cindy off to bed so they would be rested for school the next day.

Tom didn't come home at all that night, and this had never happened before. A time or two he had stayed out until after midnight, but never the entire night. The next morning she got the children off to school, did her morning cleanup chores and decided to go to Haymaker. Once there, she went straight to Sheriff Ashton's office.

"Why, good morning, Miss Carrie," Sheriff Ashton greeted her, rising as she came through the door. "How are you this fine sunny day? Everyone alright?" He pulled out a chair for her.

Carrie took a deep breath. "I'm not rightly sure if everything is alright or not, Sheriff. I may just be silly, but I'm worried, too."

Sheriff Ashton sat down on the edge of his desk facing Carrie. "I know you well enough to know you don't have a silly bone in your body, Miss Carrie. If you are worried, then there's got to be a good reason."

"Tom didn't come home last night," said Carrie. She might as well just get to the matter.

"Is that something he's done often?" asked the sheriff.

"No," replied Carrie. "That's why I'm worried. He's come home around midnight before, but in our entire marriage he's never stayed out all night."

"Has anything been troubling him lately?" asked Sheriff Ashton.

"Well, things have not been good with Alice and Luke's wedding being called off and both of them leaving town," answered Carrie. "But Tom hasn't been mean, just withdrawn and quiet."

"I'll tell you what," said Ashton. "I'll go over to the railroad office and see if he's working. If he is, I'll get word to you. If not, I'll start looking for him. How's that, Miss Carrie?"

"Thank you, Sheriff," she sighed, rising to take her leave. "I hope I'm not wasting your time, but I just can't escape this uneasy feeling."

By afternoon Carrie had received no word from the sheriff. At two-thirty Cindy arrived home from school and handed her mother a note. "Sheriff Ashton asked me to bring this to you, Maw. Is something wrong?"

Carried smiled weakly. "I hope not, Cindy. Get you some cookies and milk and then get on to your homework. Then you can help me with supper."

Cindy went toward the kitchen and Carrie opened the note.

Dear Miss Carrie,

Tom was not at work. No one seems to have seen him since he left work yesterday. I went by your sister Lily's place but she hadn't seen him. I have some other men helping me look for him.

Troy Ashton

Carrie's heart began to pound. Where on earth could Tom be? He had never done anything like this before.

At four thirty Clay came home with a worried look on his face. Sheriff Ashton had told him the problem. "Maw, I'm sure he'll be home any minute." He tried to sound reassuring. "He probably just had some things to do."

By six o'clock there was still no word. Carrie, Clay and Cindy tried to go on as if nothing was wrong, but each wore a worried look as they went about their chores. At eight o'clock there was a knock at the door and Carrie's heart gave a lurch. She opened the door to see not only Sheriff Ashton, but Beanie, Joe, Ady Rose and Willy. Immediately she knew it was bad news.

"Come in," she rasped.

The girls went straight to their mother. "Maw, sit down," said Ady Rose, quietly.

"What has happened?" asked Carrie, in little more than a whisper.

"Miss Carrie," said the sheriff, "there's no easy way to say this. Tom is dead. We found him in the river about an hour ago."

"In the river?" cried Carrie. "What was Tom doing in the river?"

"There was a big lump on the back of his head," explained Sheriff Ashton. "We think he fell and hit his head on a rock or something, then fell in the river and drowned, if he wasn't already dead from the lick on his head."

"But what was he even doing at the river?" asked Carrie. "Tom never goes to the river, especially on a work night."

"No one seems to know, Miss Carrie," replied the sheriff. "That's something we may never know."

Carrie sat in silence, trying to make some sense of it all, but it made absolutely no sense. None of this was like Tom.

"We've examined the body," offered Sheriff Ashton, "but nothing seems to suggest that it was anything other than an accident."

"Thank you, Sheriff," said Carrie. "I know you have done all you can do and I really do appreciate you taking your time to come here and tell me."

After a few more words, Sheriff Ashton left the little family to return to Haymaker. A short time later Jessie arrived, but said little except to console his maw. Carrie couldn't cry. She had no tears for Tom. She just felt this awful oppressive sadness for all that Tom could have been but never was. She insisted that Ady Rose and Beanie go on home with their husbands.

"There's nothing more you can do here," she said. "We will have some busy days ahead of us, so we'd best be getting some rest tonight."

Though objecting, the girls and their husbands took their leave. Jessie insisted on staying the night and for the next few days. That night he sat up with Carrie for a long time.

"I just don't know how things went so wrong in our marriage, Jessie," confided Carrie. "I loved your Paw so much when we were married, and I was sure he loved me. But I guess he didn't, since he was already being unfaithful to me. Do you think he just didn't know how to love?

"I don't know, Maw," replied Jessie, with a sigh. "I just never did understand Paw. It was like he resented us kids. He wouldn't let us get close to him...not even the girls. To be truthful, I never tried to get close to him. I've hated him for as long as I can remember, and there ain't no use for me to try to say otherwise. I hated him and I hated the way he always hurt you."

"I wish you could have known what it was like to have a loving Paw, Jessie, like my Papa Silas," said Carrie. "All of us children knew we were loved. He was such a good God-fearing man."

"At least you didn't have half-brothers and sisters all over the place so people could make fun of you," said Jessie, the anger showing in his eyes. "Everywhere I turned there was Loose Lizzie's boy, Ballard, staring at me, and it was like looking in a mirror, he looked so much like me."

Carrie paused a moment. "You said half-brothers and sisters, Jessie. Do you know of others besides him and Alice?"

"I don't know anything for certain, Maw," he replied. "You know how other kids like to say things to hurt you. They said one of Loose Lizzie's girls was my half-sister, then I overheard Lorris Tyler talking to Maudie Keller in the mercantile one day. She said one of Lily's boys was the spittin' image of Paw. But that's just talk, Maw. I don't know how much of it is true and how much is just people running off at the mouth. I guess it don't much matter and we won't have to worry about it anymore. He's hurt us for the last time."

At eight o'clock the next morning, Sheriff Ashton and three other men arrived in a wagon with Tom's body and a coffin.

"Miss Carrie," said the sheriff, "I took the liberty of getting a coffin so you wouldn't have to go to the trouble. I hope you don't mind. I know you will have your hands full the next few days."

Carrie placed her hand on his arm. "I'm obliged to you for that and so many other things, Sheriff. You've been good to us. I don't know what my children would have done without you and Martha. I can't repay you, but there'll be a reward for you in Heaven, I have no doubt."

They carried Tom's body in and placed it on the bed. Except for Cindy, no one cried.

"Miss Carrie, do you want me to send someone over to prepare the body?" asked the sheriff.

Jessie spoke up. "That won't be necessary, Sheriff. If Joe and Willy can help, me and Clay will prepare it."

Carrie was taken by surprise, but she made no objection.

Sheriff had some papers for her to sign, and then he took his leave. The little family was alone. The boys set straight to preparing Tom's body while the women prepared the house. Brother Nathaniel from the Primitive Baptist Church came by about noon to ask if he could help. Brother Jonas, though still living, was old and feeble and could no longer preach, so Carrie asked Brother Nathaniel to preach Tom's funeral. At two o'clock Clay brought in the sawhorses and after the boys placed Tom's body in the coffin, it was placed on them. Tom was being buried in the only suit he owned, and as Carrie looked down upon his lifeless body, she marveled at what a handsome man Tom still was, even after all these years.

By late afternoon, neighbors began arriving with food as they offered their condolences to Carrie and the children. She noticed that not a one tried to offer any word of praise for Tom.

Nora arrived, going to Carrie immediately to wrap her arms around her. "I'm so sorry, Sister. I wish I could help you in some way."

"Just having you here is a great help," answered Carrie. "You have always been here for me, Nora, through all the good times and the bad."

By six o'clock, all of Carrie's siblings except Lily and Ellie had come by. All of them knew about the reason for Alice and Luke's wedding cancelation as they had known for years about Tom's philandering. Sile J. had been coming by at least once a week to lend a hand and a good listening ear.

Eliza and Widow Thomas arrived with baskets of food. "I hope you know how much I love you, Miss Carrie," said Eliza. "You don't deserve all of this hurt, but I know that God loves you and He has a purpose that we can't understand. You have taught me many things in my life, but most of all you taught me about love. Tom Swank was the luckiest man on earth and he didn't have the sense to know it."

When Jessie could get Carrie aside, he asked, "Maw, where should we dig a grave for the burial?"

Carrie thought for a minute. "I can't bury him in his paw's cemetery," she said. "Paw Charles wouldn't have wanted that. I guess I'll bury him with Mama Cynth and Papa Silas if my brothers have no objections. That's where I want to be buried someday."

"I'll go ask Eb and Sile J.," said Jessie. "They're still out on the porch."

He returned to say that Carrie's brothers had gladly agreed, and they also said that they, along with Will and Charles would see that the grave was dug first thing in the morning. Many of the neighbors spent the night, following custom. At ten o'clock, Ady Rose and Beanie insisted that Carrie go to bed and get some rest. Carrie agreed, and as she left the living room she motioned for Cindy, who could barely hold her eyes open.

"Come, my sweet girl," said Carrie. "Let's you and me lie down and get some rest."

The next day and night were much the same. People came by, brought food, tried to think of something appropriate to say and then went on their way. Then on Thursday, at eleven o'clock, family, friends and neighbors gathered for the funeral. Will's wife, Sally, again sang the old hymn *Rock of Ages*, and Brother Nathaniel preached the funeral. Carrie knew it was a difficult funeral to preach. There weren't too many good things that could be said about Tom, but Brother Nathaniel surely did try.

"Life is short and full of troubles," Brother Nathaniel began. *"Some have a life of trouble and some cause a life of trouble, but we are not to judge. Only God can judge man who is born with this sinful nature. Our brother lying here before us has raised a good, loving family and has as good and Godly a wife as any man has ever had. That speaks to his benefit..."*

Carrie sat beside his coffin as the funeral was preached, a deep, dark, unexplainable sadness wrapping its claws around her. At that moment she could not have explained her feelings to anyone...sadness, relief, loss, pity, anger...so many different feelings. Mostly she felt regret for a life wasted... regret for a family that wanted to love him but couldn't...regret for a man who could have been a wonderful husband and father, but couldn't control the demons in him.

When the funeral ended, the coffin was loaded on the wagon. Those going to the cemetery climbed into their wagons and followed, as the trip to Tom's final resting place was about a mile and a half. Several women stayed behind to prepare a meal to be served later.

At the cemetery Sally sang one last song before Brother Nathaniel would pray the final prayer and the coffin would be lowered into the grave. Carrie's family gathered round her except the boys, who stood at the foot of the coffin. As Sally sang *Amazing Grace*, Carrie sat, dry-eyed and emotionless. Suddenly she felt eyes upon her, and as she looked up, her eyes locked with Jessie's. It was odd. His eyes seemed to be telling her something. And then she saw an ever-so-slight curve to his lips, as though in a smile. She had to be mistaken. He wouldn't be smiling on a day like this. They looked at each other for a moment. Then Carrie's eyes were drawn back to the coffin with a jolt. She stared, eyes wide, at the coffin, not able to breathe. Her entire body began to shake violently and she looked at Jessie again as the words came back to her,

"HE WILL NEVER HURT YOU AGAIN, MAW. NEVER AGAIN."

The sweat poured from her shaking body...and then blackness prevailed.

A MOUNTAIN WOMAN'S LAMENT

There's a buryin' on the hillside
To lay her man to rest.
No tears, no mournful weeping,
Just a heart of emptiness.

As she gazes at the coffin,
She takes stock of her life,
For the days of a mountain woman
Are weighted down with strife.

Back-breaking work, calloused hands,
Dreams long swept asunder.
Where has it gone and gone so wrong?
No answers...but she wonders.

But through the valleys and on the mountains
She knows God has a plan.
What is it, Lord? And she raises her eyes
To watch them bury her man.

With shovels of dirt they cover the grave
And everyone goes their way.
The mountain widow rises, bent and tired,
For tomorrow is another day.

— *Brenda Crissman Musick*

ABOUT THE AUTHOR

Brenda Crissman Musick was born and raised in Southwest Virginia in the small town of Honaker, the third of three children. "We were poor, I suppose, by the world's standards," she says, "but there was too much love to consider ourselves as such, and there was always plenty of good garden food on the table (although I sure hated weeding those onions)." She had a wonderful childhood, playing in the clean streams and skipping rocks, going barefoot, playing cowboys and Indians, and just enjoying nature.

From the time she was a child, Brenda loved to read and to write stories. She taught school in the Russell County School System for nineteen years, one of the most rewarding times of her life. Throughout those years she continued to read and write, teaching both. She taught creative writing classes for middle school students and conducted writing workshops for teachers. Upon retirement, she devoted herself to genealogy research, teaching Bible Studies, writing children's books and reminiscent writing. In 2000 she published a children's book, *The Dolls on the Old Stairway*. In the spring of 2013, she taught Memoir Writing at the Appalachian Heritage Writers' Symposium at SWCC. Her dream, however, was to write a novel, and this book is the culmination of that dream. She is a member of the Appalachian Authors Guild and the Reminiscent Writers of SWCC.

Brenda and husband Jimmie live on a small farm in the Big A Mountain section of Honaker, where they enjoy the peace and tranquility of the country life they have always loved. They have three children, seven grandchildren, thirteen cows and a bull named Rufus.

Contact Brenda at: musickb@jetbroadband.com or facebook.com/brenda.c.musick

Look for the follow-up to

ONE-EYED TOM,

as Luke and Jessie Swank attempt to get beyond the sadness and hate of the past and make a life that counts. Will that mean marriage, or has Tom Swank forever "soured" them to that idea? Will it mean a life in the hills of Appalachia, or a place far away? Watch for

A PLACE TO BELONG.

CPSIA information can be obtained at www.ICGtesting.com
Printed in the USA
BVOW07s0749170913

331378BV00001B/2/P